1

Blurred sounds begin to emerge: a humming in his head, with distant voices: shouting, women's screams. It makes no sense. The humming becomes drumming. Then, far above, a mesh of blackness writhing against pulsing crimson. Gradually the blurred forms come into focus, turn into treetops tossing wildly, with the night sky alight beyond.

Wind off the blaze blows hotly on him as he lies staring up, incapable of movement, while increasing waves of sensation slide through him, intensify, sharpen to pain. Real pain. It has no centre. The pain is all of him.

Moaning as he tries to sit up, he rolls first on one agonizing hip. His knees are torture. Kneeling there, head bowed, he knows he must get to his feet. They're lacerated, bare and bloody, but he has to get out of the wood, has to meet up with those frantic, distant voices.

There's a roaring from outside his head too, a great Niagara. But not water. And, with it, a mechanical rhythm that perhaps isn't his heart's pumping. He stands swaying; for a moment holds on to the rough bark of an

1

oak, and takes his first steps on to twigs and brambles. He wills his piston legs to get working; stumbles against saplings and over tree roots. His body is robotic once he's begun, under compulsion to keep going. The world outside him shudders and thumps.

The wood is thinning. The devouring crimson lurches ever closer, grows immense, filling the foreground; the heat overwhelming.

As he leaves the last shelter of the trees a despairing groan comes from the dying house ahead. Powerless, he stands and watches as the whole central roofing sags. It hangs, then drops like raw pastry cut off the edge of a pie dish.

It takes an age to fall, crushing the lower walls under it. With its final horrendous crash a sheet of orange flame shoots up in a giant fireworks finale, showering back as a thousand floating fragments of blazing fabric. A wall of heat rushes out across the trampled lawn.

A hoarse voice is shouting. Something about an assembly point. He's partly deaf or else stupid. The words don't quite join up. There's no sense to them. He wants to sit down, lie down, not be there. Someone emerges from the swirling crimson and black, running towards him.

'Eddie! it's you?' Rough hands seize him.

'It's OK, man. Thank God! We thought you were still inside!' Uncle Matthew, his face streaked with tears and soot.

A clumping of heavy boots as he sways, mesmerized by the inferno. Somebody is grasping him under the arms. 'Last one's out,' he cries, almost euphoric. 'That's the lot!'

He glimpses a cheerful, blackened face thrust at him from under the yellow fire helmet. And taking his full weight as he crumples, the man repeats as if to a stupid child, 'Last one to leave, mate. You bin lucky.'

More voices nearby, and then, 'Straight to the ambulance.' Shufflings and jostling. He's half-blind, his face crushed under some kind of mask. He's becoming weightless, adrift again.

Once more he blunders along an interminable corridor of smoke, seeking a way out, surrounded by closed doors that change first into trees, then to a Grecian frieze of grotesque human figures. Scenes shift, come in and out of focus. Finally it all dissolves in a fog of grey.

★   ★   ★

The fireman's voice was still in his head when he came to, alone, on a hospital trolley. 'Last

3

to leave!' *Last out, turn off the light*, he thought. But nothing was going to douse that hellish inferno. It was taking over the world.

And *last* was wrong, because he seemed to remember how it had been: he wasn't the last out. More like the first.

He'd come awake to an urgent knocking. Not from the door, but somewhere beyond his feet. It took a moment to remember that he'd reversed himself in the bed; stuck the pillow at the bottom and pointed his legs towards the dormer window. That was to get what light escaped the feeble central bulb. Old Carlton was notoriously tight about expenses, which included electricity. That was hard on someone used to reading himself to sleep — a hangover from schooldays, finishing his prep by torchlight, under the bedclothes.

The knocking redoubled in urgency. He sat up. It was the bloody radiator, vibrating now onto the tubular metal of the old-fashioned bed which he'd rammed close.

Overheating in late Spring? That was hardly on: it was stifling enough up here under the eaves. If he knew his miserly old uncle, not even in the most Siberian of winters would the temperature be boosted above 65 degrees.

So what mad family jokester was playing

4

the prison communications game and rattling his, Eddie's, cage?

He stormed out on the landing to trace the knocking down. There was an acrid smell of smoke.

No joker playing tubular bells then, but something real. It accounted for the stifling heat. Running back, roaring 'Fire' at the top of his lungs, he'd snatched his coat, rammed feet into slippers and hared out again to rouse the house. He'd banged on doors as he passed, shouted names, not recalling whose any room was.

Yes, that's how it had been. A fire breaking out in the kitchen quarters had reached the old boiler. It could have given up, split and leaking. The air trapped inside would ultimately blow. The house could go up like a bomb.

So wouldn't he have been the first out? Memory gave out right there. He could account for nothing later. Why all the damage — the gashed head, the pain? OK, so his feet were cut about because somewhere along the way he'd lost his slippers, found himself in the wood behind the house. Must have panicked and run like a scared rabbit; left the others to burn. Some hero.

At some point he'd fallen, or run headlong into a low branch and knocked himself out, which was why he couldn't get his brain straight. He did remember lying on his back under trees, and by then the blaze had taken a strong hold. He must have been out for quite a while because back at the house a fire team had arrived and set up, but too late to save the building. Thank God none of them had been left inside.

'Right, let's be having you then.' In a luminous white void an over-cheerful woman doctor swam into view with a young male nurse in tow. 'What have we here?' She lifted a clipboard off the foot of his trolley. 'M'm, yes. Yes. Multiple injuries; smoke inhalation. How'd you gash your head? Did the roof fall in on you? Let's take a look.'

She removed a temporary pad that was meant to stem the bleeding. 'Martin, clean this up for me, will you? There's probably plaster in it and splinters. Then send him off for X-ray. I'll take another look before you do the sutures. The rest of him can wait.' She breezed off, officious and efficient.

'So how *did* you?' This time an answer was required. The peroxided no.2 haircut bent close over him, the young man's brow furrowed. 'No carbon in the gash. Plenty up your nostrils. Your hair's full of leaf bits and soil.'

Eddie pulled the mask loose from his nose

and mouth. Now in the airy whiteness of the hospital he still burned inside, choked, vomited, couldn't find words to demand *what about the others?*

But hadn't someone shouted they were all out? The family was safe. Only there was something from way back that disturbed him. Something happening before the fire, was it? A dream, then? His mind was too blurred to bring any of it back. He thought he'd been involved with someone he didn't quite trust. And surely Jess had been there too. But then Jess often got into his craziest dreams. Due maybe to their being twins. No, whatever it was it had gone now.

From the moment of smelling smoke a few fresh blips of memory began to flash up, out of sequence like jumbled frames of film. Across them the nurse's low voice went on, murmuring reassurances. He couldn't stay to listen. He was off again into grey-white mist; but different now, floating and blissfully alone. Away from the insistent bleeping machine behind his head, the rushing confusion.

Gradually some kind of order established itself, but by then he felt hours, even days, could have passed. He grew to recognize the apparatus he was wired to, could identify the sighing of the ventilator, the hard, gagging object depressing his tongue, and the IV tube stuck in his wrist. He wasn't even allowed the dignity of pyjamas or to control his own bladder.

Time was measured out by regular tests and fresh dressings. Eventually they explained that one of his broken ribs, piercing the right lung, had caused respiratory failure. So he'd been operated on at once. He'd been lucky they caught on to it.

Lucky old me, he told himself wryly. That's twice I've been told that. Glad they think so!

By the time he was disconnected and wheeled through to a small side ward he'd discovered the extensive bruising on his chest and abdomen. There was more at the back where he couldn't see it, and it meant there was no position he could lie in without some pain.

They dosed him to make it easier, which made him stupid, and he had difficulty understanding when the police came asking questions.

Cousin Robert was his first family visitor. Not surprising, because he was the pushy one. Having recently got engaged to a Dr Marion Paige, he'd now be an instant authority on medical matters. He came in leaning heavily on a stick: been bloody clumsy doing heroics on the roof, he explained. Eddie took the story with a measure of salt. Robert seemed peeved that there was a pert little WPC present throughout his unnecessary inquiries after his health.

'How'd the fire start?' Eddie managed to get out, since even Robert needed occasionally to draw breath.

'They haven't said. The Fire Officer's report is with the police but there's a bit of investigation still going on. The insurance people won't get off Uncle Carlton's back, poor devil. Some fuss about the sprinkler system not having been activated.'

Well, bully for Carlton having splashed out on that. Eddie had actually noticed the points in the main downstairs rooms. 'But what caused the fire?'

His bumptious cousin looked at a loss. (A first time for everything.) 'Wish I knew. We're all being hectored and harassed over it.' He glared at the inoffensive little policewoman. 'You'd think being a smoker was equivalent to high treason. Not that it started upstairs. Everyone was asleep in bed, of course. Probably faulty electrical equipment in the kitchen. Nobody could accuse old Carlton of wasting money on updating that great barn of a house. Still, that doesn't explain how fast it took hold. Maddie insists she smelled petrol.'

The WPC coughed gently and rearranged her attractive legs. As if at a signal a nurse looked in through the doorway and suggested the visit had overrun the permitted five minutes.

Eddie was floating off again. 'Everyone all right?' he managed to get out.

'Sure. Apart from my ankle, you're the only casualty in here,' Robert declared airily, but his eyes were shifty. The nurse was bearing down on him and he edged away.

'Cheers then,' he said in the doorway and raised a hand. 'The others'll be in, given time.'

What was keeping them? Robert wasn't the one he'd been most anxious over. The words caught in Eddie's throat and refused to come out. *What about Kate, my mother? And Jess?* And old Carlton: how was he weathering the unexpected way his eightieth birthday celebration had taken off? Why hadn't redoubtable Aunt Claudia insisted on wheeling him in as the front-line visitor?

'Tell Jess to bring me some books,' Eddie whispered after his cousin's retreating back. Robert waved again without looking round and never shortened his stride.

★   ★   ★

10

When he next awoke the police questions recommenced. 'Look, this is irrelevant,' he said. 'I didn't stay to see what happened.' He explained how he'd been first, not last, to leave the burning building.

The two plain-clothes constables regarded each other warily. One flicked back a few pages in his notebook. 'We have statements from two separate witnesses,' he said, 'that after you roused all the residents on your corridor you ran downstairs and tried to fight your way into the kitchen.'

The other read from his notes: 'A Mr Augustus Railton said, 'I couldn't hold him back. He disappeared into the smoke. Then a door was opened somewhere beyond and a fireball roared out. It knocked me off my feet. I never saw Eddie again after that. I thought the young bugger was a goner, poor devil.' '

'Gus was wrong,' he told them. 'That wasn't me. Why would I do that? I just chickened out and went hell-for-leather for the great outdoors.'

'He said you shouted something about the cellar, and tore out of his grasp.'

Cellar? Eddie shook his head, then winced at the pain that stabbed back.

'Perhaps you don't remember things very well,' the first DC suggested. 'You had an almighty crack on your head. How do you think that happened?'

'I have no idea. Hit a tree or something, I expect. I was a long way into the wood when I came round. How could that be if I'd got trapped in the cellars?'

'You were there all right. We found how you got out. You took a coke hammer to the oak doors over the old coal chute. The hasp was rusted half away. The whole structure broke up.'

'Somebody was watching me?' It was meant to be sarcasm but it came out feeble.

'Your cousin Madeleine noticed a figure staggering off from the rear of the house and making for the wood. At that point things were pretty disorganized, so one more was ticked off as having got out. Are you still saying that wasn't you?'

'Does it matter? I'm out, that's all I know.'

'It matters,' the man persisted, 'because you were all *counted* out, not ticked off by name. And it looks as if you were counted for a second time when you staggered out of the wood later. So the new number tallied with the list of residents.'

Eddie stared at him in disbelief. Even in his doped state he saw the significance.

'You mean an over-count? Someone was still missing — left in there? Oh, my God! Who then?'

12

'I'm sorry, sir. I have to tell you we haven't been able to find your sister, Miss Jessica Dellar.'

★   ★   ★

He is running again. Same corridor, same wood, only now, ghostly to either side are gauzy white drapes floating in the wind. He's fleeing someone? Seeking someone?

Trees dissolve into people. They stand over him, demanding answers as he lies on his back staring at the sky burning behind waving treetops. Questions he doesn't know any answers to; can't find the strength to find.

An exasperated voice — 'Don't you care what's become of her?' A vague memory of disaster stirs in his befuddled brain.

'Become of who?'

'Of your sister. Can you tell us where she went?'

Jessica. My twin. That's who I was searching for.

But in the cellar?

And why doesn't Kate come? Mother, where are you?

Then he knew it was all beyond him. He was dying, perhaps already dead.

2

Stumbling away from the burning house, the roar of flames and hoarse shouting, Kate's first worry had been for Carlton and Claudia. Such an appalling shock could have destroyed them. Then her brother-in-law's voice reached her, fluting away beyond a wall of rhododendrons. She rounded them to find him seated on an artistically prone Greek *pithoi* with Claudia's tartan cloak over his shoulders, his wife standing ramrod straight behind him like some Victorian ghillie posed for a photograph with the local laird.

For a moment Kate thought Carlton had shaved off the right side of his wild white beard. But it was there all right, flattened to project ridiculously, like an airfield's windsock, from the farther cheek. It was the way he'd slept on it, adding to the mad Don Quixote appearance of his scarecrow figure.

Claudia was drably austere in a charcoal velvet housecoat, her iron-grey hair in schoolgirl plaits. She turned stiffly to face the other woman. 'Ah, Kate, this is a grim business. Most disturbing for everyone.'

In total control. If she was aware that her

home and everything in it was likely lost, she gave no indication. Her voice of doom was the one she normally employed for everyday observations.

'Just look at that,' piped her elderly husband, staring upwards into the fiery reflections on the underside of billowing smoke. 'What incredible colours. You know, my dear, we don't appreciate the night sky enough. When did we last come out and truly look at the dark?'

Unsurprisingly she didn't answer. 'I'm so very sorry,' Kate whispered, leaving her to guess whether she referred to the fire or to Carlton's increasing dottiness.

Claudia drew an audible, deep breath. 'It's fortunate we increased the insurance cover.'

That was startling. 'All the same,' Kate couldn't help saying, 'to lose so much that you've built up over the years . . . '

'Accumulated,' Claudia corrected her.

Had she regarded all Carlton's valuable acquisitions as so much encumbrance then? While it shocked the other woman she stored it for consideration later. 'I wanted to be sure you were both all right,' she said. 'Robert's rung for a minibus to take us all to the Greythorpe Hotel. Naturally it will catch them on the hop, so some of us may need to share rooms for the present, but at least there will be beds for the rest of the night.'

She offered her arm and between them the two women raised Carlton to his feet and got him moving in the right direction. As they passed round to the front of the house the full heat struck at them again. Three fire appliances were present and a battery of hoses was being directed on the house, already reduced to a glowing shell. It seemed impossible that such devastation could have happened in so short a while. Piles of smouldering débris lay where thrown from windows in a panicky attempt to save what seemed precious. They had to pick their way through it all to where the family had been herded together, a phalanx of stunned strangers in oddly assembled garb.

An ambulance was pulling away, circling what had been a reasonably tidy stretch of lawn before so much trampling, and just then the promised minibus, bright yellow, appeared at the far end of the drive.

They were dragooned into a semblance of order, oldies first, and, busy with getting Carlton's stiff old legs to cope with the high steps, Kate hadn't time to look around for the twins, assuming they'd be equally occupied with organizing their elders and board last.

A trio of firemen clumped across to the bus. One wearing a soot-smeared white helmet put his head through the bus doorway. He had a list on his clipboard. 'Mrs Kate Dellar?' he accused her, as though she might have denied it. 'Could I have a word, please?' So she climbed down.

Then, as the others were driven off, he told her: Eddie had been injured. He was on his way to High Wycombe Casualty Unit. And, after a recount of survivors, one was missing: her daughter Jessica.

Eddie? Jess? *Both* her children? 'But they said everyone was safe!' she shouted at him.

A policewoman, fair hair straggling from an untidy bun under her crushed uniform hat, took her arm. Kate shook her hand off. Then the full horror exploded on her. She stared back at the collapsed frontage of the still glowing ruin. Jess — somewhere inside that inferno? No, no! Impossible.

'We'll drive you to the hospital,' the policewoman offered.

But how could she leave? There might, by some miracle, be just a chance that . . . But then Eddie — badly hurt? She was torn apart.

In a daze she let herself be manoeuvred into the rear of the police car. The girl climbed into the driving seat. Kate was aware of the dark outline of a man beside her. He turned briefly to look at her as the siren crudely broke out after the doors slammed. He had a round, expressionless, puppet face with a sharp nose.

'Cut that row,' he ordered the girl, and leaned across to silence the siren and switch on the windscreen wipers. Twin jets of soapy water spurted up to dislodge the film of black detritus that had settled. The flip and slick of the blades on glass were the only sounds now above the low hum of the engine.

The car swung out of the driveway and into leafy Windmill Lane, headlights stabbing the dark through a tunnel of golden trees. Nothing was real. Kate felt her heart beating up in her throat. She closed her eyes, hugged her chest tight, desperately hunting for the words of some prayer.

There had been no point in their rushing. Eddie was no longer in the Casualty department.

'Gone to theatre,' a doctor explained. Kate had a ludicrous vision of a floodlit Edwardian proscenium, all gilt plaster and cherubs. The ruby velvet curtains were closed, like a crematorium chapel's after last viewing of the coffin. She found herself retching. A nurse brought her a chair. They were handling her like a Friday night drunk.

In the surgical ward Eddie wasn't expected back for at least an hour, and even then not

18

awake enough to talk. Come back tomorrow, she was told: not too early.

She wanted to insist she'd just wait there, not be in their way, simply hold his hand when he returned; but it was fear of her son's embarrassment that held her back. Over-imaginative and by nature protective, she'd always forced herself not to fuss, never let the twins feel she smothered them. Even more so since losing Michael.

She hadn't known that one day she'd need them there so badly for herself.

'I have to go back to the fire,' she said after they insisted that Eddie, with his injured head and chest, was in the safest hands possible. She believed they'd do their best, but had a fatalistic premonition. Distraught, and so recently widowed, she saw her little family being picked off, one by one.

She was barely aware of being helped into a taxi. When it stopped she found she'd been delivered to the Greythorpe Hotel. She stood outside shivering on that early May morning as dawn slowly broke, and knew she couldn't yet face the others.

There was too much grief. Not only her own. Carlton had lost the home where he'd been born and lived in for most of his eighty years. If the reality of it hadn't yet reached the old man, Claudia, totally aware, would be

19

indomitably in command of both herself and him. Kate did not trust herself to be with them for now.

She told the driver to take her to the Monkey Puzzle. From the pub she'd ring the family and explain she needed to be on her own at present.

Which was far from the truth. But who was there now to be with?

★   ★   ★

The Monkey Puzzle was named after the monstrous tree in its forecourt, which lodged the dust and traffic pollution of almost a century. Desiccated and hang-dog, it was shamed by the sprucely painted version of its kind on the inn's swinging sign.

The pub boasted a second tree at the rear, where it dropped confetti-like blossom on the little square of lawn referred to as the Beer Garden. A cherry tree, it had gone wildly leggy, the productive part of it isolated aloft like a ship's crow's-nest. Lower, it could have had nets thrown over in the fruiting season, but skied up there on its pine-straight trunk it was only a drop-in for scavenging blackbirds and pigeons. Whenever she thought of the pub, even before the casky beeriness of its smell and the dim, smoky interior swam into

20

her mind, she remembered those two overgrown trees.

For all its unpretentiousness, or perhaps because of it, she was fond of the place. This was where she'd stayed weekends in her late teens when Michael, very much the youngest of the three Dellar brothers, used to steal away from the manor house to meet her. She was supposedly in college and, skint as students always are, they could afford no plushier venue for their secret meetings.

The then landlord had long departed, replaced by a disabled ex-midshipman from the Royal Navy, whose name remained over the door while the main work fell to Duncan and Lily Crick, his brawny son and motherly young daughter. For two decades now Kate and Michael had established the habit of dropping in, once she'd become an almost-accepted member of the Dellars' extended family.

The Cricks made her warmly welcome. They had woken to see the fire reflected in the sky. It was only half a mile from Larchmoor Place if you went straight through the woods, although three miles round by road. Duncan had rung the house, found the line down and then contacted the local police for information.

With surprising tact they refrained from

21

questions. Lily showed Kate to a comfortable room under the eaves, bringing up a tray of cold cuts and salad with a half bottle of good Merlot. She declined the food, poured a glass of wine, showered to get the stench of smoke off her body and hair, then climbed into bed wearing a kindly-lent outsize nightdress.

Determined to sleep, she found it impossible. Against her will, incidents of the past day ran through her mind time and again, as if in a loop of film. She was forced to relive all that had happened since her taxi drew into sight of the house — her husband's home until the day they'd eloped together.

She'd come a long way since then and considered herself a pragmatist. She knew that in his family's eyes she remained little more than an outsider, valued only for having provided a brace of junior Dellars. But, released from close socializing since being widowed, she felt that she could withstand any disdain the family chose to display towards her. Or had done, until this moment.

Loyalty to Michael's ghost had made her accept old Carlton's eightieth birthday invitation, although she hadn't looked forward with any pleasure to the family gathering. She knew Eddie had felt much the same. About Jess — always the rebel — she wasn't sure, and she'd been uneasy on seeing her daughter across the drawing-room, partly because of the circumstances of their last meeting.

That had been when the girl told her she intended living openly with Charles Stone. Kate knew him only by reputation, a wealthy married man who had made a name in the City. Despite her determined policy of non-interference, she'd had to speak out against him.

'It's what we both want,' had been Jessica's excuse.

'That isn't reason enough, Jess. Marriage *means* something. He has a duty to his wife. Have you thought what you'd be doing to her? And the monster you'd be making of him? How could you ever trust him yourself, if he could walk out on the woman he'd solemnly promised to love and protect for life?'

'Mother, you should just hear yourself!' she jeered. 'I wish, I really, really wish I'd a tape recorder for this moment. You sound like something out of the ark.'

'Because I'm looking straight at what you're thinking of doing? Be honest, Jess. Admit you're valuing sexual attraction above loyalty. It's downright shoddy.'

Jess's face flamed. For a moment she looked almost ugly. 'You're a Dodo!' she'd screamed. 'We love each other and that's what we mean to do. What we're doing already. I should have known better than to mention it to you at all! You go on and on about how you loved Pa, but I was there, remember? It wasn't some great heroic passion that changed the world. You only think that now because you've lost him. If he was alive today, who knows . . . '

And then Kate had slapped her. A stinging blow across her cheek. She left her standing there, head bowed, hands hiding her eyes and her chestnut hair tumbling about her shoulders.

Ashamed because she had never before raised a hand to either of her children, Kate stumbled out of the narrow-boat. She almost ran, with the wind in her face, along the canal towpath until weariness took over and she found herself at unfamiliar lock gates. A man leaning over his elbows on the bar advised her to go a quarter mile back and cross by the bridge, where a short walk would bring her to a railway station with a taxi rank.

She had arrived home exhausted, fell into bed in broad daylight and slept for ten hours. They had never quarrelled like that before. There had never been cause to. Other dramas had been cautiously steered clear of crisis. Not this time. It seemed — if not the end of

24

the world — a point passed to which they could never return: something both needed, now irrevocably lost.

Jess didn't ring to apologize. Nor did she. Neither of them had been in touch since.

★　★　★

When Kate arrived at Larchmoor Place they were all assembled indoors for afternoon tea, except Eddie who couldn't just slope away from work after Friday lunch. She had taken a week's leave from the library, unsure how long she was meant, or was meaning, to stay. Whatever free time was left over would be profitably spent getting her little garden in order.

If Carlton or Claudia had changed since she'd last seen them it was only to have become even more what they were before: he a frail *guru* figure and she utterly daunting. Thin and erect, she had beautiful bones under the tightly stretched parchment skin. Her dark eyes in hollowed sockets were matched by the sepulchral tones of a contralto voice which could imbue the most banal of remarks with momentous significance. Besides her early legal career she had been an amateur singer of some note, but now for several years had restricted herself to public recitations of her husband's verses. She was, Kate knew, fifteen years younger than Carlton and would have carried her years well if she hadn't always dressed in cobwebby draperies of black or grey. Eddie, as a little boy, had called her the Spider Lady.

Carlton's surviving brother, Matthew, had been born after a gap of six years, and Kate's dear Michael much later, the only son of their father's second wife, Lorna. Had he lived he would have been almost fifty. She was four years his junior. The twins had been twenty two this St. Valentine's Day.

If you counted Matthew's step-grandson, the assembled family covered three generations. Matthew was a widower, Joanne having died of typhoid fever on her return from a dig in Egypt when Robert was seven and Madeleine only five. Now fifty, Madeleine was married to Gus, with a stepson Jake who had arrived that day with due biker panache on a Kawasaki and flaunting the company's matching leathers. He'd dared to park his mount opposite the house's double front doors. Jake was three or four years older than Kate's two, but there was little come and go between the younger folk.

A family member easily overlooked was the-late-produced daughter born, to general amazement, some thirty-odd years ago to

Carlton and Claudia. Daringly christened Miranda, she'd failed to live up to her name, once she'd miraculously survived. She had almost made the Guinness Book of Records for low birth weight, had three times stopped breathing and three times been resuscitated in hospital before eventually being brought home, puny and ailing, in the care of a nursemaid who'd been kept on as nanny until the child was eight. She'd been a solitary little girl, almost autistic, dumpy and without charm; an enigma to most of the family, not least to her parents.

The last member of the party, an outsider who had yet to become acclimatized to the impact of a full Dellar assembly, was Dr Marion Paige. An unknown factor as yet, she was engaged to marry Robert as soon as his divorce was made absolute.

As Kate slid in, the murmur of greetings only momentarily broke the conversation. Robert, robust ego that he was, had been centre-stage.

'That book you left lying around . . . ' said Claudia accusingly.

'Oh, did you see it?' Impervious to any attempt to deflate him, Robert preened himself. 'An advance copy. It comes out next month. Rather a good cover this time, I thought.'

Nobody rushed to assure him he was right, but then none of the family shared his enthusiasm for science fiction. They doubted, in fact, whether Robert could be much of an author. If pressed into reading the things as they came out year after year they might have felt obliged to give an opinion on his efforts.

'It's very large,' Madeleine ventured, to fill the gap. Its size alone had been too much for her.

'For the American readership,' Robert claimed. 'They demand a big book.'

'I remember — ' fluted old Carlton, his nose lifting like a police dog on a waft of cannabis — 'I remember when editors edited. They discussed the content, advised one what to cut.

'Nowadays,' he complained reedily, 'it's like putting money in a chocolate machine. Typescript in, hardcover out. No discussion, no editorial foreplay, no delightful West End lunching. All haste to get a profit. Automatic as phoning the quack for a repeat prescription.'

'Mine's not like that,' Madeleine sighed. 'Doctor, I mean. I have to wheedle and cajole like some courtesan in a cinquecento Italian intrigue before I'm allowed the weeniest amount of pain relief.'

'Then he's the rare, old-fashioned sort.

Nowadays, once you hit fifty they've decided what to put you on, key it into the sacred computer and it's set that way for the rest of your natural — or thereby *ruined* — life. More of the chocolate-machine reaction,' said Matthew, backing up his elder brother whatever the cost to his embarrassed daughter.

At the mention of age, scoring its menopausal bullseye, Madeleine had jumped up, scarlet-faced, and started fussily rearranging Claudia's white lilac in a vase on the grand piano.

'Oh, do mind the drips!' Miranda burst out; then, covered in confusion, put both hands over her mouth.

Everyone stared pityingly at Maddie's back except Robert, stung by his sister's disparaging attitude to his book. 'Oh hard luck, Sis. Dad forgot you'd just hit the sensitive half-century.'

'You're looking well, Kate.' Gus Railton moved across with a freshly poured cup of Earl Grey tea. She thanked him, conscious of all eyes swinging to read something into his effort to turn attention off his embarrassed wife. Poor Gus had a reputation for half-hearted womanizing. He had the unfortunate good looks of a melodrama villain: lean, smooth cheeks with high colour under the eyes, which were of a piercing blue. Elsewhere his porcelain complexion contrasted with the sleeked-back gloss of jet-black hair. He even had the fine, smiley moustache of a thirties Hollywood star. Possibly there's a Sir Jasper gene, Kate had thought, which also includes a weakness for gambling. In an old Western, Gus would've been the one with the figured silk waistcoat.

'I've been gardening,' she said to explain her slight suntan. 'It provides a welcome break from working indoors all the time.' She looked around and saw that apparently the ball was still in her court. She had to slam it back to keep the game going.

'Actually I've seen a copy of your new book, Robert,' she told him. 'It's on our order for June.'

'At the library, yes.' He eyed her shrewdly. Like the others he considered her occupation a pathetic effort, but never failed to call on its uses. 'Did you happen to see how many copies the county's taking this time?'

'Er, no,' she lied. It was only eight. Last year they'd gone for twelve, but all departments were economizing at the moment. The cut could have been simply for that reason.

'Won't you introduce us, Bobbo?' asked the thin woman in lime green who'd been on the outer edge of the standing group.

'A million pardons. Forgive my crude manners,' Robert babbled, putting an arm about his fiancée's waist. 'Darling, this is Kate, my late Uncle Michael's er, wife.' He had shied off from using the word widow. Kate supposed none of them was accustomed to it yet, but his hesitation had made it sound as though her legitimacy were in doubt. She found herself smiling ironically as she took Marion Paige's hand.

'I should have known who you were,' Marion said. 'You're so like your lovely daughter. Same eyes; same sweet smile.'

Kate dared then to look straight across at Jess. Gone was her erstwhile mouse-nest neglect. Instead, the long, chestnut hair was twisted high into the glossy coiffure of a Roman matron. Under it a row of little circular curls appeared stuck flat across her brow. Her hair and skin shone. She looked wonderful. From student grunge to Caesar's wife in one leap.

'I hardly think she'll find that a compliment,' Kate couldn't help saying, then wondered if that had been Marion Paige's intention.

With the removal of the tea things the atmosphere eased a little and they were able to move about, trickling through to the terrace and fanning across the lawn. Kate found herself again in the company of Robert's intended. 'Have you picked on a date for the wedding?' she asked.

The woman gave a lean grin and Kate decided she might actually be quite fun. 'His divorce isn't absolute yet. When it is — ' and she darted Kate a sideways look — 'I think we may just go off and do the *fait accompli* thing.'

'Cheat us of another family gathering?' Kate suggested, almost innocently.

Marion chuckled. 'Could you bear that?'

'Just about.' They turned at the end of the shrubbery and started walking back towards the house. Robert was talking to Claudia in the doorway of the room they'd just left and waving his arms extravagantly. Dr Marion Paige regarded them both, head tilted. 'He's not too bad an old stick really,' she said dispassionately.

Kate was impressed. The newcomer had acuity and humour, a rare coupling. On the spur of the moment she dared ask, 'What have you got against my daughter?'

'Ah, that,' Marion said sombrely, not denying what Kate had intuitively picked up. 'That is another story entirely.'

3

Marion never answered Kate's question but turned to smile at Robert as he advanced on them alone. 'That woman!' he complained. 'Boadicea had nothing on her.'

'A little opposition can be good for one occasionally,' his fiancée murmured mischievously. In Robert's case Kate doubted it. His face was turkey-red and he seethed with indignation.

'What has Claudia done now?' she inquired. 'Had swords fixed to the wheel-hubs of their ancient Daimler?'

'She's only sold off most of Grandfather's library.'

'I'm sure she was well advised on its value first,' she suggested.

'That isn't the point. There were books there which he'd always meant me to have.'

Marion faced him with her lopsided smile. It entirely changed the severe expression of her straight, leathery face. 'You can still get them, if you discover which dealers they went to.'

That, of course, would mean reaching into his pocket, and Kate was quite certain that

Dr Marion Paige was by now as aware as she that this action was painful to her intended. Kate doubted that their coming marriage would prove entirely comfortable. But certainly interesting. As Marion had herself said, a little opposition can be good for one occasionally.

'What are you grinning at, Kate?' he demanded, scowling.

'I've been enjoying your fiancée's company,' she said, 'and finding we've a lot in common. Contemporaries and all that, you know.'

'Yes.' He considered that a moment. 'Silly, isn't it,' he told Marion. 'Kate's husband was born so much later than Carlton and my father that here she is, my aunt, and I'm actually her senior by six years.'

'Fascinating,' Marion lied. 'Now come and show me round the garden. It must be simply vast.'

'A wilderness.' Robert went off still complaining. 'If they were short of cash why didn't they get rid of a few acres, instead of the books?'

Kate left them to explore together and turned back towards the terrace where Jessica was standing alone by a clematis pillar. It was time, perhaps, to bury the hatchet.

Warily Jess watched her mother approach.

When she was close she darted her a cool glance from under the fringe of flat curls. On near sight they reminded Kate of those little gilt coins Mediterranean girls sew on to their veils: intended, perhaps, to allure. She wondered who among this family party her daughter intended to work on. She hoped it wasn't Old Carlton, with venal motivation?

Had she hopes of a major mention in his will? However much she dazzled him with her vibrant youth and beauty, she'd hardly succeed there, with Claudia standing dragon-guard all the time. Jess would get as short shrift as her cousin Robert had over the books he'd coveted. Kate was realist enough to accept, and forgive, that the young couldn't avoid an occasional view of the elderly as eventual treasure-troves.

'Is Eddie coming?' Jess brusquely demanded, breaking into her mother's thoughts.

'I understood so.'

'Good. I need to see him.'

It was Kate's turn to be spiky. 'He's been perfectly visible for the past few weeks. You could have looked at him then.'

'I know,' she admitted, suddenly almost humble.

Kate was reminded of that later, because the first thing her son asked when he finally arrived, somewhat in a lather after the first gong for dinner had sounded, was almost the same question.

'Is Jess here?' he asked, having dutifully kissed her.

'Very much so,' she said dryly. 'I suppose you suddenly need to see her?'

'Something like that,' he replied; and although it came out lightly, his eyes were deadly serious.

She hadn't stayed long in her daughter's company that afternoon because Jake, divested of his biker gear, had come out in T-shirt and daringly brief Robinson Crusoe denim shorts with frayed edges, to monopolize the girl.

Expensive Wild West-type fringed leather Kate always found amusingly elegant, but ragged grunge had raised her ire ever since Jess's teenage flares threatened her clean carpets with their sweepings from the street. 'I won't have dog crap in with the rest of my washing,' she'd warned her.

Jess hadn't spoken to her for four hours after that, profoundly wounded. Then she'd hand-laundered the offending jeans and thereafter wore them rolled ostentatiously high whenever in the house.

Smiling at the recollection, Kate passed on from the young couple to Carlton, alone for once and stretched out on a rattan lounger, exposing scraggy bare arms to the welcome sunshine.

'How are you, Carlton?' she asked her elderly brother-in-law.

His washed-out blue eyes almost twinkled. 'Do you really require an answer?'

'Yes: I don't waste words. Not many, anyhow.'

'M'm.' He considered how to reply. 'It's a strange thing, this relationship with one's body — like having an old acquaintance yoked on. From habit and with any luck, most of the time you don't notice it's there, then gradually things start to happen to it: small accidents, deficiencies. You begin to feel it's letting you down, being disloyal.'

He waved a hand airily. 'Not that you've ever done much for it yourself. Often the opposite; taken chances and dragged it along. Then, irritably, you have to realize it's fallible. You start to feel some pity for it, a little guilt. Eventually, I suppose, you're relieved to be rid of the damned thing.'

His piping voice, high for a man's, ceased and he smiled dreamily into the distance. 'Though I don't particularly care to have mine done with yet.'

He had almost implied he believed in a separate soul, or at least a personality independent of its physical shell. An avowed agnostic, maybe towards the end he was at least considering an alternative. Teasingly she put the possibility to him.

'The individual's essence? Ah, solve that little puzzle if you will.' He was in a whimsical mood now, pleased with himself and the opportunity to tease back. 'I'm delighted to have stimulated your curiosity about me.'

His puckishness didn't deceive her. She'd read his most recent book of verse, *The Century's Done*, published for the millennium. Had read it, actually, more than once. He'd used the same coy style he affected now, but in fact he was a seeker after truth. What had the twentieth century — his lifetime — been about? Scientific discoveries; extension of earth's physical boundaries; labour — and time-saving devices; but to what end? Perhaps — after the nineteenth's advocacy of Duty and Acquisition, had come the Pursuit of Sensation. Wisely, he'd not settled for summing it up in a single phrase. But the book had left her thinking. 'Solve that little puzzle,' indeed.

'They should have made you Poet Laureate,' she said, and meant it.

'Wrong brand of politics,' he disallowed. 'I don't speak the language of New Labour. They consider me outdated, like landed gentry. But it's interesting, you know, how fast these socialists become what they deride. Remember Wilson, Bevan, Healey, the Old Guard, how, once in power, they couldn't wait to become gentleman farmers. So, deliberately ignorant of the countryside, where will this new lot finally go with their self-congratulatory life peerages?'

His voice was growing slower. Kate touched the fine skin on the back of his hand, smiled and wandered off, leaving the sunshine to claim him. Next time she looked across he was asleep, chin on chest, his wild, white beard shivering with each expelled breath. He tired easily, after rare moments of sweetness and wit.

That evening they toasted his eightieth anniversary at dinner. 'In advance,' he overrode them rather pettishly. 'I didn't make my entrance until almost midnight: not that I've since embraced nocturnal activities.'

Nevertheless he accepted their gift-wrapped offerings at coffee time, and had them set out on a table in the drawing-room. 'If you'll permit me I'll leave opening them until tomorrow morning, when I'll be fresher,' he said. 'It has been a long and exciting day. I thank you all for making the effort to come.' After which he withdrew and Claudia guided him to bed.

Kate had vaguer memories of the evening

after that. There was music because Matthew had prevailed on Robert to bring along his CD player and a variety of disks. When Claudia had returned they joined her for Bridge with Madeleine as fourth. The rest helped themselves to drinks, wandered in and out of the open french windows, smoked on the terrace or strolled in the garden until the last of the light went. Twos and threes formed, re-formed and broke up again. Conversation was desultory and lethargic. Even Marion Paige was trying to hide yawns behind one thin, brown hand.

Kate wondered where she had achieved such a rich tan so early in the season, then decided she had a touch of foreign blood, perhaps Mediterranean. She had seen features like hers when on holiday in Turkey and Greece.

She left her in Eddie's company, discussing some recent show at the Tate Modern. As she said goodnight she could hear Jess laughing with Jake and his father somewhere out in the dark garden. Suddenly missing Michael so badly just then, she knew she wasn't good company, and so withdrew.

Although there were single rooms available, previously servants' quarters on the top floor, Claudia had put her in what had been Michael's big bedroom overlooking the neglected rose garden. It was airy and old-fashioned. On her marriage, twenty-four years earlier, a double bed had been installed and the furniture was still the same as when, on visits, they used to hug and whisper there under the covers, fearful of the ancient springs broadcasting their lovemaking.

Carlton and Claudia now occupied the suite across the landing, which had then been Michael's father's. Matthew, already widowed, shared a home near Ascot with his horse-loving daughter and journalist son. They had seldom visited and never before stayed overnight.

Kate thought about her twins, aged twenty-two and the youngest Dellars, accorded single rooms up under the eaves; and she fervently hoped Jess wouldn't be entertaining Jake there overnight. As Gus's son by his first marriage, Jake wasn't a blood relative, but he struck her as too willingly sucked into the Dellar family culture.

Not that Charles Stone would be anyway preferable as her daughter's partner. At least Jake was of the same generation as Jess and single. So, reflecting gloomily, she slid into sleep, hugging the feather pillow where once Michael's head had lain beside hers.

It was shouting that woke Kate, then a thunderous knocking on her door which instantly burst open. Gus hoarsely cried, 'For God's sake wake up and get out, Kate. The bloody house is on fire!'

She didn't doubt him. Already smoke was billowing into the room. She threw on her travel coat and shoes and grabbed her leather grip; looked wildly round for whatever she could snatch and stuff in. She reached the door, then 'Handbag!' she told herself.

It was somewhere on the floor by the bed but had overturned and spilled out her reading spectacles. She'd be helpless without them. She scrabbled under the rumpled covers, found the specs case, then a couple of loose credit cards. That was all she had time for.

Leaving, she shut the room's door firmly behind her. Contain the fire; cut off oxygen. She knew that from library fire drills. Where were the twins? She ran to the servants' staircase. 'Top floor's cleared,' someone sang out. At the far end of the passage Robert was standing with a hand on the banister rail, waiting to help her down the main stairs. It seemed she'd been the last to wake.

Smoke was rolling up at them through the

square stairwell, and as she hesitated it was shot through with flame. 'For God's sake, woman, move!'

But it was too late. They were cut off. 'The kitchen roof,' she shouted. 'We can get through a back window . . . '

'Kitchen's gone,' he yelled back.

'The front porch then.' She started running in that direction. The smoke was less dense there and it might offer a way down.

As they threw themselves through the doorway of the upstairs library, she heard flames roaring behind them, leaping up to where Robert had stood waiting. One of the library's two high windows already gaped open. As they fled past the other she noticed bare shelves on two sides of the room. Claudia must have sold Carlton's books by the yard rather than the title.

Robert was leaning out over the pediment to the front porch. 'It's about a fourteen foot drop to the flat bit once you're over the sill. Then hang on till someone brings a ladder. You first, Kate.'

Looking down scared her, but fire was the immediate hazard. She dragged on the heavy brocade curtain beside her and the old fabric tore, coming away in her hands. She threw a great bundle of it out, then got her legs over the sill and jumped after it. The fall still jolted her and she rolled, barely able to grab at the edge. On the terrace below people were milling about in panic. Then Robert called down and someone waved back. 'Stay there! I'll get help.'

In the distance Kate heard the *hooh-hah* of a fire tender. Then Robert crash-landed somewhere behind and fell against her shoulder, nearly sending her off the edge. He was swearing between gritted teeth. 'I think I've broken my fucking ankle.'

She managed to climb down a ladder brought from the garage, buttoning her coat and wishing she'd gone to bed in her knickers. Robert was less lucky and could not manage the ladder with his ankle, having to stay crouched up there, with the flames breaking through behind, until a hydraulic platform arrived with a fireman to cart him off like a sack of potatoes.

She abandoned him to Madeleine who was sure he'd only a sprain, and set off through the mêlée to look for Carlton. He'd seemed so frail last night and she feared what the shock might do to him. Not one for nocturnal activities, he'd said.

It was then she came on him guarded by Claudia behind a rhododendron hedge, gazing up and burbling about the sky.

Recall of what happened beyond that point

would have been to re-live sheer nightmare. Mercifully Kate was asleep before reaching it.

★ ★ ★

At the Monkey Puzzle she slept until almost noon when Lily looked in to say a policeman was below, wanting to speak with her.

'It's a Detective-Sergeant Beaumont. He said he met you last night.'

'Did he?' It must be the one alongside the WPC who drove her to the hospital. *Hospital!* The nausea suddenly returned. 'Is there any news? Of Jess and Eddie?'

Lily couldn't say. She helped Kate find a few clothes to put on. It was DS Beaumont who told her that Eddie had been awake and was removed from Intensive Care to a side ward. There was nothing new on her daughter.

Kate had guessed right about the policeman. He was the wooden, puppet-faced one who hadn't spoken except to order the siren silenced. He wasn't all that conversational now, uncomfortable about distressing her with questions. She explained she'd gone up quite early, leaving the others downstairs. She'd assumed her children had been given single rooms under the eaves, while she'd been on the floor below.

But could any of the young people have shared rooms? he wanted to know.

'Why ask me?' she retorted, hearing — and shamed by — the barb in her own voice. 'As their mother I'd be the last one they'd have discussed it with.' And no, she'd not glimpsed them later in a corridor. She really wanted to help but he must question someone else.

'When I retired there were several of the family still downstairs: our hostess; my brother-in-law Sir Matthew; my nephew and niece, Robert and Madeleine; Dr Marion Paige; Maddie's husband Gus and his son Jake, as well as my two. You need to ask who saw them after the fire alarm was given.'

Then DS Beaumont explained how Gus had tried to stop Eddie entering the kitchen, but he'd broken free and rushed in, saying something about the cellar. Almost immediately an explosion had blown Gus off his feet. He'd feared Eddie was killed, but by some miracle he'd reached the cellar and escaped by the old coal chute, despite his injuries. But nobody had seen Jess since all the young people went up to bed at about midnight. Her brother and Jake Railton had left her at her door.

'Was her bed slept in?'

'Young Railton flung on some clothes and looked in on your daughter. She'd already

46

left. Her bedclothes were rumpled and her wardrobe door left open.'

'So there's no reason why she shouldn't have gone outside to where the others were assembling?'

He waited for her to take it all in and go one further.

'Jess — my daughter — can be very impulsive, sergeant. Unpredictable. It's not beyond belief that she simply walked out on the situation. I mean, just got in her car and drove off.'

'Except that, like yourself, she arrived in a cab, and the other cars are accounted for. Would you care to say why both of you, as drivers, chose to turn up by taxi?'

So Kate explained how fussy Claudia was about cluttering the driveway. At the rear there was only the old coach-house, where they kept their ancient Daimler, and very limited hard standing for parking space. Even in dry weather the grass was out of bounds.

'There was a motor cycle,' she suddenly recalled. 'I wouldn't put it past Jess to . . . '

'That was Jake Railton's. He later rode it to the hotel where they're all staying. It's still there.' DS Beaumont recrossed his legs and treated her to a prolonged stare. 'The others expressed some surprise that you chose not to join them there after visiting your son.'

47

'I'd meant to phone and explain. Somehow, with all that happened, I forgot.'

That didn't appear to satisfy the man. His stare continued.

'Look,' she said, 'they can be a very daunting bunch. I couldn't face them just then. So much had gone wrong. Overnight my brother-in-law had lost his home and everything in it. I could have lost — both my children.'

He seemed to understand then and closed the questioning. She saw him to the pub's door, where he turned up his jacket collar against a sudden downpour of rain. 'Too late,' he commented. 'We could have done with this on the blaze. Try not to worry, Mrs Dellar. Your daughter's not answering her mobile phone, but you may find she's at home before you are.'

But Jess didn't live at home any more. It was five months since she moved out. He could thank the family for being behind on that item of news. Kate had chosen not to relay the fact that, after dropping out of university, Jess was living like a water gypsy on a canal boat near Denham.

Kate nodded grimly. And that, of course, was where she must go now to catch up with her, after checking on Eddie.

4

The detective sergeant left, no further forward. He had offered no suggestions on how the fire started or spread so rapidly. While Kate waited for the taxi service to answer her call she tried to clear her memory of Claudia's stoic acceptance of their disaster; and of how she'd recently sold off so much of the valuable library. In a dark corner of her mind there remained a chilling suspicion. Could she believe Claudia had actually planned the fire and was ultimately responsible for Eddie's injuries?

Duncan Crick made Kate cancel the cab she'd just ordered, insisting on driving her to the hospital. He apologized for the state of the car's interior. They had only the one for pub and private use, so there were wooden boxes and cartons of food and drink in the rear, roughly covered by a plastic sheet.

After the sudden shower a brisk wind had scattered the clouds to reveal a beautiful afternoon, but she was chilled through and glad of her coat on which Lily had attempted to smother the stench of smoke with a generous spray of cheap perfume.

49

She dreaded what the doctors might tell her when she arrived; but it seemed that the news was good — at least to their minds.

In the tropical atmosphere of a side ward Eddie lay almost flat under a single sheet, his chest bare and sporting a line of hideous dark stitches like a beginner's first efforts on a leathercraft course. A square of padded gauze was taped to one side of his head and his eyes looked weirdly absent. She guessed this was due to painkillers.

They hardly talked at all and, after the bleak smile he gave as she walked in, his mood was sombre and unfocused. She couldn't be sure he knew that his sister was unaccounted for, so she didn't dare mention her. She stayed only twelve minutes before Crick drove her to Chorleywood to pick up her own car.

There was no sign of anyone having visited the house. She threw the post — mostly junk mail — on the kitchen counter, checked that the only message on her answerphone was from the decorator due next week to repaint her spare bedroom, and drove out to Denham. She parked as near as she could to the narrowboat. The grassed track that led to the towpath was slippery after the rain and rutted by bike tracks. She avoided the puddles as best she could and stepped up on the metal box that formed the doorstep. The padlock was missing from the small double doors in the barge's centre. Hopefully she rapped and called Jess's name. There was no answer, so she pulled the doors open and climbed through.

It was dark inside, all the curtains having been left closed. 'Jess,' she called again, 'it's Mother.'

The three steps down inside were wide and shallow, giving directly on to the galley. As her eyes became accustomed to the gloom she could make out a clutter of dishes in the sink. When she moved forward her shoes crunched on broken china.

She reached for the light switch and nothing happened. Either the bulbs had all failed or the generator wasn't working. So, turning left, she picked her way over an assortment of obstacles to the main room and drew back the curtains. Then she saw. It wasn't slovenly housekeeping. The place had been trashed.

Jess had neighbours moored to either side, separated by half the narrowboat's length to allow for pulling away into the mainstream. To get here Kate had passed an odd, home-made looking craft not unlike a Noah's Ark in shape. A trickle of smoke had been issuing from its stovepipe chimney and she'd caught the scent of burning logs. Now she went back and knocked on the door.

'Be with yuh,' a hoarse voice offered, so she waited. There was a deal of clumping and banging before the door swung outwards only just missing her face. The man staring up at her was like a garden gnome, red-faced and puffing round a blackened pipe clamped in the centre of tea-stained greying whiskers.

'Ah,' he greeted her. 'You 'er Ma, ain't yuh? You'll be looking for our Jess. Well, she's away. And just as well she is, so there! There's been some nasty folk around 'ere last day or so. Come in.'

It was kindly meant. He moved aside to make room while she climbed over the door's ledge. Then she saw he was missing the lower half of one arm.

The boat had only one room as far as she could see. A half partition cut off the tiny galley, and she guessed the plastic curtain, figuring gulls, curlews and cormorants on an electric blue background, would hide the heads and shower. For a bed there was a low divan under the open square window on the water side. Opposite it was a small gate-leg table with two stacking chairs slotted together. Everything was neat and clean. 'You must have been a sailor,' Kate couldn't help saying.

'Was a *hable* seaman once,' he boasted jokily. 'Til I got me arm blown orf. Still, better luck than some of me mates.' His ruddy face creased into a grin and he suddenly thought to remove the pipe, which she saw now was empty. 'Well, sit down ma'am, do. You'll 'ave a cuppa, won't yuh? Kettle's on.'

It was starting to sing, on top of a grill-fronted stove from which the wonderful scent of burning wood issued. She sank on to the divan to which he'd waved her. 'I'm a little worried about my daughter,' she confessed. 'Have you seen her around at all lately?'

'Las' Satdy,' he said promptly. 'She said she 'ad a job to do up north, and she left me 'er key like she allus does.'

'I shan't need to borrow it,' Kate said grimly, 'since somebody's broken in. The place is a mess.'

He nodded, his kindly eyes serious. ''Appened las' night. If I'd bin 'ere I'da seen them off. Kids, like as not. I went to water 'er pot plants s'morning and gotta shock. Thort I'd better leave it all that way 'til she'd seen it.'

'I saw her yesterday,' Kate began, and realized she didn't want to admit Jess was missing. The possibilities were too appalling.

Then suddenly she found she was sobbing and the old chap was leaving her to it while he warmed the teapot and spooned in the tea.

'I'm so sorry,' she said eventually.

'Why don't yuh tell old Marty all about it?' he suggested, balancing a large mug beside her on the divan.

'I will,' she told him. 'Only I think I ought to let the police know about the boat as soon as possible. You see, she — there's more besides. Do you know if there's a phone box anywhere near?'

He sat and stared, seeming to be debating something in his mind. Then he got up and lurched to the rear of the boat, to come back, miraculously, with a mobile phone in his hand. 'This do?'

She plunged her hands in her pockets. The detective had given her a card with his number. She hadn't expected to use it, but it was there. Why do they print the important things so small? Small isn't beautiful for anyone over forty-five. She'd need her reading glasses.

It was a woman who answered the call. 'Regional Crime,' she said, and gave a Polish-sounding name.

Kate asked for Sergeant Beaumont and explained who she was. 'It concerns the fire last night at Larchmoor Place.'

54

It seemed that the other sergeant was busy elsewhere, but the one speaking was his partner, and she offered to help. So Kate explained where she was and why.

'I'll be with you in twenty-five minutes,' the woman detective promised. 'Meanwhile, don't touch anything.'

'Good,' said the old sailor. 'Now drink your tea.' He slid a plate with a buttered scone on it alongside the mug. 'Afraid I don't do jam. Last year was bad for wild raazbries.'

Kate drank the tea. So much kindliness helped. And she'd liked the sound of the young woman detective. It was the 'five' after the 'twenty' that gave her confidence. Such precision. And it must mean she knew the district, how long it would take to park and walk along here.

Kate and Marty talked, and she forgot to check by her watch if the policewoman's estimate was exact. She told him about the family party and the fire. He spoke of his life at sea and in port, only ended by 'a bit in the Falklands'. The fire on his ship, made nothing of, must have made last night's outbreak seem small beer. But then, he didn't know about Jess. Or Eddie.

He heard the woman's approach before she did. 'Your copper's here,' he announced, and opened the door before she could knock.

Fortunately she handed Kate her card and pronounced the name clearly. Zyczynski. Well, she'd be used to explaining herself.

Kate took in her appearance before she seated herself alongside on the divan. She was of medium height, in her middle to late twenties, slim and erect, pretty, with dark brown hair worn in a close cap of curls. Her voice was low, with warmth in it, not in the least foreign. 'I've asked one of our civilian experts to take a look at your daughter's boat,' she told Kate. 'It may be some local juveniles who broke in, but it's as well to make sure. Did you see any graffiti? Urination? Deliberate spillage from kitchen cupboards?'

Kate wasn't sure, but then she'd not examined the boat closely. 'Marty — her neighbour here — may be able to tell you more.'

'Yes, thanks. I was just coming to him.'

Her questions were as precise and pointed as they had been to Kate. While she felt some confidence in having her there, Kate hadn't missed the fact the fact that evidence of hooliganism — which Marty too denied noticing, apart from the emptied cupboards and broken china — would have set her mind more at ease. It began to sound as if the break-in had been something other than teenage vandalism. More, perhaps, like a deliberate search. Which seemed frighteningly personal.

Sergeant Zyczynski went outside to use her phone and came back to announce that a forensic examiner was already on his way. She felt she must remain on the spot until he arrived. 'In case of further interference, since the boat is left open,' she explained.

Marty plunged head and shoulders into a cupboard built under the galley sink. He emerged with a small toolbox tucked under his truncated arm. 'Ere, take it,' he told her.

While she held it he clicked it open and with his left hand produced a padlock with two linked keys attached. 'That'ny good? The lady 'ere can take charge of it, then you can be on yer way, girl. Got better things to do with yer time than 'ang about 'ere on the off-chance, eh? I'll see she comes to no 'arm.'

The sergeant smiled, showing splendid white teeth. 'Let's fix it then.' They went out together and their voices faded along the towpath.

Left alone, Kate felt reluctant to leave the rough comfort Marty had offered, although by now matters here were out of her hands. Shakily she reached for the teapot and refilled her cup. The universal panacea, she thought bitterly. But what else was there?

57

Well, there was the family. The alien Dellars. They were all assembled and expecting her to return to Greythorpe Hotel. She assumed her overnight bag was there too, since she'd bundled it into the minibus along with Carlton's tartan rug. As soon as the man arrived to examine Jess's boat she would have to move on, pick things up from where she'd left them. Visit the hospital again. And the burnt-out house.

Then face them at the hotel.

The Dellars were expecting her, patently avoiding bothersome questions. They talked all through dinner, cleverly, some of them. But really said nothing.

At first, with an effort, Kate tried pretending things were normal, this no more than another challenge by the family to pull herself up to their level. She even offered the story of the small girl returning her library book who'd demanded, 'I want some four-letter words now. I've done all the three-letter ones.'

The corners of Madeleine's mouth had twitched. Robert snorted. Matthew, all donnish and pettish, had complained that libraries had mostly given up on books. 'Cluttered up with all these wretched computers. God knows what *research* such people are doing, coming in off the street.'

'We get some unlikely-looking people,' Kate admitted, 'but at least they show interest. Some are really IT literate.'

'Getting their fix of porn,' Jake suggested, grinning. 'Little old men in dirty raincoats. Kids wary of leaving evidence on their own computers at home.'

'Some, but they're not usually like that,' she defended. 'And we've an automatic cut-off system which diverts them to children's programmes. You get to recognize the frustration. Some furtive hulk, usually a man, complains he keeps getting the Teletubbies.'

Claudia made a sharp grunt of disapproval.

'That sometimes happens to innocents too,' Kate rushed on. 'We had a middle-aged couple who were keen gardeners. They'd been looking up Fuchsias, but they dropped a typo in.'

She'd thought it mildly funny, but it sank without a ripple. Perhaps they didn't understand, restricted to a *nice* vocabulary, even to be poisonous with.

Having tried, she gave up and subsided into silence. The talk went on as though her unconsidered efforts had never interrupted more weighty matters. All talking; none listening.

Blankly she watched their faces, inventing

inner conversations at variance with their words. Gus, choosing a peach, stroked its downy buttocks, smiling dreamily. His mind spoke through his fingers.

Claudia's great, mourner's eyes surveyed them eating, still her guests although transported to alien territory. 'The venison was from Chalberry's,' she announced, and behind the words were calculations of cost and a warning they shouldn't stay on too long running up bills she might be expected to pay.

Matthew, his womanish lips drawn tight like purse strings, ceased bemoaning the lowering standards of the public examination system and turned his attention to a bunch of white grapes which looked suitably sour.

Kate rebuked herself for lack of mental charity, sighed, resolved to abandon her own apartness. Let it all happen. What did it matter what any of them thought of her; how disagreeable as a group she found them? Even as a diversion from present worries they had failed her. She laid her dessert knife tidily alongside the discarded core and peel of her apple, leaning back to allow their words to stream past, meaningless and unaffecting.

The room they'd been given to dine in was small and claustrophobic. Despite the partly opened window there was no air. Outside, the dusk had a sense of heavy permanence. She felt herself drifting, had to reach out for something to hang on to, and there were only voices rolling over her, snatches of words from one side or the other, unrelated like dream sequences.

' . . . so he resigned, of course. Nothing else he could . . . '

'And then I told him straight, it just won't . . . '

' . . . unless they offered me a more serious bonus. So . . . '

'But then, the fellow was a queer.'

' . . . whether Coriolanus had intended it or not.' This in Carlton's high-pitched bleet.

' . . . hit oil and skidded across my path, the sod.'

'I'm not sure that they do.'

That last was Eddie, cautious, doubtful.

No, how could it be? Eddie wasn't here. She'd drifted off, imagined his voice. Starting awake, she looked around at the others. No one had noticed her momentary absence; why should they? — each so self-sufficient, so insulated.

Across the table someone leaned towards her. 'Kate? Kate, are you all right?'

The face thrust at her was out of focus for a second, then settled into Marion Paige's straight, leathery features. Ah, the other outsider.

'Oh, fine,' she managed to get out. 'Just that it's rather stuffy, don't you think?'

'So we'll get out of here. Come along.'

As Marion rose, Gus, next to Kate, came suddenly aware of her need, pushed back his own chair and reached for hers. She steadied herself against its back as she stood, then lurched forward towards the door. Marion met her there, put a firm hand under her elbow and steered her out. They reached the hotel's garden exit and Kate drew a long, cooler breath.

'Thank you,' she said, like a polite child. 'Of course, you're a doctor.'

'Not a medical one. My subject's Geophysics.'

An academic, like the others. An achiever. So maybe not an outsider at all. Just a newcomer, tailor-made to become one of them. 'As a librarian,' Kate said, 'I rank with them alongside a supermarket stacker.' A sour little smile tugged at her mouth. 'Not that I'd have balked at that if it allowed me to stay solvent.'

'You were a historian. Robert told me.'

'To make me sound respectable. I didn't get far with it. A second-year dropout.' Kate had no idea why she bothered to explain herself. Perhaps because just then the other woman seemed the only living thing on the planet.

But she wasn't prepared to reveal more. That was sacred ground. At the time it had been her only choice. They'd been so much in love, and somebody had had to make the money for them to live on. Michael had gone on to get a First Class in Mods, then his doctorate, while she typed for a solicitor and mugged up at night for her library exams.

It stayed a necessary source of income in his early years as a lecturer at King's College London, ending only at the birth of the twins. There had been no help from his family because they disapproved of the alliance, and her own widowed mother was dead by then.

'How about turning in now? You must be exhausted,' Marion suggested.

'I need first to ring the hospital.'

'There's a phone by Reception. Take a seat there while I get the number.'

'It's here.' Kate pulled a slip of paper from her jeans' pocket. (Lily Crick's jeans, she was reminded by their unaccustomed, baggy feel.)

Marion got through to the ward Sister. 'Mrs Dellar for you,' she said and handed the receiver across.

The voice on the other end had lost a little of its cool. 'We've been trying to contact you all afternoon,' she said. 'I'm afraid your son is — has had a relapse. He's in surgery at the moment. Would you like to come in?'

'Surgery? But they've already operated. He . . . '

'That was to save his lung, Mrs Dellar. It appears there's an aneurism. I can't tell you more at the moment. Perhaps you should have a word later with Mr O'Keefe, the neurosurgeon.'

'I'll come at once.' Kate laid down the phone. She was barely aware of the other woman beside her. 'What did you say?'

'I'll drive you.'

'I have to go in. They're operating again. The head injury, I think.'

Marion nodded. 'Yes, I heard.' Neurosurgery. It sounded critical; could be final.

★   ★   ★

As the family moved from table to downstairs lounge Robert paused by the landing window. He saw the two women running out from the hotel doorway. 'Now what?' he demanded. 'I really don't see why Kate must drag Marion into her affairs. It's been a strange enough introduction to us, what with the fire on her first night and then bivouacking here.'

'You can't blame Kate for being nervy,'

64

Madeleine reprimanded. 'Her son injured and that madcap girl gone off heaven knows where.'

'Or with whom.' He lingered to light the cigar which Claudia's dominant presence had prevented until then. 'She was always a law unto herself, that child.'

He watched the silver Nissan reverse rapidly and make for the main road. 'It looks as if the same baleful influence is working on Marion now. She's gone off without a word. It really is rude of Kate.' His tone was petulant.

Madeleine watched her brother puff at the cigar, then pluck with the free hand at his upper lip, making the little beak she remembered from earliest childhood. Then it had been as prelude to a crying fit when she'd deprived him of a toy or sneaked some titbit from his plate, safe in the knowledge that as younger pet she'd be free of nanny's chiding.

She guessed that he was put out because, in place of easy access to his fiancée, last night he'd been obliged to share a twin room with his father. And she herself was the one to double up with Marion; Gus and Jake being accommodated on settees in the lounge.

'Tomorrow, first thing,' Robert threatened dourly, 'we'll be on our way. I shan't forget

Uncle Carlton's eightieth for a very long time.'

The birthday boy himself was displaying unaccustomed obtuseness, demanding that after decaffeinated coffee they should all drive over to Larchmoor Place and survey the remains. Claudia found that for once her veto was to be overthrown.

'It will only distress you,' she insisted. 'And if you'd wanted, you could have gone in daylight. By the time we get there it will be dusk and quite unsafe to go walking around among all the debris. I can't imagine why you should want to feast your eyes on the ruins of our home.'

'I want to see how much is left,' he declared. 'That is the positive approach. It isn't enough to accept what we are told by strangers.'

'Loss adjusters and fire damage examiners,' she insisted, 'are professionals, of a kind. We must leave it to them, Carlton. They should know what they are about.'

'Claudia acknowledging a higher authority,' Jake whispered, nudging his father. 'How's that for a first?'

But Carlton was already demanding transport and for once the outcome wasn't in doubt. The hotel's courtesy coach was pressed into service. In their assorted loaned or rescued garb, all climbed aboard with the exception of Jake, who sped ahead on his Kawasaki. Unsurprisingly his matching leathers had survived the previous night's calamity.

He met them as they rounded the curve of the driveway, grinning as they became shockingly aware of the activity ahead. There were dark figures moving under an erection of arc lights. A crane had been driven over the desecrated lawn and a mechanical digger was parked by a rear corner of the collapsed building.

'You can't go any farther,' Jake told them as they prepared to alight. 'There's police tape everywhere. I said we were the owners but they warned me off. A Crime Scene, forsooth.'

'Crime?' Claudia questioned. 'What utter nonsense.'

The air was foul with the acrid smell of wet ash and an added unpleasantness of diesel exhaust. A man came towards them, lifting the blue and white plastic tape to pass under. His eyes sought out Carlton's bent form supported on Claudia's arm. 'I'm sorry, sir, but I must ask you to stay away at present. The site is unsafe. We are merely carrying out instructions. If there is any possibly that a . . . a missing person — ' (he skirted the word *body*) — 'is still inside, we have to preserve the scene.'

'Who's missing?' Claudia demanded. 'You can't mean Kate's girl. She's simply gone off somewhere. It's the sort of thing she does. Her mother was sure of it.'

'Desperately hoped,' old Carlton murmured.

'And what do they mean by a *crime scene?*' Claudia pressed the man. 'The fire was an accident. Everything points to it.'

'I'm not authorized to answer questions,' the man said. He turned away, moved off a few paces, then swivelled to watch them as they hesitated before dispersing.

'Look,' Gus said, pointing, 'the old coach-house is still there.'

At a distance of some hundred yards from the house, it had survived with only the loss of the roof and blackened beams. Inside they could just make out the dark hulk of the Daimler covered by sooty debris but possibly intact.

It was the only reassurance they could take away with them. They moved off, still protesting about officialdom, still unwilling to accept any need for the further depredation of the house's remains.

'What they haven't already ruined with water they'll hack up with their little hatchets,' Matthew accused, as though they might be wilful children.

Back at the hotel no one felt settled enough for bed. Carlton protested quite firmly when Claudia attempted to shuffle him off upstairs. 'I prefer to stay down here until the other two return. Marion is a guest, and Kate needs our support at this time.' He closed his eyes, indicating that the subject was closed.

'Whatever the outcome,' he added sombrely.

They ordered drinks. The hotel duty manager provided playing cards and a set of Monopoly. They sorted themselves into two groups and grimly applied themselves to play.

At twenty minutes past midnight a car drew up outside. Robert sprang up and went to remonstrate with his intended. They came back without Kate. 'It's bad news,' Marion said shortly. 'Eddie's had brain surgery. He's in a coma.'

'Where's Kate now?' Carlton quavered.

'She's picked her car up and gone home.'

'Just as well,' said Claudia. 'There wouldn't be room for her here.'

5

Superintendent Mike Yeadings, immersed in a welter of paperwork required asap by Crown Prosecution for an aggravated burglary which included rape and GBH, had barely raised his head to glance at the early reports coming in of the fire at Larchmoor Place. It was later, shrugging on his jacket prior to going home from a Saturday sacrificed to Thames Valley matters, that he paused to take a second look at printouts of statements taken from family members who had been rescued during the night. He rang through to the inspector dealing with the event.

'George,' he said, 'has this missing young woman turned up after your local fire?'

'There's nothing in yet on that, sir. It's the family's general opinion she simply got out and ran off. They're trying her mobile phone but it must be turned off. You expecting this'll turn into a Misper? She's not a juvenile, sir. Twenty-two years of age, with a bit of a fly-away reputation by all accounts.'

'Is that the parents' opinion?'

'There's only a mother, sir. Name of Kate Dellar. She's in a bit of a tizzy because her son's been injured. We haven't had a good chance yet to find out more from her.'

'Best make that a priority. And keep me posted. From what's been passed to me the whole thing sounds a bit dodgy.'

'Will do, sir.' He dropped the phone. 'Old Yeadings is sniffing for a new case for Major Crimes,' he complained to the duty sergeant as he passed through. 'I bet my new boots he gets on to the Fire Chief himself, over my head.'

Better make sure, Yeadings thought. I'll drop in on the scene on my way home. Someone will be there, looking over the remains.

He wasn't disappointed. Fire Officer Barclay was on site accompanied by a familiar squat figure Yeadings knew from the past. So it appeared Special Branch had got the same whiff off it as himself.

Now that the fire's physical stench reached his nostrils as well he felt sure that this scene of desolation was more than a family misfortune. There were too many oddities involved.

His main unease was confirmed by Percival's first words. 'Ah, Superintendent, I thought Sir Matthew Dellar's name might set your antennae aquiver. It seems he didn't often visit his brother, and this was a special family get-together.'

Yeadings greeted the two men before agreeing. 'The Judge hasn't been retired very long. There are some villains due out about now who once felt they'd a score to settle. He'd be a sight more vulnerable here than at his place at Ascot.'

He turned to Barclay. 'I'll be interested to hear what your Investigators turn up. How soon will they be tackling it?'

'Tomorrow, from daybreak. We could work with lights now but it needs to cool. There's nothing to gain from digging through the night.'

'Even with someone missing?'

The Station Officer thrust his hands deep in his pockets and kicked at a scrap of burnt-out fabric on the grass. 'If the poor lass was in there, another ten hours'll make no difference. I have to protect my men. Anyone under there, White Watch'll find 'em tomorrow.'

'Let's hope there isn't, then,' Yeadings said fervently. 'What are the chances it wasn't arson?'

'We'll know when we've identified the accelerant. It still just might be accidental. You'd be amazed the stuff people store under their own roofs with never a thought. It was an old couple lived here. They may have overlooked the usual precautions.

'Well, gents, I'm off if there's nothing more I can do for you. There's a lookout posted just in case. Not that there's owt left for anyone to make off with.'

Yeadings watched the tall, lean fireman pick a way back to his car. 'Have you eaten?' he asked the Special Branch man. 'I thought we might drop in at the Monkey Puzzle and eavesdrop on what the locals are making of it.'

In for a penny in for a pound, he thought. I've blown my Saturday anyway. Might as well see the rest of it out and glean some current gossip from another branch of the force.

★　★　★

He let himself quietly into the house at a few minutes before midnight. Nan Yeadings came out on the landing in her nightdress to meet her husband.

'Well, well,' she breathed in a low voice so as not to wake the children, both of whose bedroom doors stood open. 'Nice that you remembered where your home is — eventually. I feared you'd started week-ending away.'

Mike Yeadings looked stricken. 'Didn't Zyczynski phone you?'

'Of course she did, love. I just fancied seeing how it felt — the rolling-pin welcome.' Her next words were lost in his bear hug.

'Whassat?' He sounded weary, pushing his hair off his forehead..

'I asked if you'd eaten. There's some chicken korma in the freezer I could microwave. And Sally shelled some early peas specially for you.'

'Thanks, but I had to take a visitor to supper.'

Nan recognized the tone. 'An unwelcome one? Who's being investigated?'

'It's nothing disciplinary, thank God.' He hesitated, but Nan was the soul of discretion, so he admitted, 'Special Branch.'

'So what are they hunting on your patch?'

'It may be nothing, but it seems they've an interest in last night's fire at Larchmoor Place. Or in someone who'd been staying there. They're pressing the investigation of origin and cause. Station Officer Barclay has already dropped a hint there'd been acceler-ant used.'

'Larchmoor Place. Who lives there?'

'It's a case of who used to live there. The house is destroyed.' Yeadings emptied his pockets on to the bedside table and started stripping off his suit, allowing Nan to insert the hanger.

'It's the same family who've owned it for generations, reduced now to an elderly couple and their unmarried daughter. Name of Dellar.'

'Not Carlton Dellar, the poet? I heard he lived somewhere round here. There was an article on him in the *Bucks Advertiser* a couple of weeks back.'

Yeadings, bending to deal with his socks, straightened. He must have missed that issue. Normally he followed the local news with interest, as indication of the social temperatures that nourished crime. From tiny acorns did mighty oak trees grow. Thames Valley police covered the three counties of Berks, Bucks and Oxfordshire. His special interest covered the whole area.

'Nan, did the article give any hint of where the house might be?'

'It must have done, because I realized it was only a few miles away, although I didn't locate it specifically. Are you thinking it put burglarious ideas into someone's head? I thought poets were notoriously poor?'

Yeadings sketched a balancing movement with his hands. 'Everybody has something more than somebody else. But it seems the old chap had organized a family get-together for the weekend. Among the guests was his brother Sir Matthew Dellar, less publicized

75

than Carlton, but once one of the most successful, and therefore most scum-threatened, of this country's senior prosecutors; and subsequently a Queen's Bencher. As a QC and a High Court judge he sent down some pretty vicious people. We've had to provide security for him on a couple of occasions.'

'Was he hurt in the fire?'

'He wasn't, but his nephew's in a serious condition in Wycombe hospital. There's also some doubt about the young man's sister. She'd been given a room, and it seems she slept at least part of the night there, but she wasn't counted out with the others.

'Uniformed police have spoken to the family. Their general opinion is that the girl left in the early hours. But she hadn't her own wheels. So either she went on foot or someone came to pick her up.'

'Or else,' Nan supposed slowly, 'she stayed on and was overcome by the fire. That's what's worrying you. Isn't it?'

'It looks as though that could have happened. As soon as the ground temperature's dropped we'll send a dog-handler over to the site.'

Sobering thought. Nan watched her husband's taut face as he ambled towards the bathroom. He was weary, right enough. It had been a week of long hours, with a hoax terrorist warning for Windsor Castle and a violent racial attack in Reading, but she detected a new unease in him; one he shouldn't go to sleep on if she could prevent it.

'We were thinking,' she murmured innocently when he returned, 'of taking a picnic lunch to Chiltern Open Air Museum tomorrow. But if you're tied up with this missing girl . . . '

Mike grunted. 'Don't see why I shouldn't join you. One of my sergeants can cover it. Whichever has a taste for Sunday overtime. And on Monday DI Salmon will be back from leave, cracking the whip over them.'

With that care sloughed off, Yeadings reached for his pyjamas. Having buttoned the top and with the trousers in one hand he turned sheepishly to Nan. 'D'you know, I think I will take up that microwave offer. Percival had to drive on to Fishguard, so we ate at six-thirty. There's been time since to produce a rumbling void.'

'Right,' she said. 'I'll bring up a tray. Only, heaven help you if you're snoring when I get back.'

★   ★   ★

On Sunday it was Sergeant Rosemary Zyczynski who drew the short straw, but she welcomed the excuse to cancel a previous engagement. Her only surviving blood relative, the aunt who'd been her guardian from the age of ten, had invited a number of friends for Sunday lunch to mark the forty-fifth anniversary of her marriage. The company would be almost uniformly elderly and feminine, gossipy and inquisitive. Rosemary's career choice and her unmarried state would be laboriously commented on, loudly, within her hearing. The few men present would be one-time cronies of her uncle and embarrassed by his unresponsive state since the most recent of three debilitating strokes.

With a shade of guilt, she admitted to herself that the prospect of a more lively hare to chase raised her spirits considerably. The Boss had phoned the previous evening to announce Special Branch's interest in the case and she was happy to hang around while Fire Officer Barclay and a senior man from High Wycombe oversaw sample-recovery. She wandered into the plastic tent erected to house exhibits recovered from the fire scene for initial examination. A civilian forensic scientist representing the police interest was also present, but the insurance company's loss adjuster had already left after a fleeting visit to what he'd described as a god-awful mess.

Flat boards balanced on decorators' trestles had been set up and covered in sheets of clean newsprint. On them a fire investigation officer was developing an indexing system for samples of debris as each layer was exposed. To Zyczynski's unpractised eye there was little to distinguish one blackened chunk of material from another, but those bending over them were warming to the task. Under their instruction she was willingly pressed into donning latex gloves and bagging exhibits as labelled.

At a few minutes before midday a dark van appeared and a trolley was wheeled close to the excavation. It was still another half hour before the body could be lifted on, lightly covered with green plastic sheeting. The more usual mortuary bag was unsuitable due to the fragile state of the charred flesh.

The Coroner's Officer informed Zyczynski that Professor Littlejohn was week-ending in North Wales, but he had been in touch with the pathologist by telephone. A post-mortem examination was already fixed for 10am next morning.

'I'll let the Boss know,' she told him. 'I'll be attending, but he may want to look in too.' She turned to the Fire Chief. 'Is there any hope of a fire report to read along with the Prof's findings?'

'How can you doubt it?' His sarcasm wasn't wasted on her. He cast his eyes upwards on the lookout for aircraft. 'Trouble with these pigs is you must duck when they're flying over,' he said drily. 'No. It'll take Divisional experts a day or two. But one thing I can tell you, off the record.'

He looked across to fresh plastic screens being set up. 'We're fixing a roof over where we brought the body out. That's certainly the location where the fire first started.'

He sucked in his cheeks and added a cautious proviso. '*One* of the places it started, anyway.'

'Thanks. The Boss'll want to know. We'll keep that under our hats till it's official.'

She supposed she should go back and check on Mrs Dellar and give what comfort she could, but there was no answer when she phoned the house at Chorleywood. A second call, to the Greythorpe Hotel, confirmed that she wasn't there either. So perhaps she was lying low at the Monkey Puzzle pub, among friends. Best let it ride until tomorrow. The last thing the woman needed was to have police bothering her in her grief. Time enough when they'd identified the body.

With the departure of the mortuary van, Z

had a word with the constable left on duty and phoned base explaining she could be reached at home, where she'd be writing up her report. Then, thankful that she had avoided Aunt Alice's tea party, she turned the car towards Ashbourne House.

The move into her apartment there was recent enough to bring a comfortable glow at the prospect of relaxing over a chilled jug of crushed lemon, and mooching around in a state of undress with the windows open to a cooling breeze off the river. The early morning's haze had turned by noon into a cloudless heat that built by the hour, making her grateful she'd exchanged city streets for open fields.

Circling the house, she saw a green sports model parked by the open door to her garage, so Max was here. He wasn't in her flat, which meant he'd be downstairs with Beattie, catching up with gossip on the other residents.

Two of the seven flats were for resale since the double murder[1] in the house the previous winter. Potential buyers had visited and been put off by the crime's bad odour. Other visitors with a taste for scandal had for a while been attracted by the notoriety, roamed

---

[1] A Meeting of Minds.

the rooms and gazed their morbid fill before going off furnished with a gloating subject for social chat. But by now even that interest had waned.

Only the ground floor flat opposite Beattie's had received a second visit and an offer from a bank manager impressed by the exceptional security arrangements. Z had grown accustomed to the apartment opposite her own remaining empty. Until now the suicide jump from its balcony had out-weighed the low price which the estate agent had twice felt obliged to reduce.

Z, untroubled by ghosts, since her work desensitized her to such fancies, welcomed silence across the landing. Now, having showered and changed, she prepared to go down and discover why Max hadn't instantly appeared when her car swept past Beattie's windows.

★ ★ ★

As she double-locked her door she paused at the unaccustomed sound of music. An old Eric Clapton recording, surely coming from the unoccupied apartment. And the door stood invitingly ajar.

Closer, she listened for a moment, could detect no movement, then knocked quietly.

She heard chair legs slide against woodblock flooring and someone padded in sock soles from the direction of the drawing-room.

'Hello, my sweet,' Max greeted her, grinning like a monkey. 'Come in and tell me what you think.'

The room was transformed. Gone were the silks and velvet-swagged drapes, the peachy creams and thick pile carpet. Exposed wood flooring gleamed like pale honey. Here and there the bare walls had been daubed with tester shades of matt paint.

'You're not serious,' she accused him.

'It's an idea I had. It came over me gradually, after I suggested to Dr Fenner it would make a better sale if it was brought up to date, with all the flimmery flammery removed.'

'When did you see Dr Fenner?' she demanded, suspicious.

'A couple of weeks back. I had a job to do in Cambridge. He dined and wined me in College like a prince.'

'And you kept it under your hat! You're telling me he gave you carte blanche to take over the redecoration?'

'And have all the furniture removed. Yes, with a view to considering its potential for myself. I am sometimes allowed to make decisions on my own, you know.'

He was all wide-eyed innocence. 'I still haven't quite made up my mind. If you've any objections to me as a neighbour, naturally I'll call it off, hoping he likes the alterations.'

She walked past him to sit on one of the wide windowsills. 'It's unexpected.'

'You don't have to say straight off . . . '

'I thought things were fine the way they were, that's all.' She sounded uncertain. Then, 'You want to move your toothbrush out, I take it?' It was an attempt to sound unaffected. A dab at weak humour.

'Oh, I could just about afford a second toothbrush. And the lease will be up on the Pimlico place in September. The truth is I'm not sure I want to go on living in London. But I can't impose on you all the time. Being close neighbours seemed the best way out.'

But not as close as being with her in the same apartment. She seemed to hear warning bells. He was making it sound like building something more permanent between them, but at the same time it was a physical distancing. Wasn't it?

'I like having you drop in,' she told him.

'But I need somewhere permanent as well. If I give up in Pimlico, this would suit me well. The Prof isn't asking its full value. A snip, you might say. And who knows, you might get to like seeing me on an almost daily basis. As a run-up to taking me on as a full-time husband.'

She couldn't suppress a smile. 'Infiltration?'

'Something like that. I shall go on proposing, of course, if I see any signs of your relenting.'

'Ah, that reminds me,' she said brightly, glad of a sideways shift of subject. 'We've been sent a wedding invitation by Paula Musto. It's for next Saturday. Short notice, owing to Angus getting special leave from duty in Kosovo. They're taking a four day honeymoon in Scotland, then he has to go back and finish his commitment out there.'

'So he's pulled it off at last! There's hope for me yet.'

'We don't have to act like lemmings,' she said sharply and caught the flicker of some emotion cross Max's face. 'I'm sorry, sorry, sorry. You know how it is. It's just the idea of marriage, being hobbled; the sameness, the dreariness that must inevitably creep in with familiarity. I don't want that ever to happen to us.'

He stood there considering her, his head tilted to one side. Then with an index finger he pushed his spectacles up the bridge of his nose in the familiar way. And just then she felt familiar wasn't such a bad thing.

Quite endearing, really.

'You've witnessed too many bad alliances,' he said sombrely. 'I have too, but I believe we could make something good out of it. However, I see that now's not the right moment to start asking you again. Meanwhile, how do you feel about my taking on this flat? As a half-measure.'

'You must do as you wish,' she granted ruefully. 'As you said, you're sometimes allowed to make decisions of your own.'

'But your reaction is part of what I have to take into account.'

Up until then they hadn't touched. Now she rose and went across to him, put her arms round his neck and kissed his cheek. 'I can't imagine anyone I'd rather have living next door.'

This was his cue for kissing her more thoroughly. From which he finally extricated himself, took a deep breath and demanded in mock-husbandly tones, 'So, where's me dinner?'

Back in her own apartment, while she dealt with the steaks he'd left in her fridge, and Max dribbled vinaigrette into tossed salad, she explained what had taken her into work on a Sunday.

'Tomorrow,' she added, 'DI Salmon's back from leave and the reign of terror will recommence. Meanwhile we're free to make hay or whatever. That's my life. So how was your week?'

Settling to an evening of quiet companionship began to lessen her unease. Nothing appeared to have changed. Max was his normal gently droll self delivering anecdotes of newspaper life in the city, and if the alarm bells still sounded they seemed to have become less urgent and more distant.

She had as good as told him to go ahead with his plans to move in next door. If it meant that her own apartment threatened to become sadly empty, at least it wasn't immediate. He was here now and would be staying on tonight. She switched off all interest in the job to concentrate on the present.

★   ★   ★

DS Beaumont was shrugging on his jacket to take the dog for its evening walk — euphemism for a pint at the local. When the mobile phone buzzed in his pocket he knew in his bones it was work. And of the worse kind, because DI Walter Salmon had flown home from his holiday in Brittany and required his immediate company for a visit to Mrs Kate Dellar.

It could surely have waited for tomorrow. But, on the other hand, it was himself the DI had preferred to call in, and not Z. Any opportunity to get a step ahead of his rival DS had to be seized. So how far had Salmon acquainted himself with the case as it stood? He must have dropped in at the incident room already being set up, and helped himself to such reports as were logged.

Brought that much up-to-date, the DI had phoned Mrs Dellar and made an appointment, catching the lady as she returned home, actually walking in through the door. Wrong-footed, she'd not had the wit to insist that a meeting was inconvenient.

Beaumont returned the basset hound to the kitchen and flung the end of its lead to his son with suitable instructions. Then he walked to the road's end and waited to be picked up by the Great Uncouth himself.

He found Salmon unchanged but for a hectic band of scorched skin across cheeks, nose and throat, which ceased abruptly on his brow where some kind of headgear had been pulled down for protection. Beaumont pondered its likely nature: cricket umpire's panama hat; baseball cap; beret? No, he looked more the old-fashioned knotted-handkerchief type, paddling on the sea's edge with rolled-up trouser legs and twanging red braces; the sort of belly-bulging, middle-aged man you used to see on saucy postcards, surrounded by fat women and jeering kids. However inappropriate that image, he'd been keen to return a day early to duty.

At Mrs Dellar's cottage, while they waited for her to answer the doorbell, Beaumont sized up the other man. He was big. The width of his shoulders and the short car coat made a cube of him. The head on top was of much the same shape, with gingerish fair hair close-cropped like a Victorian convict's. His large, knobbly features were all squashed into the lower three-eighths of his face, and the coarse-lipped mouth stretched almost the full width of his heavy jaw.

Not a pretty sight, but the man himself didn't appear to hold that opinion. He had, in fact, a mighty conceit of himself.

He hadn't given any hint of his immediate intentions. Perhaps it was his idea of a charm offensive, familiarising himself with the main players before the game got properly under way, and impressing bystanders with his being in control of the case.

It might not come amiss to warn him. 'The lady's very upset, sir,' Beaumont ventured, deliberately avoiding the term 'guv' which was reserved for the absent Angus Mott. 'She seems the sensitive sort.'

Salmon's eyes flicked sideways to put him in his place. 'All the better to gauge her reactions,' he said shortly. Like Little Red Riding-hood's wolf, Beaumont noted, and was visited by a second unflattering image of his senior officer, in a granny's flannelette nightie, peering over the bedclothes.

The door opened. Kate Dellar stood there, white and strained. 'Is there any news?' she asked anxiously.

There was no attempt to lead her indoors, to soften the blow.

'I have to report that a body has been found, ma'am,' Salmon announced baldly. 'At the scene of the fire. A post-mortem is to be carried out tomorrow and we can tell you more then.'

It took a moment for it to reach her. Beaumont had time to step forward and catch her as she swayed.

6

Refreshed by Sunday's family outing, Superintendent Mike Yeadings had returned home to find three messages on his answerphone. The first assured him that his DI, Walter Salmon, was returning for the Larchmoor Place case and would attend the post-mortem on a body found at the scene of the fire. The second was from DS Zyczynski, bringing him up to date on the findings and giving the time of next day's post-mortem as 10am. The third produced Professor Littlejohn himself, cheerfully complaining about his long weekend being curtailed.

'I can't get a decent fly on my rod but you have to drag me back by the short and curlies, eh?'

In view of the pathologist's increasingly bald pate Yeadings found this barely apt, and smiled at the man's deviousness. He hadn't missed the weather news about torrential rain in North Wales giving rise to flash floods. Under the circumstances it wasn't surprising if Littlejohn had, so to speak, found better fish to fry nearer home.

It appeared that matters were satisfactorily in hand for the next day.

★   ★   ★

On Monday Kate Dellar awoke in her own bed to the sound of light rain. After last night's appalling news she had felt emotionally wrung out. Walls and ceiling threatened to close in, crushing from her the ability to breathe. When the two detectives had left she leaned, stifled, by her open bedroom window and tried to suck in the last of the day's used air. The tablets she'd taken — twice the normal dose — did nothing to help, only made her less able to cope. When eventually she stumbled to her bed she had left the house exposed, doors unlocked and casements gaping. And now, while it continued to rain, there seemed no point in doing anything about it. She supposed she would mop up the water later. If it ran down and damaged the wallpaper — too bad.

She experienced no sudden shock of memory returning. It had been with her all night, blackly threaded in and out of fantastic dreams, situations where she had been lost, or searching for others lost, always devastated and alone. The twins had appeared fleetingly on the edge of her vision, as young children oddly diminished in size, running hand-in-hand into a dark tunnel or between close-packed, twisted trees where she couldn't follow, paralyzed with horror.

Now, with the menace of a new day, she wearily supposed habit would make her get up, shower, dress. Then what?

Wait, perhaps, for the next blow to fall: for the last of her family to be taken from her.

It wasn't as if she could *do* anything. Nor had she the energy to try. Fighting demands in her head all night, for the moment she was incapable of more than staring up at the shadowed ceiling.

Above the patter of raindrops against glass she was aware of tyres hissing on wet tarmac as the morning rush-hour built. Then a new sound emerged, a bruising thud of heavy plastic against metal, followed by a torrent of tinkling.

Monday: so lorries had come to empty the bottle banks, a row of sturdy green containers with gaping mouths, labelled *clear, green, green* and *brown*, in which local residents posted their empties for recycling.

At least the sound had human implications. Despite her torpor she made it to the window, rested her elbows on the wet sill and leaned out. Rain fell cool and soft on her hair and forehead. Through the sparse branches of her neighbour's young pear tree she glimpsed the bulky lifting device in the public car park. As she watched, the mechanical arm swivelled, angled, and gently lowered the first of the green containers to the ground. The grab released it, groped for the next container, slowly raised it several feet, tipped it and delivered a further shower of glass into the open rear of the transporter. This second load sounded different, less shattered, as though the green glass, mostly wine bottles and usually more robust than the clear shards, had poured out whole.

Wine bottles. She visualized again rank on rank of shelving in the Larchmoor Place cellars, as she'd first been shown them years ago. Old Frederick, Michael's father and dead for fifteen years, had fancied himself a wine connoisseur. He'd put claret down to mature as an investment. She wondered how much of his treasure remained — had remained until this disastrous fire. Maybe a considerable amount. Carlton hadn't been unusually self-indulgent, and seldom brought up the best stuff for such entertaining as he and Claudia went in for.

If green bottles were so much more robust, maybe some of the Dellar collection, close-packed and horizontal in their sturdy shelving, could even now have survived the upper storeys' collapse. Or would they be long gone, sold on by Claudia like the best of the library, to cover expenses in her and Carlton's final years?

Kate wondered if that possibility had occurred to Robert, so enraged by being denied his grandfather's books or some share of their value. And had Matthew, his father, been secretly a party to any liquidating of family assets? Perhaps Claudia had allowed him to take a cut.

Kate moved away from the window, leaving the rain still pattering in. For a brief moment she had resented that Michael's portion as third brother could be overlooked and her little family deprived. But how trivial, to be considering vintage wine's survival, when a precious life has been taken! In any case the heat would have made it undrinkable.

Her present reality overwhelmed her. She had no one, unless Eddie miraculously pulled through. And if not, what use had she for anything else?

She reached for the phone, dialled the hospital and waited while someone responsible was called to answer her demands.

Sister informed her there had been no change. Eddie remained in a deep coma.

It meant there was still hope, of a kind. Jess was another matter. Today they would be holding a post-mortem. Kate refused to let her mind travel so far into the blackness.

★   ★   ★

Yeadings, having first stopped off at Kidlington to pick up and read the PR office's digest for the day, was an hour late reaching the mortuary. Littlejohn was in mid-flow, dictating his progress into a mike clipped to the front of his green plastic apron. The others had gathered and were uneasily waiting as he sliced, sawed, removed, then handed wrinkled organs over to steel bowls for the necessary weighing. There was a new mortuary assistant, small, male and Asian. Possibly Burmese.

Harsh overhead lighting, thrown back by white walls and gleaming steel, united with the heavy, airless smell of death insufficiently masked by disinfectant, producing for Yeadings the customary unease below his belt. This was by no means a normal dissection, the cadaver less resembling a human form than some charred and twisted tree trunk. The limbs, barely recognizable, were distorted and shrivelled. It was doubtful whether even Littlejohn would manage a reasonable assessment of the body's original size and general appearance.

Since the facial damage was so severe that no next of kin would be viewing the body, Littlejohn had reached the clenched teeth by removing both jaws. This meant peeling back skin from the lower face to reach and detach the masseter and temporalis muscles at the mandible, then sawing through at nose base level towards the joint before the ear. This he had skillfully achieved once photography and radiography of the area was completed.

Yeadings was conscious of DI Salmon's hard stare from across the room, but declined to make any excuse for his presence. Admittedly there was no need for him, since the DI was accompanied by the coroner's officer and one of the team's detective sergeants but, because he would ultimately carry the can for how the investigation progressed, Yeadings was taking no chances. Salmon had yet to prove himself adequate.

Z's presence indicated that she was the one who'd covered yesterday's excavations on the spot. Salmon might otherwise have consigned his female DS to less front-line business — not to spare her feelings, but from gender prejudice. The man had the sensitivity of a wild boar. And this morning, Yeadings considered, he looked not unlike one, add the odd whisker here and there.

Littlejohn had paused in his work to look

up. 'Good to see you, Mike,' he growled expansively. 'More the merrier. Must press on, though. Young Z's been taking notes if you want to catch up. Take a look. You might be quite surprised.'

Yeadings walked across and took the notebook Z offered. He scanned the first shorthand page, made out the usual description of circumstances and site of the finding. The body's external measurements noted must be of purely academic interest owing to the exceptional heat distortion, and pretty useless in this case. Nevertheless they had been scrupulously noted because minor changes would certainly occur later during protracted refrigeration.

Littlejohn was now examining the state of the teeth. To Yeadings' lay mind they sounded nothing out of the ordinary: a few small fillings, a single eyetooth capped; no denture. Salmon shouldn't need reminding that a match with the missing girl's dental record would be necessary to ensure identification. Requiring the mother to view the body was quite out of the question.

'We'll be going for DNA,' the pathologist murmured.

That did startle the superintendent. Surely no need for that added expense if the teeth had sufficient work done for her dentist to recognize them. So maybe they hadn't.

Well, it'd be nice to find out who it is we've got here, eh?' Littlejohn remarked with a fierce grin. 'And why the funeral pyre.'

Yeadings assumed that the pathologist had so recently arrived back that he hadn't caught up with all the information available on the Larchmoor Place survivors. But 'pyre?' he questioned. Wasn't that an unnecessary touch of macabre imagination?

'Pyre,' Littlejohn repeated. 'Oh, very much so. Our deceased friend here got the full Maid of Orleans treatment. I'm sending off parts of the underside to the chemi lab for analysis together with samples of the vinyl kitchen floor. They appear to have — er, much in common. Melded, in fact.'

It was unusual for him to be so mealy-mouthed. Yeadings saw clearly enough what the man meant. 'So it's definitely not a natural or accidental death?'

The pathologist straightened stiffly, rubbing at his lower back. 'Nothing natural or accidental about the cremation of a human body. But we'll need a great deal more time and exploration to determine whether the victim was alive when the fire began. Or, if dead, from what cause. You haven't brought me an easy one this time, Mike. In fact it's quite a teaser.' He sounded delighted.

Yeadings didn't want half the team hanging about for hours. Zyczynski had done her bit yesterday, witnessed the body's retrieval, ensured continuity. DI Salmon could manage from this point on his own.

'Right, Z, you can knock off here. I'll see you back at the incident room. Bring your notes. We can leave this with the DI now he's back.'

'Sir.'

He observed Salmon's slack mouth tighten to match a black stare. 'Let me know when you've finished here,' Yeadings added mildly.

'Going, Mike?' Littlejohn paused, scalpel raised. 'You're going to miss all the fun bits.' He grinned fiendishly. 'My best regards to Nan and the kiddos.' Then he plunged back into the charred flesh. Yeadings and Z withdrew. Salmon turned sourly away from the exploration.

★   ★   ★

At a few minutes before eleven Kate Dellar heard a car draw up outside the house and waited in trepidation for the doorbell to ring. She lived in a quiet road. By 9am most mornings the traffic flow outside had stopped. It wasn't a kerbside people chose to park by. Few tradesmen called because most of the neighbours commuted daily to London.

Even expecting the bell, she started as it shrilled. No, she told herself. Nothing more. I can't take it.

But she moved into the hall and tried to make out who stood beyond the glass panel of the front door. The head's outline was irregular. It looked like a woman's. Then it turned in profile and Kate recognized the knob of dark hair low on the neck. Marion Paige. An envoy from the family?

The letterbox flapped and the visitor peered through. 'Kate? I know you're there. It's Marion. Please let me in.'

Back in the shadows Kate stayed still, uncertain. Of them all this woman had been the only one to offer help. She could hardly turn her away. She moved forward into the light, let herself be seen as she opened up. But still she couldn't speak.

'Kate,' the other one repeated. 'You look like a ghost. Have you eaten?'

'I — I . . . '

'Come on. I'll make you something. You shouldn't be here alone. I hoped you'd ring or send for one of us. Haven't you any neighbours who could come in?'

She bustled past, slid off her jacket and hung it on the newel post, then almost pushed Kate towards the kitchen with scooping motions of her hands. 'You'll feel better once you've got something inside you.'

Just like I used to do with the children, Kate thought; when they couldn't face school. She let herself be propelled towards the breakfast bar. A stool was pulled out and her elbow held firmly while she allowed herself to be seated. I shall be sick, she warned herself, at just the smell of food.

But Marion had the sense not to attempt anything greasy. She found wholemeal bread in the crock, sawed off two slices and dropped them in the toaster.

The warm, yeasty smell that arose reminded Kate she hadn't eaten since toying with the hotel food the previous evening. 'No butter or spread,' she warned the woman scrabbling in the fridge.

'Marmalade, then. You can't eat it dry.'

Kate supposed she was right. Dry, the toast would lodge in her throat. There seemed to be a lump there already. 'Just a smear,' she allowed.

She stirred herself to fill and switch on the kettle, aware of Marion watching under lowered lids. The effort of moving made her feel less light-headed. Something like anger pulsed inside her. She resented the woman

102

regarding her as spineless. 'I am not a victim,' she said shortly. 'There's just so much that anyone can take at once.'

'It's the uncertainty,' Marion suggested. But that was just parroting. Everyone knew that was what parents said when their children went missing.

Well, Kate's children had gone missing. Hadn't they? Not in the same way, though. The thing she confronted was death, still in the balance in one case. In the other . . . no hope now.

'Have the police been back?' Marion asked.

Kate shuddered, remembering the detective inspector's face; the crude message delivered on her doorstep.

'Not since last night,' she admitted once she could find words. Grim-faced she fetched two mugs, the cafetière, milk and sugar bowl, lined them up on a tray, then forgot what next.

'Ground coffee?'

'Packet's in the fridge door. It keeps fresher that way.'

Her words were cut across by the phone ringing. As with the doorbell earlier, she started, felt her body thudding with shock, and all energy instantly drain.

Marion Paige held out one hand towards her, but was moving in the opposite direction.

'No!' Kate shouted. 'Don't answer it. I'll go.'

The phone was in the hall. In the seconds it took her to get there she forced herself to take control. 'Hello,' she whispered; lifted the receiver and repeated it aloud.

'Mrs Dellar?' It was a woman's voice, not Sister's, so nothing important after all.

'This is Sergeant Zyczynski again, Mrs Dellar. From Thames Valley CID. I heard you were at home and wondered if there's anything I could do. Is there someone with you?'

Not a friend exactly, but the young woman detective who'd come out to Jess's boat. 'I'm all right. There is somebody here,' Kate admitted.

There was a short pause, then, 'I don't want to bother you, but there are one or two things we need to know, Mrs Dellar.'

Kate wished she wouldn't keep repeating the surname. It made her sound like one of *them*, in parallel with Claudia. 'Is it something I can answer now, without you coming round?'

'If you prefer. It's just that we'd like to know the name of your family doctor.'

'I told them at the hospital. My GP's Dr Finnegan at the Medical Centre. But my son has someone else in London now. A Dr

104

Santer, but I don't know his address.'

'Yes?' The policewoman appeared to be waiting for more.

'Is that all?'

'Perhaps I'd better have your dentist's name too.'

'We use the Park Clinic, but . . . ' She was going to say that maybe she was the only one registered there now. The children would have joined another list when they moved away. Then the reason for the request struck her. Neither of the twins, nor she herself, had any need for dentistry at present.

They needed to know, for an odontologist to identify the body. They would check with Jess's records and there would be no escaping. It would be certain then. No way of going back, of keeping the frailest hope alive.

But she'd known since last night, hadn't she? A body found in the ruins. Only one member of the family missing. There was no one else it could be.

Blindly she reached out the receiver. It clattered down in place. 'They're identifying the body,' she told the woman hesitating in the kitchen doorway.

'At least you will know then for sure.'

'I don't want to know,' she wailed. This was Jess they were talking about: Jess, once her darling baby.

Back at Carlton's, when they'd been first introduced, this woman had made an odd remark about Jess. After Marion had said how alike mother and daughter were, Kate had had the momentary suspicion that there had been a tinge of malice in her voice. And later when Kate had rashly demanded what the woman had against Jess, she'd brushed the question aside, saying enigmatically, 'Ah, that's another story entirely.'

An interruption had occurred at that point, so she had never explained herself.

But she could now.

'You'd met Jess before seeing her at Carlton's, hadn't you?' Kate accused her now.

'Yes.' Marion sounded casual. 'Michael introduced us. I'd called in at King's College and she was in his Faculty office.'

So she had known Michael too. The academic world was a small one, but if Marion's department at UCL was Geophysics, why would she need to consult a historian?

This must have happened almost a year ago, maybe more. Michael's fatal mugging down by Temple Underground station had been in October. At that time Jess hadn't yet dropped out of Engineering, hadn't become infatuated with Charles Stone.

'I see,' Kate said; but she didn't. Any idea

of this woman offering comfort was shaken now. She'd been an acquaintance whom Michael had never troubled to mention: someone on first-name terms with him. And any animosity between her and Jess could have started from that moment of first meeting in his office at King's.

So what were the circumstances of it? Kate looked away from her, wishing she would go now and leave her to grieve alone.

★ ★ ★

Zyczynski had returned to the Area CID office and was re-reading her shorthand notes on Kate Dellar. 'I should have gone to see her,' she regretted, almost under her breath.

Beaumont was perched on a corner of her desk, working his way through an apricot Danish. 'It's done now. At least you say she's not on her own. Do you want me to go and pick up the dental records?'

'If you've nothing more pressing. Better telephone first or they'll leave you hanging around.'

'Right, then. Tell the Boss where I am if he asks for me.'

'Will do.' She watched him stand, brush the fallen flakes of pastry off his shirt-front, wipe his fingers on a scrap of printer paper and make for the door, conscious that this left him one up.

Zyczynski gave a wry smile. When Little-john's notes on the body's teeth arrived Beaumont would be there, star pupil, to produce the matching chart from Jessica Dellar's dentist and win any acclaim.

She shrugged. Scoring points should take second place in a case like this. And it didn't matter that she'd handed him that one on a plate. Their detailed track records weren't so important at the moment in the race for promotion. Walter Salmon was installed again as their DI and looked likely to remain until such time as Angus was permanently back: which she was sure he would be eventually, now that the wedding was definitely on.

She'd bet almost anything that Paula had finally surrendered, agreeing to quit her Law practice in London and seek a place in local chambers; even switch from legal defence to join Crown Prosecution. Which surely meant the pair of them would be setting up home here in Thames Valley.

She settled to transcribing her notes on the computer, reflecting it might now be a good thing that Max was taking the apartment next to her own. Good flats were hard to find at a reasonable price, and much as she valued Angus as her immediate guv, she didn't need him on her doorstep after the day's work was done.

She printed out her report, dropped a copy off at the incident room and took another to leave on Yeadings' desk. She found he had just returned and was on the phone. He waved her to a seat.

'DI Salmon's still at the PM,' he said when the call was through. 'I want you to follow up some of Sir Matthew Dellar's judgments. He's been retired from Queen's Bench for over four years, so you'll need to dig way back. Make a list of any disgruntled old lags released in the last three months. Special attention to anyone with a taste for arson who made a death threat against him. It's often no more than hot air, but just once in a blue moon some obsessive will make an attempt on the judiciary.

'That'll do for the present. If nothing of significance shows up we may need to go even further back, to when he was a QC. No, on second thoughts I'll put a DC on checking among long sentences from that period.' He entered a note to this effect in his log.

'Yessir.'

'That's to say, after we've tried this new Italian coffee you brought in. Where's Beaumont?'

'Chasing up Jessica Dellar's dental records.'

Yeadings looked up from his pouring. He looked thoughtful.

'Ah, yes. Littlejohn thought we might have to go for DNA. There hadn't been much work done on the body's mouth.'

'Well, she was young. Probably took good care of herself.'

'Until the early hours of Saturday morning,' he said dryly. He paused. 'I'd very much like to know what she was doing downstairs before the fire had gone out of control.'

'And if she was the reason her brother rushed to get through to the cellar,' Z suggested.

They drank their coffee hot, both keen to get on with the inquiry. Z departed, seeking an expert in legal archives and a terminal for access to High Court case records. It was more than an hour later that she was paged to return to the Boss's office. She found Beaumont already smugly installed. A copy of the girl's dental chart from the Park Clinic was on Yeadings' desk.

'Do they match?' she asked. 'Has Littlejohn's report come through already?'

'Your notes from the PM are sufficient,' Yeadings said sombrely. 'According to Jessica Dellar's dentist she'd broken off two upper front teeth in a riding accident when she was thirteen. He had rebuilt them himself and said the work was distinctive.'

He looked from one of his sergeants to the other. 'So, there's no way our body could be Jessica. And there's nothing to suggest who else it might be. Even DNA will be useless until we have something to compare it with.'

He waited for his announcement to take its effect, then, 'It means we have an extra case on our hands. Because now Jessica Dellar is officially a Misper.'

'It's a reprieve for her mother,' Z said instantly. 'I'll go round and let her know the good news. She'll be so thankful.'

'It may not be such good news in the end,' Yeadings warned her. 'Although it's unlikely they'll find another body in the burnt-out house, we have to consider the vandalized condition of the canal narrowboat. That may have been part of an unsuccessful plan to injure or kill her earlier. And, as reported, it occurred in the same hours of darkness as the torching of Larchmoor Place. It's possible whoever was out to get her was successful with the second attempt.

'Jessica Dellar may still have been a victim of murder or abduction. And since the Senior Fire Officer has decided the outbreak was arson, our original case looks like premedi-tated murder with criminal disregard for the lives or safety of others.'

111

7

On Sunday, ignorant of all that had happened at her uncle's after her departure, Jessica Dellar rested her elbows on the balcony's rail and gazed out across the lagoon. It was immense, stretching west and east until lost in early morning haze, and so vast that she could imagine that at either end it sloped downwards as the global horizon.

The water's surface barely stirred, limpid and almost colourless beyond the fish-traps' black verticals staked out in receding horizontal rows to the west. And directly across from her, the distant shoreline, with the Doge's palace and San Marco miniature and unreal, was a shimmering thread of opalescent light.

From the end of the balcony she could look down into the convent garden next door. Above the ancient, stained terracotta of the roof rose a demure little square bell-tower of bleached wood from which a bell tolled a single note, calling the faithful to early Mass, sounding medieval in its mixture of secure orthodoxy and irksome restrictions.

Mother still went defiantly to church, but it

was something Jess had given up after Dad died. She supposed all the Dellars would be trooping off as customary to the village service, Claudia dominating the choir's contraltos and Miranda, the *idiot savant*, performing prodigiously on the organ: Dellars en masse pretending to recognize a greater power than the Family!

She turned back to the lagoon panorama. What a place to be sent to. But not to stay. Venice was too rich and romantic for everyday living. To stay was surely to remain entranced, slowly sink with it almost imperceptibly, millimetre by millimetre, back into the sucking lagoon.

Last night the water had looked infinitely deep, inky dark, the boat's bows cutting out a violet-white curve that flew along the gunwales. She had thrilled to the choppy movement as they sped through the blackness, stopping only at Murano for a few passengers to land. It was a stageset, a night scene from Barcarolle except that the stone buildings looked menacing, each ancient block sparsely lit by a single globe high under the roof, the glow scarcely reaching to the shadowed water. This was a place for masked assassins and poisoners and vendettas. She'd been bound for another island: Lido, which, she remembered, was quite different.

All the same, there was no knowing what lay in store for her ahead. Already, over the past twenty-four — no, thirty-six — hours she had found herself increasingly out of her depth. Too many instant decisions. Certainly too many obscure instructions. Used to flouting convention, she preferred to have control over events. This time she'd obediently leapt in, eyes closed. She didn't really know how deep the water might be.

She supposed events were bound to get out of hand when she accepted old Carlton's invitation to his birthday weekend. She hadn't intended going, but Charles Stone had insisted, although it meant turning down a better alternative. Still, she'd thought Eddie might be there, and she'd something important to ask him, tell him, whatever.

In the event there hadn't been an opportunity, because Jake was being such a weedy limpet that she'd played him along, and it took a rise out of Ma to let her see that. She'd thought there'd be opportunity enough to talk with her brother next day.

The essential thing was that Eddie should be told before he returned home. But things had got out of hand, happening so fast, without warning: so still he had no idea.

She had let Charles Stone have the last word. 'Keep in with your family,' he'd as good as ordered. 'When all else fails in life, a family is still there for you. In any case I need to be sure where you are for a few days. Stay until Monday. I will be in touch.'

At the time she'd taken it at face value, but later she realized that the cliché about family was totally un-Charles. And then she'd been sure: he was up to something. But, of course, when wasn't he?

That had been on the Tuesday, so when Eddie rang next morning to ask what she intended doing about the family rally, she'd said, 'I guess I'll go. What are you giving the old boy?'

'God knows,' he'd said. 'The coffers are almost empty, and anyway we've few tastes in common. Maybe a book.'

And because she didn't trust the phone line she hadn't simply warned him then.

Clever-clogs Eddie. Empty coffers or not, he'd turned up at Carlton's with a superb first edition copy of *Three Men in a Boat*. The stick insect uncle had almost clasped him to his bosom.

Her own offering, a silver paperknife, was more modest and lay still unopened with all the other gift-wrapped presents on the octagonal table in the drawing-room. The plain brown paper bag containing Eddie's offering had so clearly revealed the shape of a book that Uncle Carlton couldn't resist opening it there and then. Full marks, Eddie. Give the boy a scooter.

Not that Eddie was the sort to curry favour. He simply enjoyed others' pleasure. If she'd been able to choose a sibling from everyone she'd ever met it would have to be Eddie. Steady Eddie, so unlike herself although they were twins. Even Ma felt comfortable with him, whereas her own escapades put an almost permanent strain on mother-daughter relations, Kate trying so hard, and so obviously, not to be openly judgmental.

So how had the 'party' evening scored overall on a scale of one to ten?

Barely four-ish. Uncle Carlton and Aunt Claudia had been in their element, of course, holding court. Their nephew Robert, only slightly less bouncy than usual, had plugged his new book and successfully presented his new love. His widowed father, Matthew, had drifted through the necessary greetings-and-eatings in a mild-mannered way until the bridge table came out, and then he reverted to the natural predator he'd been for half a lifetime as a QC, seeing it as his divinely bestowed function to fill Her Majesty's prisons with his rivals' clients.

The others of his family sprig had mingled

in their several different ways, daughter Madeleine over-conscious of her hot flushes, her husband Gus from habit buttering up the ladies, and her stepson Jake peacocking away as though he'd been brought up in a corridor of mirrors. For herself, she'd had only a brief word with Eddie, frozen off Gus, been a trifle provocative with Jake and had the satisfaction of turning him down at her bedroom door despite his beseeching spaniel eyes and hand-on-heart gestures behind Eddie's back.

About the outsider Marion Paige, Jessica had yet finally to make up her mind. They'd met before and she'd admit to strong prejudice. And she hadn't cared for the hard stare she'd given poor Miranda, who'd been no more negative than she customarily was.

At least it hadn't rained to keep them penned mustily indoors. As she'd sat that night at her open bedroom window the pleasant breeze of the afternoon was turning into a sneaky wind tugging at fronds of Virginia creeper which encroached on the window panes. The old shutters had started to rattle in their iron hasps. She had turned away to undress and became aware of a square white envelope pushed under the door.

That idiot Jake doing the Romeo thing, she'd supposed; opened it and found a printed message: *The pool after midnight. Magnus.*

That could only be from Charles Stone. Nobody else knew the jokey name she teased him with. Silly, really: Charle*magne*, Carolus Magnus, Holy Flipping Roman Emperor, because he could be so high-handed and needed taking down a peg or two.

So was he staying somewhere near and had sent someone to deliver the note? It was only on Tuesday he'd flown out to Washington.

At already a quarter to one the house appeared silent. Glancing again from the window she could see only three lit windows reflected on lawn and shrubbery.

A carafe of water was already supplied beside her bed so she hadn't the excuse of going for a drink. But, ostensibly fetching something to read, she could creep down to the study passage and let herself out there.

The rusty bolts were stiff and she loosed them slowly to keep down their screeches. Two more bedroom lights went out as she crossed the cracked flagstones of the terrace and circled to the house's rear. Here all the windows were in total darkness, and the moon, in its last eighth, gave her little light through the archway of overgrown trees.

Towards the end of the semicircular path she could make out a gleaming surface which

118

would be the pool. Not water, she found, but the shabby, bleached blue plastic which covered the empty hole for eight months of the year. At near sight she found it was stained with mould, sagging under an accumulation of twigs and leafy rubbish from recent rains. The whole scene was creepy, dingy and deserted.

The little cabin, once used for bathers to change in, was in sad disrepair, with a fallen branch lodged in the broken thatched roof, and the edges of the hole black with rot. For a secret tryst the place was ideal for privacy; but so dismal. It was impossible to imagine the immaculate Charles making love to her here.

Cautiously she circled the little ruin. Nobody stood waiting under the thatch's overhang, but a whisper reached her as someone lying on the bench beyond sat up and started uncertainly to rise. In dappled moonlight she made out the thin form of a young man, little more than a boy perhaps, and he staggered as if in pain. She reached him as he swayed on the point of falling.

'Who are you?' she demanded. 'What are you doing here?'

He shook his head, grasping at her wrists for support. 'Hide me,' he begged. 'I work for him.'

'For whom?' she insisted.

'Your husband. Charles Stone.'

This was no moment for arguing her status. The man was clearly ill. 'Look, sit down. What's wrong?'

He slumped again on the bench. 'I was shot at, coming here. From a passing car. They got away. It's only a flesh wound.'

She looked at him in disbelief. His eyes were sunken in deep pits of grey, and a sheen of sweat beaded his forehead. She doubted he'd make it on foot as far as the house, and she couldn't support his weight alone. And, of course, she'd left her bloody mobile back in her room.

'We must get you to hospital. Can you wait here while I call for an ambulance?'

'No ambulance. No hospital. See. I'm padded.'

He meant bandaged. His English was adequate but the accent was foreign. She began to doubt him. He'd made that mistake about herself, so he couldn't know all that much about Charles's affairs. On the other hand his injury wasn't an act. As he pulled back one edge of his green knitted jerkin she could see the open shirt and the blood-stained handkerchief below the right shoulder. So who had fixed that for him but not informed the authorities?

'Hide me,' he said again, more faintly. 'Nobody followed, but if they come back, they will search.'

'Why should they?' Her voice sharpened with suspicion. 'You know who they are, don't you? It wasn't random.'

'Enemies. His. I come to help you. Secretly.'

She stared at him a moment. Quandary-bloody-plus.

So she did the obvious thing and ran for Eddie. His was the one light still on, and he rose from reading in bed as she knocked and entered.

'Jess, what now?'

She said she'd gone out for fresh air and there was this injured man in the garden. He'd sworn someone was after him and he had to lie low. He was too ill to walk unaided and she couldn't get him into the house on her own.

Stated baldly like that it sounded crazy, but the full truth, with mention of Charles, would have been worse. And Eddie knew as well as anyone that she was always getting involved in harebrained situations.

His reaction was instant; terse and sceptical. 'It's the police he's running from, idiot. And he expects you to grant him free entry to rob the house. We'd best go down and see how far he's got with it.'

He reached under his pillow to arm himself with a heavy torch. It looked the business, and she began to feel all options might be covered. If this nameless young man really came from Charles she'd somehow make Eddie help him. And if he was a phoney . . .

The unknown boy was still stretched out on the bench. 'What's your name?' her brother demanded, bending over him and shining the light on his haggard face.

'Nicholas. I am shot.'

It might have been *Niklaus*, she thought. A more or less international name. He certainly wasn't native English.

'Let's be having you then,' Eddie offered unexpectedly. 'Where's the wound?'

Jess pulled back the edge of the crumpled shirt to reveal the bloodstained area. Her brother made a soft humming sound. 'Can't risk a fireman's lift then. Jess, are you up to helping with a bandy-chair?'

He steadied the man on to his feet and they slid their arms behind, fingers locking on to each other's wrists. Gently they eased him into position so that he sat on their hands, his left arm reaching for Eddie's far shoulder and the other lying useless in his lap.

'What now?' Jess panted as they re-bolted the door, gained the study and closed the curtains. She switched on some lights.

Eddie had the young man laid out on the floor. 'Does Claudia have a First Aid box?'

'I've no idea. There used to be one in the kitchen, but I'd question anything in it being sterile.'

'Whatever. Fetch it. I need to change the dressing.'

She went without a word, using the torch to avoid switching on the corridor lights. In the kitchen the second of the heavy old wooden drawers yielded a circular toffee tin with a Red Cross label peeling off the lid. There was also a half-full bottle of disinfectant. She took both along to her brother.

The two men appeared to have been talking together. Whatever was said, Eddie appeared now to have accepted the young man's story. There was no further mention of police.

'He has to lie low until first light,' he said decisively. 'Then I'll get him away by taxi. In the meantime, let's shift him to the cellar. No one's going to walk in on him there. Carlton's already removed all the wines they need for the weekend. I carried them up for him a couple of days ago.'

They managed the man between them. When Eddie had fixed the new dressing and roughly arranged a low hammock out of fruit nets, Nick appeared more relaxed.

'The bullet's gone right through,' Eddie said. 'It barely touched the ribs. He'll be all right for a few hours, but to ease things, we just need this.' He selected a bottle from the claret rack, opened it with a corkscrew hanging nearby and brought it across to the other two. There was only a single wineglass for them all to drink from, so they passed it round like a loving cup, the Dellar twins only sipping, and the stranger relishing the wine as a painkiller.

'I'm also leaving you the torch,' Eddie said, 'but lie still as long as you can. I'll be back before sun-up.'

All of that had taken place in the early hours of Saturday morning. Definitely odd. Not least because of the calm way Eddie had accepted it all. And getting even odder from then on. Back in her attic room Jessica had lain down again, resolved only to catnap and be ready for when Eddie took the man away; but there was too much adrenaline at work for her to sleep.

They shouldn't have left Nicholas alone. Anything might happen and he was powerless to look after himself. Suppose he drank the rest of the bottle, then tried moving around on the uneven flagged floor. She couldn't lie here in comparative comfort while . . .

Slipping on sweater, jeans and trainers, she stole again downstairs to let herself into the cellar.

That was when the real nightmare began.

At the foot of the back stairs she felt wind blowing in from the far side of the house. Not one of the normal Larchmoor draughts. The front door had been propped open with a chair. 'Eddie,' she called softly. He must be out there waiting for the taxi.

The sound came from immediately behind her, a soft shuffle and a drawn breath. Instantly hands swept round and clamped on nose and mouth, pulling her backwards off balance. She flailed helplessly, couldn't breathe, felt herself falling back against a hard body, then a sharp kick behind the knees brought her down. Squirming on the hall tiles, she tried to tear at the hands bearing down on her face. She felt the savage satisfaction of flesh ripping under her nails. If he raped her, killed her, at least she'd marked him. There'd be evidence . . .

A low voice threatened. 'Scream and I cut your throat.' Cold steel pricked at her cheek.

She believed him. And it wasn't Nick's voice. This was one of the men who'd tried to kill him. She shivered and lay still.

8

Once he had her mouth taped he didn't speak again until he had her trussed hand and foot in the van. Then he set it gently coasting downhill towards the village road where he switched on the engine. A mile from the house the van pulled into a field gateway and he came round to open the rear doors. Jess shrank away, making little animal noises through the gag.

'Listen,' he said, easing the tape from her mouth. 'Charles wants you out of the country until he can get back. It seems you're a bit of a loose cannon. If the wrong people get hold of you they could put pressure on him. Do you understand?'

'And I'm the Pope,' she spat at him.

Then he explained. It was he, Roger Beale, who'd passed the note from Charles to Nicholas who'd handed it to Flo Carden, Claudia's hired help as she left the house after washing-up.

Nicholas had claimed it was for his girlfriend, Jess Dellar, only nobody must know. Flo, simple soul, had agreed to act as go-between in a clandestine affair. She was to go back and push it under Jess's door.

'So where is Nicholas now?' Jess demanded, still doubting.

'Back at the house. Your brother's going to get him away.'

Yes, that was what Eddie had said he would do. And Jess remembered the name Beale. She'd taken a call from him once at work and handed the phone on to Charles. He'd moved away to continue the conversation, but she'd picked up that it was a friendly one.

'How do I know you're who you say you are?' she demanded.

He sighed. 'The last thing I'd want to carry is ID. But I'll show you something.'

He threw back a canvas in the van's opposite corner. It had concealed a smart travel trolley. 'In it you'll find several outfits all correctly sized; handbag complete with makeup; a credit card in a new name, ditto new passport and a stack of euro banknotes.

'Your flight tickets are in this envelope. You'll find everything's in order. Instructions here.' He took a single sheet of paper from an inside pocket and handed it to her. 'When you've memorized that, I shall destroy it. Understood?'

She glared at him while he stared evenly back. 'I understand all right. It's just I'm still not sure I *believe* you.'

'So what — I'm a rapist? You're an item for white slave export?' His sarcasm was cutting. 'A lot of planning has gone into this; just don't go all girlie and mess things up.'

Careful planning. Yes, she could appreciate that. Who else but Charles would be behind such deviousness? Or dare to deprive her of all dignity? It bore his hallmark. And the note sent via Beale had been signed with her private name for her lover. That precaution was in case the note fell into the wrong hands. For the present he'd had to hide their connection.

The man Beale loosed her wrists and ankles. Silently she opened the envelope with the flight tickets, checked on the destination and that a return half was included, the date left open. Her name was given as Laura Nelson.

Then she read the instructions. They were brief, clear, and included restricted freedom of action until the evening flight took off from Heathrow.

It seemed to be kosher; and it did follow on from the order Charles had given her in person before his flight to Washington: that she should accept Carlton's invitation because he needed to know where she'd be this weekend.

'Right,' she said, handing back the sheet of

paper. 'You can go ahead and destroy it.' She managed a tone of some authority, head held high.

She traded a glare for the steely way he was observing her. 'There was no need to manhandle me the way you did.'

He permitted himself a sliver of smile. 'I'd no choice. You could have squawked.'

He was right. If she'd had a single second to draw breath she'd have gone off like the *QEH* leaving dock. You don't stand on ceremony when you're attacked out of the blue. And he'd never have had time to explain fully while they struggled in the corridor with his hand over her mouth.

'After Nicholas turning up like that, I should have been expecting trouble,' she admitted, sounding almost humble. Beale was one of Charles's lieutenants, after all: knew the ropes. He'd be reporting back on her. 'God knows it was a weird enough night up till then.'

Now he really smiled; a great melon slice. Nice teeth, she thought wistfully; square and glowing white in the dim light of the van's rear. She would bet they tasted minty. Nice build too. Six foot two or three. He'd look good in beach shorts.

'Ready to go further?' he demanded.

He meant the journey, of course. Her mind

had taken a different tack for a second. 'Sure. Drive on. Only keep your eyes on the road, because I'm going to change into something rather smarter.'

★ ★ ★

And so, after a long detour until he released her that afternoon at the airport, then a reasonable flight, she had landed by dusk at Marco Polo airport, Venice.

It was much as she remembered it from a student visit three years back, but, walking through towards the boats, she found the telephones had all been changed. None took coins any more. There were no translations in English, French or German, and she hadn't enough Italian to make sense of the instructions.

Forget a common agricultural policy or a common currency — why hadn't someone insisted on a common European language? Which must, she thought, of course, be English, even at risk of war with chauvinist France.

Meanwhile she had to rely on her inadequate Spanish, which locals were free to accept as Italian with an outlandish accent. It sufficed to get a response first from a youngish woman with a quantity of luggage

130

by her feet, but she too was new to the machines and appealed to a pert-looking lad of ten or so who regarded them both with incredulous scorn. He guided them to a machine that gobbled Jess's 5-euro note and delivered a small card. From this the boy nonchalantly tore off one corner and inserted the card in a telephone's slot, where it was rejected three times in different positions.

Jess watched a dull flush creep up the child's neck and spread into the prominent ears. So un-cool. She felt mortified for him. Eventually he thought to feed the torn end in first, magnetic strip uppermost. A dialling tone sounded. The child faded. The youngish woman shrugged and signalled for someone to come and dispose of her luggage.

Jess called the memorized number, was instructed where to contact her next escort, and purchased a boat ticket for Lido. Then she dragged her trolley to the jetty labelled *Ailaguno* and took a seat on the waiting water-bus.

It waited ten minutes, gradually filling, then chugged into a wide half-circle before shooting off at full throttle. White spray thrown up from the bow eased the heat of an exhausted day. Jess ran a finger under the neck of her new silk blouse and savoured the welcome chill.

Overhead, silver-blue was dimming into indigo, with a fine sickle moon that looked stuck on velvet. All along the shorelines of the islands distant lights were appearing in a denser design than the random stars above. On all sides the lagoon opened out darkly, and for the first time in days Jess relaxed, giving herself up to the throb of the engine and the hiss of spray.

After some forty minutes the boat slowed to pull in at Murano, below the museum. The island seemed dead, and when a few passengers streamed off, sight and sound of them were instantly swallowed up by the tall, blank-faced buildings lit only by occasional globes fixed high against stone walls. The very darkness of the place and the black, sucking water seemed sinister. It had all been so different before, by daylight.

The *vaporetto* reversed and pulled out into the final stage of the crossing. Another fifteen minutes of roaring and rocking before she recognized the illuminated Campari sign rising high from the water, then the wood and glass shelter of the *debarcadero* at Lido-Venezia.

Here, following her phoned instructions, she disembarked and crossed the square by the taxi rank. All down the main street opposite, in brightly lit windows, closed shops displayed fashion goods, floral arrangements, brilliantly boxed confectionery. Towing the trolley, she crossed over, passing crowded bars, *trattorias* and restaurants where diners lingered over their evening meal. A few closed shops further, and then she turned right into the broad walk of Lepanto.

Twenty steps into the pedestrian precinct a man stepped from a shadowed doorway, murmured 'Permeso?' and took the luggage trolley from her. Round the next corner a car was waiting with the engine quietly running. The front passenger door swung open. As her baggage was stowed she observed the driver, a handsome, plump woman with raven-dark hair, middle-aged and unalarming.

Reassured, but uncertain quite what she had let herself into, Jessica Dellar accepted the seat offered. The man got in behind, unseen, and without a further word spoken they slid off into the night.

★   ★   ★

She had been mistaken about the woman. She wasn't plump, but well-fleshed and stood splendidly tall, was possibly older than Jess had assumed, and certainly impressive: a sort of Maria Callas presence. Perhaps a diva?

133

Lido was a place where you expected to see celebrities.

Electronically operated gates swung open to admit the car to a short, curved drive close-walled by evergreens. The house appeared to be of white stone and they entered by a flight of wide steps.

A square hall paved with rose-veined marble had several rooms off it on both sides. At the far end, beside a small jungle of flowering shrubs and a tinkling water feature rose a slender circular stairway supported on matching marble columns.

Impressed, Jess thought ruefully of her cramped little narrowboat where Charles had seemed contentedly at home roughing it. This was a different challenge.

She determined to mind her manners as required in a well-regulated Italian family. 'How very kind of you to come and meet me,' she said, properly, to the diva. 'Is Charles here yet?'

Her hostess waved her through to a small salon where a table was laid with supper for one. She appeared not to have heard the question, and Jess thought perhaps she had no English.

'I am sure you would like some refreshments. The meals on flights are quite impossible, I find,' the diva said. Her voice was low, full-toned, with a hint of laughter in it. The Italian accent was barely detectable.

'Aren't you joining me?' Jess ventured.

'I dined earlier, thank you; but a glass of wine would be pleasant while we get to know each other. My name, signorina, is Giulia. You may call me that. I trust your journey was not too uncomfortable?'

'The return by water was wonderful. The lagoon is magic at night. So mysterious.'

'*Return*. Ah, you have been here before? Good. You must tell me how you would like to spend your time here as our guest.'

Our, Jess noted, and wondered who else was in the house. The man who had met her had vanished, gone perhaps to garage the car. With all the inner doors open, she was sure he hadn't yet followed them in.

'I'm Jessica,' she introduced herself, as her hostess removed the cover from a serving-dish.

'Yes.' Clearly this wasn't news to her. 'Or you were. Here you are Laura Nelson. Please be sure to remember that.' She waved a casual hand at the laid table. 'Fresh salmon with a lime and coriander sauce,' she indicated. 'Baby potatoes. There are various salads. Please help yourself.' She filled two glasses for the girl, one with water and the other with wine.

Although she had spoken of their getting to know each other, she stayed silent while Jess ate, sipping slowly at her own white wine and occasionally admiring her be-ringed fingers.

Despite the woman's apparent detachment once she'd done the welcoming bit, Jess was aware of her as something between hostess and jailer. On duty anyway. There were questions aplenty she would like to have put to her but the atmosphere was forbidding. For the present she must respect the level of discretion Charles's staff exercised, but if it went on too long she knew she'd be breaking out. They couldn't hold her indefinitely without providing some explanation.

She declined the dessert. It was one of those elaborately sculpted Italian confections of sponge, liqueur and icing sugar. The coffee was exactly the way she liked it, strong and unsweetened, with a hint of Mocha.

'You are young,' Giulia remarked. 'Myself, I cannot take caffeine at night. I would never sleep a wink. But I think you have had an exciting day and will be ready to retire now.'

The last sentence was spoken as a question, but with an undertone of firmness. Jess decided the woman had been an actress rather than a singer. She left no doubt about the significance of anything she said. It was still irritating that she hadn't answered the query about Charles. The omission had certainly been deliberate. As Jess rose from the table she resolved not to be put off.

'Sitting most of the day, I really need exercise,' she said. 'I think I'll take a walk before I turn in.'

'But of course. Let me show you the garden. It will be my pleasure.'

So escort duty was to be maintained. But at least a tour outside the house might give some idea of the fastness she was to be confined in.

There were dogs. As the women left by a side door into a terraced walk they appeared silently and stood watching at a distance of some ten yards. Giulia murmured a few words and they fell in behind, not at heel but maintaining the same distance, two sleek Dobermans with beautiful movement.

The garden was small, as on all the islands, but skilfully laid out with pergolas, twisting walks and steps to connect its three levels. There was the constant sound of water where it gushed from the mouths of three *putti* into a pool edged with yellow iris. The air was scented with lavender, box, and a small red flower shaped like a hop but redolent of sage. At the far end from the road the garden met a high stone wall interrupted by a wrought iron gate with a formidable-looking lock. Beyond and below it Jess caught the gleam of dark water and the lagoon's quiet slap and cloop.

As she walked Giulia brushed the surrounding shrubs with her fingers letting off fresh scents at every turn. She was far too much in control, Jess decided. 'When are you expecting Charles to arrive?' she demanded.

They had reached the end of a circuit, and light from a window illuminated the older woman's face as she turned. It was smooth and calm, almost featureless.

'You supposed you were to meet him here?' she questioned. Her elegant shoulders rose as she shrugged the possibility away.

'No, signorina. It is not for an assignation that you have come. It is to prevent your being killed.'

9

Last night, after the garden tour with Giulia, they'd returned to the drawing-room and she'd met the two men. Stefano, sprawled on a *chaise longue*, shirt unbuttoned to expose a long, bronzed torso, had languidly waved a bare leg towards Giulia, then sprung upright at sight of their guest.

'Signorina,' he'd said with extravagant adulation, and mocking her.

Then, on being introduced, she'd recognized Franco, (stolid and stocky while the other one was willowy) as the almost silent young man who had met her at Lepanto. He advanced from his chair and offered a firm handclasp. 'It is a pleasure to have you with us, signorina.' His English was almost perfect. She guessed he would be about eighteen and possibly Giulia's son. They had the same high, wide forehead and slightly hooked nose, but he was shorter by some three or four inches.

'Can I get you a drink, signorina? Mama?'

'Laura?' Giulia prompted, raising an eyebrow.

'Thank you. A mineral water would be lovely.'

'And a sambuca for me, then.' She moved across to a sofa by the open window and arranged herself theatrically while her son poured and Stefano brought their drinks to them. Close to, Jess saw that he was some ten years older than the other young man, so perhaps the woman's lover? Certainly his casual informality suggested something close.

'My son and my nephew will be delighted to entertain you, Laura,' Giulia said silkily, as though she had guessed what was in the girl's mind. 'Between them they must know all there is to know about the islands, and unless you stop Franco he will lecture you until you die of boredom. Also, Laura, you will find both are quite adequate at tennis and swimming. The pool here is tiny, but we have a cabin on Lido's south shore where you may swim in the Adriatic.'

'That's very kind, but I'm not sure how long I'll be staying.' Giulia was assuming too much, and Jess resented the repetition of the new name she had to go under. It implied she wasn't capable of remembering that precaution herself. In fact the whole business of her enforced removal from old Carlton's home and the journey here smacked too much of the press-gang. The moment had come when she must stand on her hind legs and make it clear she would please herself what she did.

Giulia's suggestion in the garden that her life might be in danger was ridiculously melodramatic. Roger Beale had explained that for the moment her presence in England could be embarrassing for Charles. That much she'd accept. She knew he was involved in some big, multinational deal with political undertones, and while negotiations hung in the balance a breath of scandal could tip the scales. Even that consideration seemed over-correct in these permissive days; but presumably he knew the prejudices of the important foreigners he had to haggle with.

'Let me show you the lights,' Franco had offered, cutting through her thoughts. He led her through double doors on to the balcony. Like the one jutting from her own bedroom above, it was on the lagoon side of the villa and overhung a little jetty where a small white powered craft tilted gently at its mooring.

'There are more trees in Venice than in any other city in Europe,' he told her.

Jess pictured the tortuous alleys, the *palazzi*, galleries, crowded boutiques and humped bridges — nothing green except a glimpse here and there of a branch reaching out from some secret, walled garden.

He had laughed at her puzzlement. But of course the trees were below the marble floors. They were the timber piles that supported the proud *campaniles*: underwater forests petrifying over the centuries, but still sinking, because all these islands were a continuation of the miles of offshore swamp. And the sea, that had brought Venice its ancient glory, would finally suck all its magnificence away.

Even her ghost wouldn't linger here. She had no time for nostalgia. Go for it, she always told herself: she had things to do, a life to live.

Franco pointed. 'Over there, to the left, that dark mass is the Isle of Dogs. All strays from the islands are taken there. You can hear them barking at mealtimes. And ahead is the island of the Armenian Brothers. If you wish to visit their chapel they will row across and fetch you. And those distant lights, strung out . . . '

'Are *Venezia*, from *San Marco* down to *Arsenale*, with the island of *San Giorgio* in front.'

'Ah, you know our tiny world already. This isn't your first visit.'

She was aware of having cut him off and was sorry. 'One can never know enough about such a magical place,' she granted.

'So what would you care to do tomorrow?'

She took her time answering while they stepped back indoors. There was no question what she would prefer to do: go home. Find out what Charles was actually up to. And have that word with Eddie which she'd not found time for at old Carlton's.

'Tennis?' she suggested. There wasn't a court in the garden, so it would mean going outside, testing how closely she was guarded. Maybe she could buy some postcards, send a message to say where she'd ended up.

She was conscious of Stefano and Giulia exchanging glances, then the woman's barely perceptible nod.

Stefano turned his brilliant smile on her. 'So that's what we will do, before it gets too hot.'

'Yes,' Giulia agreed. 'The forecast is for 38 degrees Celsius tomorrow. Breakfast will start at seven. Stefano shall book a court for 8.30.'

★   ★   ★

So this morning's programme had already been mapped out for her. She showered, practised speaking her new name in front of the mirror, slid into a short, yellow sundress and went downstairs. She followed voices to the large, airy kitchen. There a dumpy, fat woman looked up from filling a cafetière, her dark face one shining smile.

'Signorina, I Rosalba. I cook,' she

announced proudly. She pointed to the other, who appeared to be Chinese. 'He, Ping Pong.'

The little man bowed. 'Not true name, but it amuse people. Rosalba, that is all the English she know. She learn it for you.'

'I'm honoured,' Jess said, 'Thank you. I'm Laura.'

She took a place at the scrubbed, square table. 'Where are the others?'

'The signora take coffee in her room. The young men go sailing. Perhaps we get fish for lunch,' the man said.

Rosalba might have little English, but she was more than able in Italian. While Jess helped herself to fruit and rolls her voice went on relentlessly, passionately, with an extravagant sweeping of arms and rolling of eyes as she related some dramatic story quite incomprehensible to the girl.

'What was all that about?' Jess asked in a brief lull while the cook went to answer a bell's summons.

Ping Pong shrugged. 'Her son. He have this woman she do not like. Families, *aiiigh*!'

Before Jess had finished her coffee Stefano and Franco were back, smelling of the sea, with salt crusted on hands and eyebrows. Franco flung a hessian bag at the Chinese who peered in and declared, 'Not enough. Tomorrow you do better.'

'Two minutes,' Stefano promised, 'and we shall be ready for you, Laura.'

'He lies,' Franco said, following him to the door. 'He will spend at least twenty minutes on just spraying his perfume.' Joshing each other, they went flying upstairs.

★　★　★

The tennis courts were on the Adriatic side of the narrow island, protected by a surround of shrubbery and palm trees. They played singles, Jess the first set against Franco, losing to him four-six. She did better against his cousin who slammed the ball fiercely from the baseline but had less finesse. At six-all he declared they should leave it so, well matched.

'Now you must play each other,' Jess said, 'while I watch.' She let them battle on for a game or two, then quietly made for the gate of the little park. Before she could make her escape Franco was there beside her.

'Have we bored you?' Stefano called from the net. He had started to wind it down.

'Not at all. Please carry on. I just thought I'd have a look at some shops, perhaps get some postcards to send home.'

She'd said too much. 'We'll come too,' Franco insisted. 'Here, borrow my sun glasses. The light is too much for your English eyes.'

They let her choose the view cards, even reminded her what euro stamps were now required, but she knew she was under arrest, the wraparound shades protecting her from public gaze much as the police at home covered their suspect with a blanket. It was beginning to get to her that Giulia's warning had been serious.

They would never let her post those cards. She knew that, and she couldn't see any way she could smuggle them out. When she checked her things after breakfast she'd found that the return half of her flight ticket had been removed from its envelope, although so far the money was intact. In the villa there was always someone on duty. In the garden there were the Dobermans.

All the same, she wrote three cards during siesta time: to Claudia and Carlton, doing the thanks thing; a vague greeting to Kate; a longer one to Eddie, quoting the temperature here and warning him not to eat the cake she'd left in his freezer until she was back to share it with him.

She signed them all with the letter J, still hoping it might pass muster with her guards. But if she imagined she'd be allowed further freedom she was put right when they all met up at four o'clock for iced tea.

'My beautician is to come later,' Giulia said, stroking back her blue-black hair. 'You may wish to make use of her. With such a lovely fair complexion, Laura, have you never thought of becoming a blonde? It would suit you so well. Don't you think so, boys? A new Marilyn Monroe.'

They agreed instantly, Franco perhaps with less enthusiasm. Anyway it was clear that they'd been put up to it. Not a suggestion, but a command.

'No way!' Jess protested. 'Bleach is out of the question.'

Giulia wasn't impressed. 'Oh, but I think it would be best. More tea, signorina?'

Jess started to get up from her chair but was strangely lethargic. The heat and the tennis were taking their toll. She slid back. Giulia leant forward. Her face came so close, peering in, that her two eyes became one, like a shiny, black beetle.

Jess awoke on a sofa an hour and a half later, bottle-blonde, with an urchin cut gelled into spikes.

She was outraged, trembling with inexpressible fury. Giulia remained calm, totally in charge: Franco silent but unable to meet her eyes. Stefano kept his distance, shrugging his angular shoulders. In the kitchen Rosalba and Ping Pong carefully pretended they noticed no difference.

Alone at last in her room she examined herself in the mirror. A pert bimbo stared defiantly back. Every surface of her face had taken on a different, upward slant. When did she ever have a retroussé nose?

Her whole persona seemed changed, and surely with it her mental tectonics had realigned. She *knew* this character she now stared at, had passed her in the streets of London, been crushed against her in the Underground, shared a cloakroom mirror with her in restaurants, watching her slam on more black eyeliner. She'd be shallow, mouthy, confident, voicing secondhand judgments, her slang — like the spiky hairstyle — just that bit *passé*. If this one couldn't fix a bloke to take her out of Italy on his pillion then she'd march out as a backpacker. You could lose her ten times over in the swarm of tourists boggling at the Bridge of Sighs.

Good. So that was the way she'd leave. Her mind was made up. She had suffered the final humiliation at Giulia's hands.

Her present passport was useless. This trollop was no Laura. What 'celebrity' name would her mother have saddled her with? Patsy? Charleen?

Giulia had said nothing about updating the

passport to her new appearance. The reason wasn't hard to imagine: she had no intention of letting Jess use it again. Return to England was off the agenda. All this hoopla about instructions from Charles was beginning to wear thin. His original intention had been to protect her, or at least distance her from his present situation. Jess suspected Giulia of adorning it with her own fancies, or even of running a separate agenda in parallel. Behind that perfectly turned-out hostessing she sensed a hint of malicious invention, because under it lay instinctive hostility.

So I'll run my own game, Jess decided. However long Charles had originally intended her to be kept away, if she turned up despite all the humiliating frustrations, he'd have to admit she had initiative.

She returned downstairs for dinner pre-serving the expected mood of high dudgeon, making the cousins work hard to bring her round to a better mood. Tomorrow, Stefano said, they would take her across the lagoon and she could do the tourist round, go wherever she fancied — Doge's Palace, churches, museums, the Peggy Guggenheim Modern Art gallery. Next day Murano for the glass factories, Burano for linens. It seemed there was no limit to where she could safely go, now that she was disguised.

Even while she allowed herself to appear won round she fumed against them inside. How crass to insult her further with promises of childish treats. The ultimate indignity had been to have all choice removed: to be put under and operated on like a sick cat at the vet's. And be turned out a common bottle blonde.

She shrugged at their plans, keeping up a barrier of sulkiness. That was all for tomorrow. Tonight there was to be sea bass and chargrilled peppers followed by a pineapple torta with toffee sauce. Then Scrabble or backgammon while Stefano sang, serenading them with his guitar.

Jess endured the pantomime stiff-faced, inside coldly vowing revenge. They mustn't guess her new appearance could be turned to advantage. And there was one added point in its favour: when eventually Kate got to see it, all the air would go out of her sails. Speechless, she might forget to ask the most embarrassing questions.

★   ★   ★

Seated at Eddie's bedside, Kate was startled as one of the nurses came in quietly behind her. 'Tea, Mrs Dellar?'

She hadn't been dozing; simply trapped in

mental miasma, and it was good to be rescued from it. She took the proffered cup with a weary smile and cradled it in her lap.

She sat well back, allowing the nurses freedom of access. Although Eddie remained totally immobile there was so much to be done for him: constant checking of heart and blood pressure; drips to be overseen and kept flowing, then replaced; urine bags emptied; notes to be made up for the surgeon's round.

Only the sighing *clunk* of the ventilator assured her that he was, at least mechanically, functioning. She fixed her eyes again on his still face, the dark sweep of eyelashes lying along his unlined cheek. The five o'clock shadow that proclaimed him a mature man seemed a mockery. This was a distorted replay of how she'd watched over him soon after his birth, Eddie the later twin to be born.

Jess, ever impetuous, had thrust herself into the world, lustily crying. Eddie had taken his time, lying awkwardly. There had been anxiety that with delay his breathing would be affected. Yet he had made it to the outside.

For several weeks he'd seemed frailer, slower, with a more tenuous hold on life than his more robust sister. Even when Kate had both babies home he was the one she most often stole in at night to check on.

But with the years all that had changed. He'd gathered strength, put on weight, grown into a sturdy, thoughtful little boy. At puberty he'd shot up, overtaken his sister in height, proved himself in athletics as well as with academic work. A sensible, sensitive, kindly personality, well able to take care of himself.

And now, suddenly, it had gone full circle, so that he was helpless again, and she must watch, powerless to do anything for him. Her hurt was overwhelming, physical.

She believed that for two days she had been his only visitor. Surely there was someone else who could take a turn sitting here, talking, in the hope that a familiar voice could reach through to his unconscious mind and stimulate it into action. She wondered if perhaps it worked away inside despite his outer stillness. What kind of dreams would he be having? There was no way to read that from his passive face.

She would give anything to have Jess here alongside, chattering and teasing in the way that never failed to get him going. Others would be useless at that.

Last evening she had sat alone in her cottage and watched dusk soften the outlines of her garden until all colour was sucked away and only the white lilac remained dimly visible, floating on the dark. It had seemed like life draining away. When she spoke by phone with Night Sister she'd learnt Eddie's condition was still unchanged. But *stable*. That new word had brought a small measure of comfort.

Later the young woman detective had called in with the wonderful news about Jess. That the charred body was someone else.

Or it had seemed wonderful until she realized it was still a violent death. Some unknown mother had lost a child in her place. It seemed shameful to feel such enormous relief.

And still nobody knew where Jess had gone off to without leaving word. It was appallingly rude, especially to Claudia and Carlton. If they hadn't had their minds full of their own losses they might have been more censorious. Undoubtedly, now that she'd phoned them about the body in the burnt-out house, they would be attributing Jess's omission to bad upbringing.

More black points against me, Kate thought wearily. I can't do anything right for them. Some people have to cope with a dysfunctional family. The Dellars are some-thing else: individually *hyper*-functional, with each of them going all out to do his or her own thing, and the devil take any other consideration.

She ran through the events since Friday afternoon. With Dr Marion Paige she had felt some empathy because she too was an outsider: not a Dellar. But then, none of the family could be totally Dellar. At least half of their genes were from elsewhere, from people like Matthew's dead wife Joanna or herself; from dear Michael's mother too. She'd brought a new strain into the family, diluted the Dellar self-sufficiency. It was she who accounted for Michael having been so different, lovable and loving; appreciating a world of people outside himself.

But hadn't Carlton's and Matthew's mother been an outsider too? Maybe some of what disturbs me about the others was down to her, Kate thought; that first wife of Grandfather Frederick. We don't know enough about the past, about those who were dead before we lived. That is one way in which I really believe in ghosts — the inescapable genes that they leave to haunt us.

And then *Claudia*: also an outsider. How had it come about that she was the most Dellar of all? — almost setting the pattern: the poison in the pool. (Kate didn't know where those words came from. They sounded like a poetic quote.)

It was hard to think of Claudia as ever not having been a Dellar. She was so much the prototype. She considered no one's feelings when she spoke or acted; took no prisoners. Kate could not believe she loved her elderly husband. She was simply the dragon guarding his gate. Theirs was a symbiotic relationship, like rocks and barnacles, but Kate wasn't sure who was which.

Carlton lived isolated in his imaginings, surviving physically under her shadow. For Claudia, Carlton was her *raison d'être*, providing material security and nourishment. Little wonder then that when, amazingly, this disparate couple had produced a child she should turn out so strangely detached as Miranda.

Back to Marion Paige, no longer the new enigma. Kate believed they'd much in common. Both watched people, observed things about them, saw their strengths and weaknesses. But overnight her feelings about the woman had shifted. The difference between us, Kate realized, is that I try not to work on what I see. Particularly I've tried with my children. Marion, she was sure, picked up on others' foibles and made use of them. Her compulsion was to manipulate.

Which made her wonder quite why Marion intended to marry Robert, whom she obviously found transparent. The look she'd given him across the garden hadn't actually been doting. With new, sharper insight Kate knew then: in secret Marion despised him. Her expression at that moment had been one of slightly disguised contempt. And Robert — once-bitten in marriage, surely twice a harder nut to crack — was nevertheless in thrall to Marion, who would twist him to fit her requirements.

Kate shuddered. Oh God, she thought wretchedly; must I dislike them all? What's wrong with me? Perhaps, just now, I'm paranoid. Put it down to shock. Otherwise why should I feel revulsion for the one person who'd at first appeared to be kind?

Is there no one I like?

Old Carlton: yes, she was quite fond of him, but warily. He could diminish one too easily. The more so if you let drop the protection of banter. Appearing so mild, so woolly-minded, he was the keenest of the lot; the most capable of withering the spirit with a word. She knew her own attitude was one of subservience: the underdog, nervously self-protective.

And Matthew was a sadist despite his courtly veneer: the legal raptor. Madeleine had little time for anything but horses. Her husband and his son Jake didn't really count.

What other Dellars were there? Only Miranda, the panicky hermit crab, poor girl.

10

On Tuesday morning Miranda Dellar was following her mother downstairs with a suitcase in one hand and the tartan rug over the other arm. She counted the eighteen steps to this lower flight, then twenty-seven repetitions of the fleur-de-lys pattern on the bottom line of the wallpaper as far as the hotel's outer door.

There had been five hundred and eighty-two square tiles in her bathroom upstairs. She felt safer if she knew.

Her lips moved as she passed over the flagstones out to the cab. Claudia was standing beside it and gave her a hard stare. Miranda closed her mouth tightly, and accidentally her eyes, so that she blundered into the open door of the waiting taxi. Her mother's breath escaped in a controlled *whoosh*.

Miranda let the cabbie take the case from her hand and tried to step in, clumsily entangled with the rug. It was snatched from her. She took the seat in the far corner of the rear. The car had eight panes of glass for its windows, including the windscreen. There had been ten clouds in the sky when she woke up this morning. Now there were thirty-three smaller ones. That was good. She didn't know why, but it made her feel better. Clouds you could have a game with, because they were always changing. Too many other things stayed, fearfully, the same.

Not Jessica, though. Like the sky, every time she saw her cousin, Jessica was different. She came and went, like a wild dog that had never had a lead on. The policeman with the puppet face had asked last night when she'd last seen Jessica, and she'd said Friday, downstairs after dinner, just like everyone else. She'd remembered, because then Jessica had been going out to the terrace wearing a necklace with fifteen shiny green stones hung from a fine gold chain.

Something she hadn't mentioned was seeing the white oblong of the letter being drawn from under Jess's door much later. That was because she hadn't seen the hand that took it in, though she had seen Flo, who worked in the kitchen, when she came back to deliver the letter. The policeman hadn't asked about her.

Miranda had been sitting on a library windowsill, (fortyeight small panes in a six by eight arrangement over its two sashes), and wondering at all the empty spaces on the shelves. Only one hundred and twenty-two books left. She wondered what had happened to the rest.

When Flo came indoors she'd silently followed her up the sixteen uncarpeted steps of the backstairs and watched as she pushed the paper under Jessica's door. Flo hadn't seen her standing back in the shadows. When Flo had gone she'd waited there five hundred and thirteen seconds until the note had been pulled fully in. But she hadn't seen Jessica do it. Then she'd felt tired and gone to bed.

Well, the questioning was past and over now, she consoled herself, as the taxi gathered speed over the short trip to the old house. (In passing she counted seventeen cows in Harper's field; then two police vans in their old driveway; a white plastic tent with five men in white overalls still examining the pit they'd dug where the kitchen used to be.)

She stepped down and waited while her mother paid off the cab. (Five pound coins and three fifty-pence pieces. No change.) It drove off, the suitcase and rug having been transferred into the ancient Daimler. Claudia backed it out of the stables. A white-overalled man came across to speak to her and didn't seem pleased at what she told him. Then, seated behind her parents, Miranda was in the soot-smudged Daimler on their way to

Cooden Beach, Sussex. To the holiday bungalow, which Mother said was all the home they had now.

The Daimler had just left the M40 at the M25 junction when a patrol car came up behind, flashing its lights. 'I was doing sixty-five in the centre lane,' Claudia dictated grimly to Carlton as she pulled onto the hard shoulder. 'I want you to stand witness to that.'

The police car pulled in ahead and a plain-clothes man got out, approaching with his warrant card extended. He wasn't one they'd met already. 'DC Silver,' he introduced himself cheerfully. 'I'm afraid you failed to inform my inspector that you were moving out of the Thames Valley area.'

'I have just informed one of your men who was examining the old house,' Claudia said icily. 'And obviously he has passed that fact on to you. Will you now kindly let us continue our journey.'

'When you have satisfactorily answered a few more questions, madam. May I know the address you're making for?'

Claudia opened her mouth to put him in his place. 'Oh, tell him and have done with it,' Carlton muttered, foreseeing complications.

Claudia frigidly dictated the address. 'It is a holiday bungalow.'

'And how long are you intending to stay there?'

'Really, young man, I don't see that . . . '

'Indefinitely, I imagine,' said Carlton. 'We have nowhere else to go at present. Fortunately we left a few of our possessions there last autumn.'

'Thank you, sir. In that case we shall be in touch with the Sussex police force, and if there are further questions we need to ask, you may expect a visit from them.'

'Is that really necessary?'

'This is a major crime, sir. An unidentified body was found in your house. We need to find out who else might have been present overnight, apart from your family as listed.'

'How on earth would we know?' Claudia interrupted impatiently. 'Obviously somebody broke in, a stranger, and set fire to the place.'

'I understand you employed a catering firm that evening, who left in their van at ten-fifteen. All are accounted for. Was there anyone else, a domestic help of any kind . . . ?'

'Florence from the village, she stayed on to clear up. I was paying her overtime. She came for her money at about ten to eleven.'

'And left straight after?'

'I assume so. She had her hat on and a bag with some leftover food.'

161

'Right. I shall need her full name and address, madam.'

'Florence Carden. She lives in one of the old almshouses down Church Lane. Either the third or fourth. That's all I can tell you.'

'The third,' Miranda muttered.

DC Silver peered into the dim rear of the old car. 'Ah, miss. Anything you can add?'

His face loomed palely through the glass like a white-bellied fish in an aquarium and startled her into speech.

'She came back. Not right then. Much later, after midnight.'

Everyone was staring. She closed her eyes and waited for the fury to burst on her, but the detective got there first. 'You saw her? Where did she go?'

'She's imagining it,' Claudia rapped out. 'She doesn't know what she's saying, constable.'

'Where, Miranda?' Carlton quavered.

'To the attics. She had a note for Jessica. She pushed it under her door.'

'And then?' Silver pursued.

'She went away. And I went to bed.'

Everyone relaxed a little. 'That would account for the girl leaving,' Claudia said sharply. 'An assignation with some lover, no doubt. And she hadn't the common courtesy to leave a note to explain she was going.'

'How do you know she didn't?' Silver asked pertly, glad to put one over on the old trout. 'In a blaze like that, what chance had a piece of paper?'

He'd have delayed them further if he could think what else to fish for. As it was, he'd have a small tiddler to take back to the Salmon. But first he'd have a word with this Flo, who just might have observed something of interest about this stuck-up family. He hoped to find more commonsense in the kitchen department.

★   ★   ★

The extended Regional Crimes team had taken over the canteen for the morning's briefing, sitting around on tables, chairs and service counter. DI Salmon planted himself opposite the mobile whiteboard which had been rolled in from the Incident Room. 'Settle down,' he growled and the conversation died.

His grotesque grin panned the watching faces. 'It's like Christmas,' he told them, 'the way crimes are being crammed into our stocking. First, we have suspected arson and the insurance adjusters sniffing round for reasons not to pay up. Second, overnight we discover an extra person gained access to the property, either by stealth or invitation. And thirdly this unidentified person is found burnt to a crisp. Fourthly, a young woman guest, Jessica Dellar, has gone unaccountably missing from the house. Fifthly, it appears she was a bit of a water gypsy. Her narrowboat on the canal near Denham has been broken into in her absence. A neighbouring boat-dweller quotes this as happening during the evening of Friday when she was with the Dellar family at the house that was torched, and the neighbour had gone to see a film in Slough. He discovered the padlock broken and the boat's contents disturbed when he went the following morning to — as he claims — 'water her plants'.

'Sixth, the young woman's brother, having escaped the fire and at present in a coma at High Wycombe hospital, has injuries consistent with being viciously attacked. While still conscious but confused, he claimed he had damaged himself blundering through a wood.

'The bruises have now had time to develop and some are quite specific. Photographs are available in the Incident Room.' Salmon grinned fiendishly, his grating voice laying on the heavy sarcasm. 'As we all know, trees don't wear boots, so it's clear he was well and truly done over. Among other recognizable marks, his ribs were kicked in. His coma arose from a blood clot on the brain.

'Some of you've had time to familiarize yourselves with the family in question. And the *question* gets more complicated as time goes on. It appears that the elderly householder, Carlton Dellar, his wife and adult daughter have removed themselves outside our authority. All further questioning must be by arrangement with the Sussex force. In view of the arson, as yet unofficially confirmed by the Senior Fire Officer, I want every detail of these people's financial affairs sifted. DC James, take a uniform officer and see what bank details you can get locally. Two estate agents have given the opinion that the property was in very poor shape and worth less than the valuable ground it stood on. Total destruction while so many were present in the house could have been an attempt to blur the issue and spread the blame.

'The family has dispersed. From today Sir Matthew Dellar can be contacted at his daughter's home in Ascot. In view of his legal background we are already checking on death threats made to him when he was a Prosecuting Counsel, and more recently a Queen's Bencher. His daughter, her husband and stepson also live at the same address. His son, a city journalist with the *Independent* has returned to London and will be in touch with us daily.

'The unidentified body may, I'm told, still yield DNA, so let's hope for a match already on our books — er, computer. There's an assumption that the body is male and fell through to the cellar with the collapse of the kitchen floor. Damage to bones in the throat indicate that he was strangled, and confirm the case is one of murder.

'Your incident room manager is Sergeant Harry Thomas. Let him have your individual reports within half an hour of return to base. You will continue in the teams already drawn up, and tasking will be arranged by your team leader. The fingertip search of the grounds at Larchmoor Place will resume immediately after this briefing. A mobile canteen will be laid on at midday. Any absence requests will be dealt with by myself. So think twice before you bother me. Any questions?'

A hand went up from a rear table. 'The missing girl. What were her relations with the others?'

Salmon scowled. 'She was family. Carlton Dellar's niece.'

'Yeah, but I mean could she have duffed up her brother and then run off? Family doesn't mean they all got on well together, and these two were twins. Maybe too close for comfort.'

Salmon grunted. 'What's your name?'

'Callow, sir. Community PC.'

Salmon ignored the titters. 'Well, Callow, you can look into that yourself and give me the answer by four o'clock. Anyone else?'

No one ventured further, and the briefing broke up. From his seat in the rear, Superintendent Yeadings folded his notes, rose stiffly to his feet and nodded across the room to Z. She would find him in his office.

He had barely gone three steps when DC Silver burst in from outdoors, red-faced and out of breath. 'Sir,' he said desperately, to cover both Yeadings and Salmon. 'Sorry I'm late. I've been chasing something up.'

'And?' Yeadings enquired. Salmon glowered.

'Carlton Dellar's daughter Miranda saw a note delivered to Jessica Dellar's room late on Friday night. It was Florence Carden, the kitchen help, who brought it, so I went and questioned her at her home. A nice old girl about sixty, she said it was from a young man, her sweetheart, who was waiting in the garden to speak to her. That is . . . '

'Jessica's sweetheart, not the kitchen help's,' Yeadings suggested helpfully.

'Yessir. And she's coming in later today to make a statement.'

'What was in the note?' Salmon demanded.

Silver looked embarrassed. 'She didn't read it, sir. She said she respected their privacy.'

'And you believed her?' The DI was incandescent. Only his superior's presence, mildly looking on, prevented his taking the naïve young DC apart. 'I'll see her myself,' he threatened. 'Get out there and bring her in right away.'

Yeadings nodded. The DI was going for the only available information on activities late on the fatal night, but he doubted his bull-in-a-china-shop approach would draw out an elderly countrywoman trained to domestic service. Either she'd be intimidated into silence or she'd resist him out of stolid independence. It seemed a good moment to step in.

'If you've a free moment,' he suggested, 'I could offer you a decent coffee upstairs.'

Salmon hesitated, suspicious but flattered by the invitation. 'Right, sir.'

'Ah, Z,' Yeadings called across the emptying room. 'You busy at present?'

'Not immediately, sir.' It was quite evident Salmon hadn't found a niche for his female detective-sergeant.

'Good. Just pop up to my office and get the percolator going, will you?' With his back to the DI he closed one eye and signalled with his furry caterpillar eyebrows. She caught on

168

to the 'woman's work' irony and smiled back. 'My pleasure, sir.'

Yeadings waved Salmon ahead. Now he'd be under control when this Florence Carden arrived for her grilling, and Z could be dismissed in advance with instructions to head her off. She would treat the woman with tact. Meanwhile, if the DI accepted him as equally the male chauvinist, too bad. He'd sort that out later, with interest.

As Z stood aside for Salmon to leave, Yeadings noticed the knot of uniform men who were waiting to ambush him ahead. They closed round the DI with requests to be taken on the CID team.

Quietly Yeadings explained his requirements to Zyczynski. He made no apology for relegating her to parlourmaid duties. She was happy to turn her hand to anything, quick to pick up that he was being devious. He then took a turn round the building, examined his front teeth in the men's room, calculated that enough time had passed and sauntered upstairs.

In his office the aroma of freshly brewed Mocha welcomed him. Salmon was already seated, with his chunky backside overlapping the straight-backed chair, and facing the paper-strewn desk. On which nothing of importance was left open to prying eyes,

Yeadings reminded himself happily. He seated himself and pushed the piles of irrelevant reports away with the sigh of a suffering bureaucrat.

Z poured two cups of dark brew and set them before the men. 'Is that it, sir?' she asked. She almost stood to attention.

'Thank you, Rosemary,' Yeadings said graciously. Salmon's small eyes flickered at his use of her first name.

'Got any milk?' he demanded curtly.

'Only Long-life.' Her tone was dismissive.

'That'll do.' He let her attend to him then nodded her away. She went out, quietly closing the door.

Yeadings relaxed behind his desk. 'Good briefing,' he approved. 'You covered almost everything.'

'Almost?' Salmon snapped alert, on the defensive.

'Which is all we can ever be sure of,' Yeadings sighed. He sounded weary, worldly-wise, almost defeated. It seemed to satisfy the other man.

Maybe I'm laying it on too thick, Yeadings warned himself. Mustn't let him lose total confidence in me. Just enough to give him his head, let him paint himself into a corner and then demand a way out.

It wasn't as though Salmon was a

permanent fixture. Give it a month or two and Angus would be back. Heaven and earth would be moved before then to ensure Mott was promoted but not moved away. He'd be wasted in any other posting than Major Crimes.

'So what hasn't been covered?' Salmon challenged.

'Ah, yes.' Yeadings sat, apparently sunk in thought. What the hell was there? Then something resurfaced. It had troubled him in bed last night. 'Mrs Kate Dellar,' he reminded the DI. 'You've read her statement together with all the others' who escaped the burning building.'

'And?'

'Something a bit odd. She was late waking, had taken a sleeping tablet. Her cousin Robert Dellar warned her off the back staircase because the kitchen was ablaze. And just then flames shot up the front stairwell, so that too was out. She ran to the library, hoping she could get out on to the front portico and attract someone's attention.'

Salmon grunted to indicate he was on the ball. 'Followed by Robert Dellar. She escaped down a ladder. He twisted an ankle or something and was given a fireman's lift.'

'Yes, but the window,' Yeadings pointed out. 'She said it was already open. In the early hours. Why was that?'

'Someone had already gone out that way.'

'But nobody was waiting marooned on top of the portico. I want you to check on all the others' statements. Ring them if necessary. Who, if anybody, got out that way? If a ladder had been used why wasn't it left there?'

Salmon treated him to an ox-like stare. 'Somebody opened it but chickened out at the height. The front stairs were still usable then. He preferred that to a jump.'

Yeadings nodded. 'Possible. But it doesn't appear in anybody's account of what happened. I want you personally to go over every report and check. We could find that that window was used for entry rather than exit. That could be the way a cat burglar got in. We do have a spare body to account for.

'Find a recent photograph of the house front, and see if there was wisteria or strong creeper growing up the pillars or wall. Alternatively, the fire may not have burnt out the roots if it was well established. Send a DC out there to look; someone who's clued up on gardening.'

Salmon's stare held a mixture of consideration and scepticism. Just the right combination, Yeadings thought, to get him moving. But moving only as far as his own office telephone: conveniently out of the way when Florence Carden turned up.

11

The ventilator kept up its rhythmic sighing. In the unnatural heat of the Intensive Care Unit it was a brutal reminder to Kate of time ticking away. As counterpoint, the nurses' soft-soled shoes made sticky kissing sounds on the polished vinyl flooring. She almost resented that they were active, while she had no contact, no control. Despite her patient summoning up of familiar topics Eddie had failed to respond to her voice or her occasional pressure on his fingers.

She slid a disk into the CD-player and left music to replace her. A Scarlatti sonata wove bright mathematical patterns of the kind he'd once delighted in. After that would come plainsong from Christ Church chapel, Elgar's clarinet concerto, the Zwingle Singers, Eric Clapton and an old Ralph McTell recording. Surely something there would get through to whatever consciousness remained behind the stony face.

Her own features grew taut. If she had failed here, there remained something else to follow up. She knew the police had resumed their fingertip search for clues in the grounds of Larchmoor Place. The Cricks had phoned early that morning from the pub to tell her, having somehow also learned the result of the dental check. Then a further call from Rosemary Zyczynski had questioned her about any of Jess's acquaintances who might help to trace her whereabouts. There was an active police operation which surely she could take some part in.

Kate had drawn up a list of one-time school and college friends. Beyond that point Jess hadn't confided who was closest to her. Except, of course, Charles Stone. Kate hadn't included his name with the others. Him, she intended to contact in person.

She had insisted on continuing her work at the library, although offered compassionate leave. Even with her hours cut to four a day, it helped to keep her mind occupied between hospital visits. She went directly there now.

During a round of tidying the reference section, she lifted down the thick red volume of *Who's Who* and looked up the name of Jess's lover. She ran a finger down the entry. Several lines of discreet description covered his interests: euphemism for wheeler-dealing, she supposed. The world of high finance was totally alien to her and she had no interest in finding out more. All she needed was his address there at the bottom: Alders, Chalk

Lane, near Maidenhead.

Kate made a note on scrap paper, looked up the relevant local map and photocopied the part she needed. She had two and a half hours more to get through before she could go and confront him.

It wasn't an easy house to find. In the end she asked at a little farmhouse. The woman who came to the door gave her directions but added that she wouldn't get an answer there. 'It's shut up,' she said. 'Everyone's away and they've cancelled the eggs till next month.' She had no idea where they'd gone.

Just the same, in case there was a caretaker left in charge Kate followed the directions and drew up at pair of closed iron gates set in a red brick wall some two hundred yards long. Behind stood quite a pretty lodge built of cream stone with a small garden. The flowers in it looked well cared for.

She could make out no movement in the rooms on the near side. There was no bell to ring, but overhead a highsited CCTV camera slowly panned the approach road. Her own car must have been caught by it as she drove up. It would be recording the length of her stay as she sized up the entrance.

Useless to remain longer, she decided. A wealthy man like Stone would surely have more than one home; and this could be the less used, to keep a check on junk mail and unwelcome visitors. She couldn't even be sure there was any house beyond the curve in the drive because the shrubbery and trees were so dense. A man so security-conscious might just use the lodge for a *poste restante*.

Dejected, she managed to lose herself in the narrow lanes and took a few minutes to find her way back to the A4094 and head for home. By now the sky had clouded over and it began steadily to rain. On reaching the motorway she realized the same pair of headlights had followed her from Maidenhead and were pacing her in the central lane.

With a wet road surface, she had been driving at a reasonable 60mph and keeping a good space from the car in front. Now she accelerated, flashed right and pulled into the fast lane. The lights behind her followed her across. Half a mile farther on she crossed suddenly back into the central lane where the traffic was denser. For a few minutes she thought she had lost the other car, but when she turned off from the M40 a vehicle two places back did the same.

There was no reason anyone should be following her. Perhaps there was an innocent explanation. There was a way she could check on it. She took the next exit, then by the village road to Ford's End and into the public car park.

The headlights of the other car, a green Land Rover, went cruising slowly past. By the time she had locked and left her own car the other could be indistinguishable from those vehicles parked farther along by the shops. It must be one of the commonest makes of car in this rural area. She started to walk in that direction, looking for a familiar face.

Barney, who sold copies of the *Big Issue*, was still there, squatting on the grey army blanket he shared with his scruffy black mongrel, his back against the wall of Parrish's the chemists. He was grinning up at some passer-by and displaying the black gaps in his crooked teeth.

'Evenin', Missus Dellar,' he greeted her as she came opposite. She dropped a coin in his cap and bent to take the newsletter he handed her.

'Barney,' she said quietly, 'it sounds idiotic, but I think I'm being followed. Would you keep an eye out?'

He winked. 'Nasty wet evenun settun in. I was jes go'un home.' He dragged the waxed cape closer round his shoulders. Rain trickled in little crooked lanes down his whiskery young face.

She knew it took more than rain to upset

him. A little harshness in the weather added to the pitiable picture. This was good business. He wouldn't quit his post until the depressive dog lifted its muzzled snout and nudged him foodwards.

Kate smiled and walked on, called in at the post office for stamps and an *Evening Standard*, then wasted minutes looking through the display of birthday cards. When she felt enough time had elapsed she retraced her steps, never looking round.

Again as she passed Barney he grinned. 'Yeah, yorrigh,' he said. 'Nasty-lookun geezer, but'e's scarpered now. You watch yerself.'

'You too,' she wished him, and walked briskly back to her car. Still nervous, she kept glancing in her rear-view mirror as she drove, but the cars that followed appeared to be changing places in a normal sort of way. Before she garaged her car she sat there in silence a while, waiting to see who drove by. Everything appeared quite ordinary.

Indoors she made tea and looked at the evening paper. On the front page was a photograph of police officers and dogs searching the grounds of Larchmoor Place. So now it was out in the open. Thank God for one thing: Jess would see it and get in touch. But she'd be furiously embarrassed.

She carried her tray back to the kitchen,

checked that the back door was bolted and the key removed from the lock, then did the same for the front door. When she had bought the cottage, after Michael died, Eddie had insisted on making the place secure for her, even fitting an alarm system which she seldom thought to switch on. This evening, however, she felt disturbed enough to need its comfort. Not that the follower, if there had been one, had continued as far as this.

So where, and why, had he given up? Why, for that matter had he taken an interest in the first place? And where had his car picked her up?

Imagination, she told herself. She was getting jumpy about perfectly normal traffic on the roads. Except that Barney had confirmed her suspicion. He was a great deal sharper than he looked, and he'd spotted the 'nastylookun geezer' showing an interest in what she was doing.

Perhaps the man had seen her from inside that empty-looking lodge and, alerted by the CCTV, suspected she was up to no good. Kate Dellar, casing the joint prior to breaking and entering? Unlikely, but how was he to know that?

So he would have driven some way to check on her. Perhaps her normal, house-wifely activities at Ford's End had satisfied him that she was just rubbernecking at the lodge. In which case she too could feel relieved.

Only she didn't.

★   ★   ★

Superintendent Yeadings directed a brief glance at the computer terminal on his desk and picked up his fountain pen. These electronic devices had their uses and what he felt for them wasn't scorn or Luddite horror: more a determined resistance. He was involved in an unhappy relationship with his own computer at home. It was a dominator, permitting no freedom of action to the human unit: fine for the nerds who surrendered their whole lives to its service, but for him there must be broader horizons.

He rolled the Parker appreciatively between his fingers. A present from Nan last Christmas, it had become his passport to freedom. He could click a keyboard with the best of the codgers of senior rank but, when it came to thinking, it took pen and paper.

The main advantage was that it carried the writer's authority, admitting personal responsibility for what the document contained. It made his log sacrosanct, inviolable to interference, with every action and proactive decision recorded, dated and timed to the minute. As far as an investigation could be faithfully recorded, this was the way he demanded it should be done, with the added precaution at each day's end of a transcript backup with electronic timing and dating.

At present, in the case's third day, there was a dearth of positive information. Each question raised led to another. 'Was it arson?' led to 'At whose hand?' 'Was the body that of Jessica Dellar?' — now proven wrong — led on to 'Whose then?' Even DNA, which he was assured could be obtained from the bones, could have no value until they'd a name to link it to.

He had hopes: that the missing girl would read newspaper accounts of the 'Mystery Fire at Poet's Home' and get in touch; that the searching of débris and grounds would yield material clues to the identity of the arsonist; that further examination of the dead body would lead to its identification; that Edward Dellar would regain consciousness and explain exactly what had been going on in the early hours of Saturday June 8th.

He read through his notes on allocation of individual personnel. His nuclear team had been well enough employed, although Salmon still didn't recognize the value of a woman DS.

By now Beaumont would have interviewed Matthew Dellar, the Railtons and Dr Marion Paige. He'd also chased up Jessica's dental chart and disproved the body was hers.

Zyczynski was regularly liaising with the missing girl's mother and had set up a search of her narrowboat, broken-into on the canal bank. She'd attended the extinguished fire and next day watched the body's recovery. She stood in at the subsequent post-mortem, providing useful notes in advance of Littlejohn's official report. She was now detailed to follow up any of Sir Matthew Dellar's judgments which could have given rise to a revenge attack.

DC Silver had followed up the Florence Carden lead offered by Miranda Dellar, whose written statement would be taken by police at Cooden Beach. He would bring Florence in for further questioning by the DI. ('Supt Y attending in person,' Yeadings wrote in, and highlighted the sentence.)

DC James had been ordered to look into Carlton Dellar's financial standing, but would probably get short shrift from that gentleman's bank manager. They might, for the present, have to work more circuitously, relying on local gossip on promptness of settling bills and any outstanding extravagances. Not that outgoings were a reliable indication of income or balance.

Salmon was over-optimistic in going all-out for the notion of an insurance scam. They were facing too complicated a web of unknown factors for certainty on that yet.

Yeadings grunted: plenty of occupation there for everyone but himself. 'More exchange of ideas essential between principal investigators,' he wrote. Then, on a fresh line, 'Query Special Branch visiting Edward Dellar and requesting regular reports on his progress. Is that young man their concern rather than Sir Matthew?'

He looked at his wristwatch, wrote 'Tuesday, June 11th, 14.20 hrs,' and passed the last two pages through the scanner. He locked the log in the top drawer of his desk and pocketed the key. The copies went into an inner pocket; just to be on the safe side, he told himself. He wouldn't have been so paranoid if Angus had been here handling the investigation.

A phone call from front desk informed him that DC Silver had just brought in Florence Carden. He summoned Zyczynski and made his way down.

In the Interview Room he complained of stale cigarette smoke. 'We'll be more comfortable in my office,' he told the visitor.

'Silver, wait fifteen minutes, then let the

DI know where we are and come up yourself.'

Florence Carden was a small, neat woman in a grey, straight-skirted jersey suit and a hat like an inverted flowerpot plus a drooping brim. It was the sort of headgear Joan Hickson had invariably worn as Miss Marple. In fact she was not unlike that character with her pale, lined face. At present the washed-out blue eyes held something of the same steely determination, but in her case from a prim distaste for finding herself inside a police station.

Yeadings hoped she hadn't been too badly inconvenienced, and explained how important her recollection of the night of the fire could be. 'I'll leave you to chat to young Rosemary here while I find someone to fetch you a cup of tea,' he offered, vaguely avuncular.

She declined both tea and coffee, sitting with hands demurely clasped in her lap and a heavy handbag hanging from one arm. 'Have you worked a long time at Larchmoor Place?' Z began conversationally.

'Sixteen years, miss. Well, nearly seventeen now. Not regular, like. Nowadays just when things get a bit out of hand.'

'How out of hand, Mrs Carden?' Yeadings inquired.

'It's *Miss*.' She struggled between discretion and a wish to oblige. 'I bin brought up to keep me mouth shut,' she informed him. 'Doesn't mean I've gotta keep me eyes and ears closed too. You wouldn't last long in service otherwise. But don't expect me to gossip about me betters. I know not to do that.

'What I mean is, a big place like that takes a lot of upkeep. But there's things you can let slip for a while and then catch up with. Things like polishing brass and cleaning rooms that aren't used. Mrs Carlton thinks she can manage on her own most of the time, but . . . '

'Things can get out of hand,' Z echoed, nodding sagely. 'That's why they rely on you.'

Florence Carden smiled at her and appeared to relax a little. 'She's very droll, Mrs Carlton. She says she runs the house on a system of organized neglect. Only trouble is, what's neglected is much harder to get right later. Housekeeping's something you have to keep at if it's to be any good.'

'Of course,' Yeadings agreed. 'Having been so long with the family, you must know them very well.'

'Not to be familiar with them, sir. But yes, I do go back quite a way. I first went there as a parlourmaid when Mr Carlton's father was still alive. He kept a very well run house in those days. There were eight staff, four of them living in.'

'And now there's only you.'

'Yes, sir. Sir Matthew sacked the lot of us when he decided not to live there. By then he had a big place in Ascot with his family.'

Yeadings cleared his throat and ventured to ask, 'But Sir Matthew was the younger brother. Why didn't the house go to Carlton Dellar?'

'The house went to Sir Matthew and the contents to his brother, as I understood it. But Mr Carlton wanted to stay on, because he didn't have anywhere else.'

'As his brother's tenant?'

'I think they came to an arrangement, sir. Mr Carlton wasn't a wealthy man and not in the best of health even then. Perhaps they thought it wouldn't be for as long as it has been. Instead of rent perhaps he was letting his brother have some of the contents. A lot of furniture and pictures have disappeared over the last year or two.'

'I see.' Yeadings looked up at a knock on the door. 'Come,' he called, and Salmon entered, followed by Silver. The office was beginning to feel crowded.

'Detective Constable Silver you've met

already. This is Inspector Salmon, Miss Carden.'

The look she turned on the man was shrewd. Yeadings doubted she gave him high marks for presentation. This woman used her eyes; could be a good witness in court.

'Now this young man you found in the grounds on Friday night, Miss Carden. It would help us find him if you could give us a description.'

She nodded. 'He was about twenty-four to twenty-eight, I'd say. Same height as me; that's five feet seven. Mousy sort of hair. He was thin, with a bony face, sharp nose and chin. He was wearing a knitted top in some dark colour, perhaps green, and black or navy jeans. He didn't have any finger rings or pierced ears.'

'You're very observant. How about his voice? Did he have a distinctive accent? Would you say he was local?'

'I took good note of him once he said he was a friend of Miss Jess. She does seem to keep some strange company and I didn't want no harm — any harm — to come to her. His voice . . . ' She paused and frowned. 'He certainly wasn't born around here. He spoke different. It reminded me of that pianist who was on television last Friday, only younger; not so growly. Finnish, wasn't he?'

She hesitated.

'There's something else?' Yeadings suggested. 'Did you have doubts about delivering the note he gave you?'

'Like I said, I didn't want any trouble coming out of it, but he seemed quite a nice young man. I suppose I felt sorry for him, and I was sure Miss Jess could take care of herself, if any young woman can nowadays. But afterwards, because of the fire, and then this body they say was found . . . '

'I don't think anyone can lay that at your door, Miss Carden. Inspector, have you any questions?'

Salmon scowled at the offer. 'Where was he when you saw him?'

'Down by the pool. He must have heard me coming and stepped out from behind the old changing room. I was startled until he explained why he was there. He had this note he needed delivering to Miss Jess. He seemed to know she was staying over at the house and he didn't look alarming.

'So I thought why not. Only I hadn't got a key to get back in. Mrs Carlton had picked me up from the village store that morning when I went in for stamps. And I'd slammed the door after meself when I left. So I'd have to go home first for me key. That upset him a bit. He said the note was urgent. Anyway, I took it, only by then I wasn't so sure I should.'

Yeadings nodded. 'So what time would it be when you delivered the note?'

'Goodness knows. Well after midnight. I hadn't fed the kittens, you see. When I got home they were crying their little hearts out. Their mother got run over, so I have to give them their milk with a gravy-baster.'

'Did you speak to Miss Jessica?'

'Gracious, no. Her light was still on, so I pushed the note under her door. She'd have seen it before she switched off. The socket's right there as you go in.'

'Meanwhile her young man was waiting in the garden.'

'I couldn't say, sir. I never caught sight nor sound of him on me way back. He could have got tired and gone home.'

Her mouth tightened like a drawstring purse. 'If he was serious he'd have waited all night. She's a nice girl, Miss Jessica, for all she has some wild ways. I suppose I thought she deserved someone a bit smarter.'

'And you weren't quite happy about acting as go-between. Something about the young man wasn't quite right,' Yeadings said softly.

She sat staring at the carpet by her feet. After a moment she raised her eyes to his. 'He smelled of sweat,' she confessed. 'I thought there was something a bit wrong with him.'

They left Silver to get a written statement from Florence Carden and then take her to the canteen for refreshments. 'Could be our body,' the DI surmised. 'Which means the girl read the note and went down to let him in. She's got a lot to answer for once we catch up with her.'

Yeadings was pondering the woman's last words. Not 'Something wrong *about* him' but 'something wrong *with* him.' Had she meant he seemed unwell? His thoughts were cut through by the internal phone's ringing. He picked it up to hear Beaumont sounding mildly exasperated.

'I've just had that Dellar woman on the phone. You'll never believe it — *complaining!*'

'Which Dellar woman?'

'Mrs Carlton. The old Daimler ran out of gas on the way to the coast and she's blaming us. Apparently it's a gas-guzzler and they always carry a can of four-star in the boot because it's never been converted to lead-free.'

'I'm amazed she can still get the stuff. Go on.'

'Well, the can wasn't in the car. So apparently it's *our* fault it got stolen. Thankfully it hasn't occurred to her to blame us for it fuelling the fire!'

'Marvellous,' sighed Yeadings. 'Does she expect us to return the can if it's found in the débris?'

12

Claudia Dellar firmly replaced the receiver and drew a long breath. Later she might regret making the call but at the moment of deciding it had brought relief.

There had really been no choice. If the can of petrol had been deliberately removed then somebody had known about its existence. And knowing that, then they might maliciously have leaked that fact to the police. The connection was there to be seized on: one of the family had used it to fire the house. And the person there who made all the decisions, let alone carried them out, was herself.

So she had had to move first: acknowledge the can had been in the car, make the point that the Daimler was never locked and the old stables left open to everyone. Let the police make something of that. It gave her breathing space.

Nevertheless she seethed inside. It had been galling to get stranded in mid-journey; and doubly so to be obliged to take measures because of it. Passing the hall mirror of the sprawling little bungalow she stopped and studied her face, watching the unaccustomed colour slowly fade, the lines of anger settle into the normal expression of supercilious control.

In the sitting-room behind her she heard Miranda open the piano and a pile of sheet music slither from stool to floor. God, now she must put up with that row as the girl worked through her scales, then the Bach which was little better. She couldn't trust herself not to go in and flay the wretched girl, so instead she marched out to the rear of the building to endure Carlton, languid on a beach lounger, babbling on about the sea.

The sea to look at; not to venture on. At best his stomach was queasy and the least hint of a swell could upset it. Even when they had travelled by air he could sometimes manage to be sick. Those adventurous days were past, however, and she missed them.

The thought of travel exercised her enough to climb up into the loft and open the briefcase with the floppy disks in. She selected from centre-batch the one labelled Holiday '95. The small room in the roof held a workstation with her computer. She switched on, booted up and inserted the disk. Swiftly she scrolled through the first pages of scenic description until she reached a blank. At that point the setup changed to columns of figures. There she found itemised the main contents of Larchmoor Place at the time of father-in-law Frederick's death. This list was the one to be printed out for the loss adjusters.

Dated some two months back, separate final pages held two columns, the first of which listed the actual reduced contents as at the previous weekend. Gone up in smoke and little regretted, she thought, smiling tightly. It was the second column that really mattered to her, and the price obtained against each item. They might have made more sold on the open market, but she had needed to be extremely discreet. She allowed herself a few more minutes to play the disk through and, feeling braced, prepared to go down and cope with her husband.

Locking the tape back into the briefcase with the others, she ran her hands over the faded surface of the leather, remembering the day her father had given it to her. It had cost him his invalidity pension for three weeks, but a daughter has only one twenty-first birthday, and they were all each other had. He had died three months later while she was still in her pupillage in Matthew Dellar's chambers, and only two weeks before she'd become his mistress.

Matthew had been her insurance then, she

thought bitterly. But he'd had his own agenda. She thought of the years of faithful service she had given, in office and in bed, and the stupid vow of silence he'd demanded, in return for empty promises. Then Joanne Blythe-Hamilton had become a client and he won her big compensation in a damages claim. With full disclosure of her financial standing, Matthew had proposed marriage to her and been accepted.

Horse-faced, four-square, stolid and stupid Joanne, with her landed gentry background and an inherited fortune made in city property. That had bought his partnership in chambers, and subsequent path to success. What chance had beauty and passion against such competition?

And I *was* beautiful, Claudia reminded herself. Lithe as a greyhound, tall, majestic, with the face of a Pre-Raphaelite saint, she used to turn heads as she swept through the law courts, ambition her inspiration. And clever. But not as clever as her heartless lover.

Not then perhaps; but the game wasn't over. Matthew was going to pay in full. Did he still think he'd done enough for her, in passing her on to his doddering older brother?

She had bided her time, letting the property deteriorate over the years because it was legally Matthew's, and exploiting the house contents, ultimately to receive double by the time the insurance money came through.

She would outlive both brothers, find someone to take over Miranda. Finally she would be free, a wealthy widow travelling the world.

She picked at a fingernail. A rubbing from the old, scarred leather had lodged under there. After so much hard use she could barely remember the briefcase in its pristine glory. Instead, she was haunted by Dadda's tired, lined face transformed by pride as he watched her open the birthday package, having so short a while left to live. If she tried she could make herself see Carlton's face with the same sickly intimation of mortality. It helped her to tolerate his awfulness.

★   ★   ★

Nobody had picked up on that phone call from Cooden Beach, Yeadings realized. There'd been some tongue-clicking and eye-rolling at the old people's lack of common-sense, then the team had gone its several ways, leaving him desk-bound as ever. It might, however, furnish him with an excuse to get out of the office and breathe fresh air.

Accordingly he made an entry in his log: *Supt Y to check on reported petrol stash at Larchmoor Place*, and noted the time. Then he borrowed a uniform constable to drive and do the legwork.

He was correct in assuming that the Dellars would have used the nearest petrol station to their home. The kiosk attendant confirmed that their 'old crate' took some filling. 'More a case of how many gallons to the mile,' he joked. 'They shoulda traded it in years ago.' They would put in just enough to get them twenty miles or so and fill a can for emergencies.

'How often?' Yeadings asked.

'Every time they called, reg'lar as clockwork. Same thing most weeks.' Their last visit had been on the day before the fire.

With a modest amount in the tank at a time, they would need the emergency can for any journey over the routine length. 'Did they ever forget to bring their can?'

The man scratched his head. 'Yeah. Once or twice. Didn't matter. They could get another from our sales department. You'd best ask there.'

'No, no. No matter,' Yeadings assured him airily. He didn't want to cast suspicion and set rumours flying. 'Old folks get forgetful. My dad's the same,' he lied.

His next stop was at the remains of the house, where he left the car and walked round to the rear, his nostrils filled with the stench of burnt debris. The old stables had a row of closed half-doors where the horses were once kept, but the double gates of the coach-house were slightly ajar. He alighted and slid through, followed by the uniform man.

A light switch gave sufficient illumination to reveal a large square interior which had once been whitewashed and grown festooned with cobwebs over the years. The worn floor, of black stable tiles, sloped gently to a central drain. There was a dark stain of sump oil where the car had stood.

Along one wall was hung an extendible aluminium ladder above a brass tap with a zinc bucket under it. At the far end an open staircase led up to a loft at the opening to which old straw spilled out, accounting for the musty smell.

'See what you can find up above,' Yeadings ordered, waving towards the loft. While the constable was absent he poked about among the cupboards' mainly rusted tools.

'Not a lot,' the man reported when he had clomped back down. 'Jest a couple of milking stools and an old pack of playing cards.'

'No fuel cans?'

'Nothing like that.'

'Right.' Of course this building had already been searched, but it did no harm to have gone over it again. Yeadings resolved to re-read the list of salvaged rubbish from the fire when he got back to the nick. The Dellars must have disposed of the old cans somewhere.

'Let's do a tour of the grounds,' he suggested and made off down an avenue of limes. At its beginning the leaves were charred and curled like Autumn, but the flowers had yet to open and weren't sticky to the touch. He followed the path to a cleared space where a dilapidated little hut had a fallen branch piercing the holed thatch of its roof. Just beyond it a faded blue plastic sheet sagged over a rectangular space which must be a small swimming pool.

He sauntered towards a wooden bench which grew flaky silver-green lichen on its soggy timber. The place had such potential. An enthusiastic weekend gardener, he was saddened by the neglect of fine old trees and once-rich soil. Even this bench had . . . He paused, bent closer and examined a thread of something dark green caught in the jagged edge of the seat. Not navy blue, so it hadn't come from any police uniform during the search of this area. It appeared to be a wool

199

mixture of the kind used in machine-knit sweaters.

Florence Carden had described the unknown young man's clothing as a darkish knitted top, possibly green, and black or navy-blue jeans. So perhaps he had waited here for an answer to the note sent to Jessica. The superintendent didn't carry evidence envelopes, but he pulled the thread free and folded it inside a laundered handkerchief. From its position on the seat it could imply that the youngster had even bedded down here, and pulled the thread in turning a shoulder on the splintered wood. A slender enough lead for identification, but it shouldn't have been overlooked before.

The constable came crashing through overgrown raspberry canes that had gone wild behind the little hut. 'Found anything?' Yeadings asked without hope.

'No sir.'

His own visit hadn't been entirely fruitless, although he hadn't high hopes of getting anywhere with the thread. It was time to return to the office and see what had come in.

As the car passed the black ruins of the house it struck him again as curious that the younger son should have inherited the family home. Why had it been left to Sir Matthew?

Because the then QC had achieved greater status? But apparently it hadn't come up to his requirements, and he'd chosen to buy a more impressive family home elsewhere, relinquishing Larchmoor Place to his brother.

According to local intelligence, the contents inherited by Carlton included some remarkable Old Masters and valuable books. So perhaps after all he'd received the better legacy. The house itself was known to have been badly neglected and barely worth restoring: of much greater value as a future building site.

Which could provide a motive for arson. So to whose benefit? Sir Matthew's, surely, but one didn't go around voicing incautious suspicions about a retired High Court Judge. (*Injudicious.* Yeadings caught himself smirking at a *double entendre* worthy of DS Beaumont.)

If Sir Matthew would benefit from the fire, so must Carlton with his fortune in art treasures converted into insurance compensation almost overnight, with none of the hassle or expense of being sold through a London auction house. Provided, of course, that the cover had been adequately upgraded over the years.

Yeadings played with the notion of an internationally respected poet as a fire-raiser for profit. There wasn't much mileage in that notion either. So, his domineering wife, or the apparently autistic grown-up daughter? Suspicion didn't have to focus on either, because the house had been packed full of family. What better occasion to get away with it and spread the blame?

Then again, the arsonist could have come from outside and the motive been nothing to do with monetary gain. Revenge would be reward enough if the rancour ran deep in someone who'd spent half his adult life in jail. Destruction of the house could have been peripheral to the real intention, which was to wipe out the judge himself. So who would have known that the Carlton Dellars would be entertaining him over that weekend?

Which brings one, Yeadings considered, to the body in the cellar. Had the arsonist gained entry with an accomplice whom he then strangled to guarantee silence? Or was the body connected with the young man lying unconscious in hospital? — because he had certainly been in a fight which might yet cost him his life.

So was Eddie Dellar the intending Good Guy who'd come on the arsonist, attacked him and killed him before escaping outside? He'd still have to face a manslaughter charge if he survived. At twenty-two was his job at the Department of Trade and Industry enough in itself to justify Special Branch's interest? That was doubtful.

So many questions. So little to go on as yet. Yeadings closed his eyes and stayed that way until the car drew up again at the local nick.

* * *

Kate Dellar had almost dropped off at Eddie's bedside while a CD of Vivaldi's *Summer* quietly played through. Last night she had spent long periods without sleep and now tiredness was rolling over her in waves. She jerked awake with a vague impression that Eddie had made some small movement. And then he spoke, quite clearly. 'Jess is all right, Ma.'

She came more sharply to her senses. He couldn't have. The bandaging gag was still in place with the clear plastic tube-holder in his mouth. There was no movement now. His eyes were still closed. She'd imagined hearing him, as she'd done once before against the Dellars' disconnected conversation at dinner.

Then from the real past the words came back. Once, when she'd been almost despairing of some new craze that Jess had taken up, he'd sensed the impatience in her. She hadn't complained out loud, but maybe she was transparent to her son just then. That's when he'd said it, and in just that voice. 'Jess is all right, Ma.'

Then it hadn't been about Jess being safe from danger. What he'd meant was that she really *wasn't a bad girl*. 'Jess is all right, Ma.'

Now it had replayed in her memory. My mind playing tricks, Kate warned herself; but it was comforting all the same. Eddie was right, and she ought to have more faith in the fact. In every sense Jess *was* all right. She would hold on to that, be more confident.

She was a ninny to have been scared by the man following her yesterday. It was a caretaker's natural reaction to someone seen hanging around the gates. Instead of bolting like a rabbit she should have confronted him. He could have told her where Stone could be found, or how she might get in touch with him. There was no call to mention Jess, in case the man was working directly for Stone's wife.

She had made up her mind. She would go back there right away, and rattle the gates until someone came; then demand to be given a phone number or some other address where she could find Stone and ask him . . .

Ask what? 'Have you got my daughter?' Was that it? Something of the sort, she supposed. But the right words would come to her when they came face to face.

She bent over and kissed Eddie's forehead. It seemed less heated than before. His breathing continued unchanged. Well, of course it did: the machine went on doing that. It governed him.

'I'll be here tomorrow,' she told him. 'God bless.'

She sat fuming in the hospital's car park before she could drive out. A green Land Rover had been parked across her nose so that she couldn't pull away. She was beginning to work up a strong dislike for that make of car. Angrily she pressed on her horn. It brought no response, except for a man in a denim suit staring back at her as he passed and hunching his shoulders in non-involvement.

After some three or four minutes she got out and went back into the hospital. At Reception she reported her difficulty and gave the Land Rover's registration. An announcement over the public address system was followed by a further wait of some five minutes before a claimant arrived breathlessly from the direction of the wards and rushed out to remove the obstruction. At last Kate was free to go on her way.

She was quicker today finding the right route, and when she drove up to the gates she

205

had still not improved on her former plan. But this time the gates stood open. She continued through and followed the driveway as far as the bend. Nosing round it she saw, some hundred yards away, an oblong, three-storeyed façade of warm red brick, late seventeenth century, with a white-columned porch.

There was scant cover in between, but over to the right was a break in a trimmed yew hedge and a view of gardens beyond. Unsure of how to approach, she opted for caution, reversed until the car could not be seen from the house, got out and slipped through the archway in the hedge. Its wrought iron gate also stood open, inviting her in.

Past this archway the garden was partitioned by hedges eight-feet high into spacious squares, all of different sizes, each with a theme and dedicated to a floral species. Kate walked past upturned soil, moist and peaty, with regular drills ready to be planted. It smelled good, black and productive.

Beyond a wall of espaliers with tiny, young fruit there extended a short walk of pergolas draped with trusses of purple wisteria. To either side, glimpsed through arched openings were other roofless rooms, one ablaze with multi-coloured gilly-flowers. Their rich scent was almost overpowering. The other was laid to grass dotted with fallen blossom. Straight, dark trunks were canopied with remnants of white ornamental cherry on branches that extended from tree to tree, giving only a glimpse through of blue sky here and there. A tethered white goat lifted its head from cropping and gazed at her. The effect was weirdly fairy-tale.

Through a gap in the next hedge came the *clitch-clitch* of someone hoeing. She went through to a formal square of bedding, with some stiff, spiky plants opening into exotic, foreign-looking flowers in brilliant jewel colours.

A man was working there, bare to the waist, his back towards her. His naked flesh shone moistly, brown with established suntan. She noticed a dark, round mole under his right shoulder blade. He straightened and turned.

No gardener. She knew him from press photographs. This was Charles Stone, the Ogre himself. Her daughter's married lover.

13

Kate stared, her eyes too intent on taking him in to be capable of speaking. But she didn't need to think of an approach. He asked immediately, 'Have you news of Jessica?'

So he knew who she was; must know Jess was missing. Anger flooded through her. She detested the smooth, handsome face, the slightly foreign features seen for the first time in the flesh. How dare he be here at home, *gardening* for God's sake, when Jess could be in danger? Because that's what it meant, if even he didn't know where she was.

'She's not with you, then?' Her voice came out a croak.

He put out a hand as if to steady her, then remembered the soil on it and his arm fell back to his side. He shook his head slowly. 'Shall we go into the house?'

'No.' That would have been a concession. She wasn't granting any.

Her mind was running ahead, trying to make sense of him, of the way she'd been given access this time and the way she'd found him. She had nothing more to say. Then doubt rushed in. Why should she believe what he'd implied? — that he wasn't hiding her daughter from her. The man knew his way about the world, a manipulator, a hard-headed businessman, a deceiver.

She knew her mistake. She should have taken up his offer, gone inside the house. She wanted to search it, room by room — dozens of them here — and shout her daughter's name until Jess came running into her arms.

She closed her eyes to conceal her emotions and get some control of herself. When she opened them she thought his face had softened, showed some pity. The gall of the man!

'The police are looking for her,' she threatened.

'Yes. I saw the English papers. So I came back.'

The garden seemed to lurch sideways and swing back. The man's face was dissolving into mist. She felt him bearing her up, then lost all feeling. It was only momentary, then with each jarring pace she knew he was carrying her up the stone steps and into the house.

She became aware of lying on a couch and a woman bending over her. She had greying hair pulled back into a chignon. Her dress was a dark red-brown. 'I'm Mrs Christie,' she said. 'Mr Stone's housekeeper. Lie still a while and rest. Then I'll make you some tea. I'm afraid the kitchen staff are all still on leave.'

'I'll do it,' a man's voice said.

Kate pulled herself upright and set her feet on the floor. Mrs Christie took the vacant place beside her. When Stone brought the tray in there were warm scones as well, oozing butter.

'I'd just been baking,' the woman said, and Kate, comforted by the mundane domestic detail, nodded weakly. Sure that she couldn't face food, she found half a scone in her hand and discovered she was ravenous.

'You haven't been eating properly,' Stone said after a while. 'And probably not getting enough sleep. You must take care of yourself, not go rushing about looking after others. I know how mothers are.'

So he was considerate, thought of a mother's feelings. That was another side to the man. But she wouldn't let her antipathy go.

He drew up a chair opposite and sat leaning towards her, hands on splayed knees. 'We must talk,' he said sombrely.

Mrs Christie collected the used crockery and took away the tray. She closed the door firmly after her.

Say what? Kate asked herself, and closed

her eyes against him. But he was explaining.

'I had to go to the US on business. Jessica told me about the weekend invitation to her uncle's at Larchmoor Place and I asked her to accept. So perhaps I am responsible for what happened.'

'Why should you want her to go?'

'Because I thought she would be safer there while I was away. I didn't like her living alone on the canal.'

'No more did I,' Kate said heatedly, 'but Jess is so independent, headstrong really, and I couldn't oppose her renting the narrowboat. That would only have made her more determined to go her own way. Nor could I ask her to share the cottage with me.'

He waited for the outburst to be over, then pursued, 'You were there too, at the family gathering. I want you to tell me everything that was said and done, because this may have a bearing on what has happened to your daughter.'

She didn't see that it could do any good, but perhaps talking would help to sort the past few days in her mind. He didn't interrupt and she forgot who was listening, simply relived the events as they'd happened. He was just another in the procession of questioners ever since the fire.

'A terrible experience,' he said at the end.

It brought her back, and her anger with him returned. 'You were right to be afraid for her living on the canal,' she said. 'Her boat was broken into while she was away. Who else knew she lived there? I thought she was keeping it quiet. She hadn't even told her brother.'

'She could be secretive, yes. Discreet.'

'But she told me about you. About being your mistress.'

He stared at her, unblinking. 'And you disapprove.' It was statement, not question.

'You must be almost twice her age. And you have a wife.'

'I'm thirty-seven. Not really an old man.' His tone was sardonic.

'But married just the same. Marriage is meant to be for life.'

He stood up and walked towards the window. When he turned and looked again at her his face had changed. It was all hard, straight lines. She was seeing the indomitable money man who dealt in millions.

'You are right. Marriage is for life — a lifetime of loyal partnership and unswerving devotion. But it was never that for me. If I've been cheated, must I accept there is nothing more? Jessica is all I could ever desire in a woman. She is honest and clever and brave. Integrity like hers is rare. Even more;

incredibly, she loves me. It is more than I hoped for or deserve. I would lay my life down for her, and for us to spend the rest of our years together.'

There was no argument against passion like that. Kate's hands trembled, remembering herself with Michael; the overwhelming love, their stolen weekends, finally his defiance of the family who had forbidden his marrying. So, still students, they had taken it into their own hands, and been cut off. With no income, she'd chosen to become the bread-winner. Those had been desperate, wonderful years until Michael was established. And finally the family had acknowledged her, after the twins were born.

She straightened against the cushions and breathed in deeply. There must be no schism this time. If her daughter was determined to go to this man she must accept it, and be there for Jess if he let her down.

'I think,' she said slowly, 'Jess wants the same. She expects a lifetime of being with you.' It was hard to say it, but she must: 'I shall not stand in her way.'

'But you are disappointed.'

It struck her suddenly then, like a physical blow, and she started up, hardly aware he'd spoken. 'But where is she? What can we do to find out . . . ' She discovered his hand was gripping her own and now her whole body was shaking. It was shameful to be so feeble.

'I will look after you,' he said fervently. 'As I should have done for her. I blame myself.'

'It's not your fault. I wanted her to go for that weekend too.'

'No. You see, it is perhaps because of me that she was taken.'

'What do you mean — *taken*?'

For a moment she was paralyzed with fear, then, 'Do you mean kidnapped? For ransom?'

'I should have protected her. Because I am wealthy there is always that danger . . . '

Kate threw back her head and howled. He tried to restrain her but she pushed him away. *Money!* That evil thing that had blighted her early years — either too little of it, or now too much.

'Listen,' he insisted. 'That has been in my mind ever since I heard what had happened. It's why I flew back and have been sitting here, powerless to act, waiting for the phone to ring or some message to come.'

She saw his agony exposed now. She understood why the Land Rover had followed her the day before. Someone in the gate lodge had been warned to look out for contact from the kidnappers. She knew the impotence and frustration that sent him out today to work in the garden. Any activity must be better than

214

waiting for the blow to fall.

'But we don't know,' she insisted. 'We can't be sure that's what happened.'

Was it worse than having no idea where Jess was? She only knew that she wasn't up to coping with this new thing. With Eddie so ill, there was no one to turn to.

All along she had been trying to persuade herself there could be a safe outcome of Jess's disappearance. There'd been that terrible moment when she heard of a body found in the ashes. Then such relief that it was someone else. And behind all the anxiety the frail, remaining hope — that Jess had simply taken it into her head to walk out on everyone.

And now she faced this hideous image of the girl threatened with a gun or a knife and bundled out of the house in the hours of darkness to be taken — where? And who had got her? What kind of people were they? As Stone had said, she was brave, but if she defied them, what might they do to her?

'We must let the police know,' she said. 'About you, I mean. That you and Jess . . . '

'I've been in touch already. They've notified the branch that deals with things like that.'

With *people* like that, she thought, huddled in fright. With *terrorists*. She was in a

215

different, mad world now. Where had normality gone?

★ ★ ★

'It's for you, Maddie,' Gus said drily, entering the drawing-room and jerking his head in the approximate direction of the hall telephone.

His wife threw down her rumpled copy of *Country Life* and pushed herself to her feet. 'I can't think why people don't use my mobile number,' she grumbled. En route she walked round her stepson's out-thrust legs as she passed the sofa. 'Jake, for heaven's sake don't lounge about like that. Can't you find something to do?'

'Haven't been searching actually.' His voice was silkily derisive.

Across the empty fireplace filled with an arrangement of pink lilies and irises Sir Matthew raised his head, silently stared over his half-moon spectacles first at him, then at his father. 'One of Madeleine's horsy acquaintances?'

'Claudia, actually,' Gus told him. 'To announce they'd eventually arrived at the coast.'

'The vulture has landed,' Jake murmured, smirking.

Sir Matthew's mouth tightened to check an

appreciative twist of the lips. The boy was a drain on one's patience, but this time he had the *mot juste*. 'Vulture' was appropriate. From a rangy beauty in her twenties his sister-in-law had turned into something between a mummified Edith Sitwell and the famous portrait of the Doge of Venice. Time had been cruel to her, and she'd masochistically encouraged its depredations.

He called up her present image: scrawny neck and shoulders, stick arms, sharp beak, deeply hooded eyes, bloodless. At seventy-six he had endured ten years more wear and tear than she, but he was in better shape.

There was a time she had been Circe, Calypso, Cleopatra; all the sirens rolled into one. He had gloried in her superb, lithe body. It was as much by good fortune as good judgment that he had finally escaped her toils. He doubted he'd have survived a lifetime in her proximity. Old Carlton must be tougher than he appeared.

He settled back comfortably, congratulating himself. Joanne had suited him better, and brought clear advantages. A plain and undemanding wife, she hadn't been clever. It was a pity the children had turned out little better. She'd been fond of hunting and travel, happy to do so alone. When she died it made little difference to the level tenor of his life.

He re-applied himself to the obituary columns of the *Times*, until a word Gus had used came back to tease him. His sharp features rose out of the newsprint. 'You said 'eventually'. What did you mean by that?'

'Eh? Oh, Claudia. They had a bit of a hiccup over the journey. The old Daimler ran out of juice. It takes a lot and you must know how she's stingy filling it, a sort of weaning process maybe. Normally they carry a spare can of four-star in the boot, and someone must have nicked it. So in the end they had to settle for unleaded. It seems to have brought on a near-terminal degenerative disease. Of the car, that is. I guess Maddie is having to endure a blow by blow account.'

Sir Matthew transferred his judgmental gaze back on to Jake who had uttered an involuntary snicker and was now looking artificially unconcerned. The boy had a thousand ways of living at others' expense, and it seemed likely that whatever drove that old bus of Carlton's would more than serve to fuel the boy's rocket-from-hell machine.

'Do you know anything about that, Jacob?' he asked mildly.

'Of course not, Grandfather.'

If he realized how much that word irritates me he wouldn't assume on a relationship of any kind, the old man considered. He does himself no good.

He shook the newspaper and tapped creases out before turning a page. 'I see old Pettigrew has finally hung up his wig,' he remarked equably. 'It was a race whether he would collapse *in media re* or in a home for the mentally deranged. Only sixty-four; he should have been good for another twenty years.'

He darted a glance at the other two and maliciously hoped he'd plunged them into despair over the likelihood of his own longevity.

Maddie came back fussing over domestic shortcomings. Her aunt's complaints had obviously stirred her to reply in kind. The Barkers had been given a week's leave, which meant she was without chauffeur and cook. Since Matthew had expected them to stay on longer at Larchmoor Place, Mrs B hadn't left enough ready prepared in the refrigerator to last them all until she was back. The freezer cabinet appeared to be stacked with unrecognizable packages which were beyond Maddie's sparse catering experience. There was no alternative to traipsing into Windsor for dinner.

This meant she'd have to drive and forgo the wine, since Gus surely wouldn't, and Jake would insist on riding the Kawasaki. Claudia, enduring this recitation of minor hardships had been insufficiently sympathetic. It had rattled Maddie and sent the blood rushing up her neck to stain her face.

Sir Matthew rose and selected a cigarette from the box on the coffee table. As he straightened he fixed Jake with a grim, judgmental stare. 'Now that the telephone has come free, you'd better ring back and express your abject apologies to Claudia for her disasters of the journey.'

'Why? What's it to do with Jake?' Maddie shrilled, momentarily defensive.

'Explain, Jacob.'

'What the hell! It's no big deal. I'd run a bit low on gas is all. So I borrowed theirs.' He knew it was pointless trying to deny a charge when the old freak homed in on a potential petty crime. He shrugged, turning his too-charming, Hugh Grant smile on his stepmother, but she was already too ruffled to be receptive.

'Right then. Do that. I'm most displeased, Jake.'

Bloody hell, he groaned inside. But she was his meal ticket. If it wasn't one old harpy it was the other. Now he'd have to cringe to Claudia who was totally charm-proofed. He'd need to hold the phone at arm's length. Or lay it down while he dropped his pants and mooned.

He sucked in his cheeks, breathed 'Sorry, Stepmama,' in Maddie's direction and tossed his head so that the wayward lock of hair fell further over his eyes.

'That's a good boy,' she said, forgiving him readily.

Claudia was another matter. Her tirade reached Jake from a couple of yards away. It wasn't all on account of his actions, he guessed. Plenty else had upset the old scorpion and he was a convenient receptacle for her spleen. Which she was no slouch at.

'OK then?' he said brightly as she paused at last for breath. 'Well, I'll send a cheque along to cover what I used. Cheerio then,' and he hung up.

With the purring phone still in her hand, Claudia crouched, shaking with anger, on the second stair up to the loft. From the sitting-room poured out Miranda's scales. Diminished sevenths. She'd been at them for over half an hour without cease.

Claudia stood up and brushed invisible creases from her skirt. She drew several deep breaths until she was again in control. Then she twisted the doorknob and went in to confront the girl. The music went on. She might have known it: Miranda was entranced.

Claudia leaned forward and shook her by the shoulder. Her hands fell into her lap and she looked startled awake.

'That bike of Jacob's,' her mother said coldly, 'what is its licence number?'

Almost automatically Miranda reeled it off.

'I thought so,' her mother said with satisfaction. 'This time he has really gone too far.'

Miranda waited with bowed head until Claudia had left. Time now to turn to the Bach Preludes and Fugues. She left the sheet music on the floor where it had spilled. She didn't need it. She raised her hands and stared ahead, starting with the first one in C.

14

The temperature on Lido was again hovering over 38 degrees at breakfast. Giulia floated into the kitchen barely covered in a chiffon negligee and languidly waving a fan of finely woven palm strips. It was shaped like an Ace of Spades, with an insistently Venetian motif of black-edged eyeholes to double its use as a mask.

'Today,' she announced, 'will be a stinker.' She emphasized the slangy word with some pride. 'So what do you young people intend to do? Venice will be teeming with tourists, all sweaty and dripping *gelati*. I should not recommend it.'

Yesterday Franco had suggested a gondola trip up the Grand Canal. They would cross the lagoon by their own motor launch moored below her window, and this for Jess had been the most attractive part of the arrangement. Her ambivalent position here as guest-prisoner needed clarification. It was time she took over and made her bid for freedom.

Whether it ran counter to Charles Stone's plans for her barely mattered now. The game had been played his way long enough. She intended to introduce her own rules. Too bad if it momentarily peeved him. He'd said he admired her independence. Let him now live by his words. She looked forward to seeing his face as she walked in on him unannounced.

Her hopes were centred on the motorboat. However well Charles knew her, these people here couldn't have guessed at her longtime love of the internal combustion engine. Father had once claimed she was born with an adjustable spanner, not a silver spoon, in her mouth. Let her once take a trip with one of the boys at the controls and she would pick up on any of the boat's special eccentricities. Later she'd choose her moment, once she'd a plan for getting out of Italy.

Her new appearance made her current passport useless. Even if she passed through Immigration by nonchalantly waving its EC cover, it could still leave a trail to her which one of the boys might pick up on. Getting other false papers was out of the question. She'd need to give some thought to going stateless.

The Italian newspapers which she'd found in the house didn't make much sense to her, but the television news was easier. Last night there had been a heated discussion about the stream of illegal immigrants landing along the eastern and southern coastlines. The boats bringing them from Albania didn't have to return empty. Surely she could bribe some needy skipper to take her along?

Once she went missing the search for her would logically start at Marco Polo airport or on the westbound roads out of Mestre on the mainland. It would take some time before it occurred that she might head east, away from the direction of home.

'You promised,' she reminded Franco, 'that you'd lend me your camera and today we'd do the tourist thing. Crowds don't bother me. It's all part of Venice in June.'

His gaze flickered to Stefano who shrugged. 'Give the lady what she wants, of course. We'll make up a threesome.'

'As you wish,' Giulia conceded. 'So I will phone the *Gritti Palazzo* and make sure you have a table for lunch on the *Terrazza del Doge*.'

'Won't you come with us?' Jess asked her.

'Thank you, no. It's cooler here on Lido. And I have little commissions to attend to. I will mail your cards for you when I go shopping. Then you needn't bother looking for a postbox. How many cards have you?'

'Four or five,' Jess said vaguely. 'I'll bring them down.' She knew Giulia would destroy them. The one that really mattered was Eddie's. She'd find some way of posting that herself.

'Comfortable shoes. That is important,' Giulia counselled, having adopted the motherly role. 'It is not all gondolas. You will walk and walk and walk all day.'

★   ★   ★

They left at a little before nine, Jess in a cotton trouser-suit of pale green, open-toed sandals and a floppy straw hat. The boys, accustomed to sunlight, wore shades, but only on the water. The boat purred away from the mooring, and Jess gave it full marks for maintenance. She had seen Stefano's hand hover over a key board inside a kitchen cupboard, but she was confident she'd be able to start the engine in any case. It would simply take a tad longer without the key.

She found she remembered the navigable lanes from her previous visit. They were clearly marked and a strict speed limit was adhered to, at least during daylight. It was only at night that, in bed, she'd heard the wide boys of Lido out racing, and the water slapping against the walls below as it sucked away at the foundations.

Stefano was cruising the waterbus lane,

passing the jetties of *Sant' Elena* and *Giardini Biennale* where small crowds waited for transport to *San Marco*. At *Arsenale* he turned in under the archway and proceeded to an inner quay where Franco leapt out to tie up.

'All history,' Stefano said sardonically, waving an arm to embrace the proud towers topped by their Venetian winged lions. 'Once from here we ruled the world, which the Mediterranean then was. In these shipyards sixteen thousand skilled workers could build and equip a galley in less than a day. Ask me what this place has now become. A show place, yet another gallery to hold things that have no purpose.'

'Art is its own purpose,' Franco rejoined without heat. It was obviously a familiar argument. He'd finished with the ropes and held out a hand to help Jess ashore.

'From now we walk. It is up to you to choose the route. I have a map here for you, but later you will get lost just the same. Probably more quickly if you consult it.' Stefano was positively prancing alongside, searching her face with dark eyes full of mischief.

She knew he was right. Everyone eventually got lost in the narrow, wriggling alleys. If she'd wanted to impress the boys with how streetwise (canalwise?) she was here she couldn't. In fact that would be undesirable.

'At risk of boring you, because you've done it a hundred times, it has to be the Doge's Palace first and then San Marco. After that there's the Peggy Guggenheim collection, the *Accademia*, Rialto Bridge, the fishmarket, *La Fenice* . . . But I think you both had better sort out the order for me.'

'I leave it to my cousin to escort you to the Doge's dungeons,' Stefano offered, 'while I sit in the piazza like an English gentleman and enjoy a Grappa. When you reach the top of the palace you may wave to me and I will deign to acknowledge you.'

'So kind,' Jess said. 'Come on, Franco. I suppose we queue to get in.'

★ ★ ★

Giulia had been right about comfortable shoes. One of the sandal straps was rubbing up a blister before they had completed the first two visits. Jess thought regretfully of her scruffy old trainers left at home in the narrowboat. A pharmacist supplied a neat dressing for her and they met up with Stefano for cappuccinos.

After crossing the Grand Canal to the *Accademia*'s cool shade she set a more leisurely pace through the lofty rooms full of Old Masters, until at a little before one they took a waterbus back to *Santa Maria del Giglio* and lunch at the *Gritti Palazzo* which overlooked the dazzling lagoon.

'I rather think,' Jess said sadly, 'the Guggenheim will have to wait for another occasion.' The combination of artichoke-stuffed turbot, *vitello veneto* and heady wine against the gentle background of Vivaldi's music was soporific. When their gondola came she was ready to stretch voluptuously on the velvet cushions and rest her head on Stefano's ready shoulder for a dream progress the length of the crowded Grand Canal. On their return journey, making way for a Japanese wedding procession in four floral-wreathed gondolas, they pulled in near the Rialto Bridge.

'Just one thing more,' Stefano insisted, brushing her ear with his lips. 'Boutiques. You cannot spend a day in Venice without shopping. It is what modern Venice is for after all. Just five steps on land and we will show you Aladdin's cave.'

Nothing could dissuade him from buying her a carnival mask which she admired: a delicate upper-face covered in white and silver sequins and edged with cocks' tail-feathers dyed peacock blue. Then Franco led her into a glassware boutique where she chose an emerald-green paperweight with an orange and black twister at its centre.

She knew that when she finally left Venice she would be leaving these gifts behind. That could be taken as an insult, which she didn't intend. For a moment, as Franco steered them back across the lagoon to Lido she was almost tempted to give up on the idea. Yet the way she was kept as an ironically honoured hostage was demeaning. She owed them for that.

Besides, just after the gondola had delivered them back to the piazza San Marco she had hit on a possible method to get away. In the little gardens where they sat a while before walking back to their boat, a group of backpackers were lying on the grass with cans of fruit juice and ice creams. Three had little Union Jacks sewn on to their gear. When two of the girls got up and moved off towards the public toilets she made her own excuses and trailed some way behind.

High partition walls enclosed the utility and she waited for them until they were fixing their makeup, screwing their mouths to take on fresh lipstick. 'Hi guys,' Jess greeted them, 'how long you here for?'

The redhead darted her a look that meant

back-off. 'Long enough to piddle, is all,' she sneered.

The other shrugged an apology. 'Leaving tomorrow,' she said. 'Heading south.'

'Would you do me a favour?'

They exchanged streetwise glances. 'It will cost you,' said the redhead.

'Just to post this card to my boyfriend in England. I gotta coupla fellows waiting outside. Eyeties, and they're the jealous kind. Here, see.'

She produced the postcard addressed to Eddie and a five Euro note.

'Ten,' said the redhead.

'You're sharp, but OK.' She handed them over. 'You travelling by train?'

'Nuh. Got offered a lift in a carrier's truck, four of us, down to Bari.' Since the commercial transaction they appeared to trust her more.

'Like to make that five? I'll pay my way with the nosh.'

Again the girls looked at each other. It's on, Jess decided. They take me for a sucker.

'Maybe. Depends.'

'On what?'

'If you can get up early. Five-thirty at Piazzale Roma. It's at the far end . . . '

'I know it. I'll be there.' This was the

231

perfect pick-up point for joining the mainland. She was really in luck.

'What about the fellas?'

Jess put her nose in the air. 'Plenty more where they came from. Same in Bari, for that matter.'

The girls grinned. 'See yuh then,' said the dark girl.

'On the dot,' the other warned, 'or we go without you.'

'Cool,' she told them and watched as they shouldered their bags and went off. She waited another two minutes, renewing her makeup, then slipped out to rejoin Franco and his cousin in the shade of the little gardens.

'We did buy you a cornetto,' Stefano said mockingly, 'but you took so long making yourself beautiful that I did you a service by eating it myself.' He showed the tip of his tongue and made a suggestive licking movement while holding her eyes with his own. Franco had turned away a moment before and missed seeing her repugnance.

⋆   ⋆   ⋆

'It's been a wonderful day,' she said as the powered boat headed back towards Lido. 'Thank you both. I shall always remember it.'

This time Franco was at the controls and as he smiled back at her his attention was taken by something beyond. Stefano, picking up on it, swivelled in his seat and grunted. 'Look,' he said, pointing back inland to distant flashes over the northern mountains. 'It's going to be a noisy night. Heat's been building all day. When the storm hits the lagoon it will be really spectacular.'

At present the water was like sheet silver. Not a breath of wind, unnaturally calm. She'd never known a storm here but she guessed it wouldn't make for an easy escape.

★   ★   ★

The distant flashing continued for over two hours with no accompanying thunder, then a little after seven it rushed down from the heights to strike with demon fury. From a breathless stillness all hell broke loose. Torrential rain lashed the lagoon and the shutters of the room they ate in clanged against the outer walls while all the candles streaked sideways and went out. Through the darkness the boys struggled to fix the shutters across and close the tall windows. They had to shout to be heard above the buffeting of the wind.

Giulia was muttering, hunched in her

chair. 'Dear God,' she said, 'this could go on all night.'

So much for my plans, Jess thought. I'd end a drowned rat to venture out in this. If I wasn't struck by lightning.

She knew that, curiously, the safest place to be in an electric storm was inside a car, totally surrounded by metal. Fibreglass adrift on water offered no protection at all. The escape had to be put off. There was no chance of keeping her rendezvous with the girl backpackers. All that duplicity for nothing. Except that they might have the decency to post that card to Eddie. Even then, in view of the relaxed Italian postal system, she reckoned he'd not receive it for another four days.

Giulia's instant reaction to the ferocious weather was recourse to brandy. She had Rosalba produce half a dozen varieties of exotic flavourings, with which their full-size wine glasses were recharged.

They remained at table, peeling fruit and becoming increasingly pi-eyed while the tempest roared outside and the house thudded with its onslaught like an echoing cliff cavern battered by high seas.

Tomorrow and for several days Venice would be awash, with duckboards in the alleys, and gondolas sailing through the piazza San Marco as the deluge drained from the mountains and the lagoon rose. With the wind's savagery, intricate tracery would be torn off ancient stonework and a little more of the elegant past would be lost forever.

Sad, Jess thought, but her main regret was purely selfish. It had been a good idea to go south and east, but now she would have to rethink her escape.

Stefano at last persuaded Giulia to retire, swearing she'd never sleep a wink, but tottering off on wayward feet. The young man leered back over her shoulder as he supported her from the room.

Franco sat on, seeming lost in depressive thought until finally he rested his arms on the table and his head sank down on them. Regretfully Jess decided there was no alternative to finding her own bed and pulling the covers over her ears.

Upstairs she found the windows had all been made secure earlier. It was only the room they dined in that had been left open for air until the storm actually struck. She lay propped up against the pillows a while, watching a sliver of light flickering where the shutters failed quite to meet. Its repetition played on her mind and, mesmerized, she felt herself drifting until her head fell suddenly forward and she jerked awake.

Outside the wind continued tearing at the house's fabric but the thunder was a mere roll of drums now, the flickering fainter. With everyone in the house asleep she might have a chance to leave, if she could brave the lagoon crossing.

Quietly she unlatched a shutter. The heavy wood with its iron hasp was almost torn from her hands but she held it wide enough to glimpse the water surging below. The overcast sky made distances uncertain but she caught the pale flecks of swirling foam and they struck at her rediscovered resolve.

It would be crazy. She let the shutter thud back into place and refastened the iron bar. It was then that she heard the creak of a floorboard beyond her door and the furtive sound of the handle being slowly depressed.

She slid behind the opening door, heart thudding, hoping that the shadowy hump of pillows would be taken for her sleeping body. Enough light escaped from the corridor outside for her to make out the man's shape as he approached the bed. Too tall for Franco.

With disgust she remembered Stefano's tongue when he spoke of licking her ice cream, and the leering smile as he led the drunken Giulia off to bed. He had been little more sober himself and she had a horror of his fumbling her in the dark.

Retreating further she brushed against something at waist height. It was the floor-based wrought iron candle-stand that must surely have come from some convent or chapel. The flower shape that held the guttered remnants of wax was surrounded by ivy-shaped leaves. Her fingers curled round the central stem and ran down until she had a firm purchase on it.

'*Carissima*,' Stefano breathed, leaning over the bed. '*Tesoro mio*.'

She hefted the heavy standard and his head half-turned as he sensed her movement. There was a split second of choice. She had a startling knowledge of what might be the outcome. But then her hand had acted. The blow jarred up her arm and the candle-stand fell to the carpet with a muffled thud, almost lost in the noise of the storm.

Stefano crumpled across the bed with a little sighing sound.

'God, I've killed him. I never meant . . . '

She knelt over him and felt the sticky oozing of blood from the side of his head. Then her fingers found his neck pulse. It was still beating. He gave a small whimper and seemed to make an attempt to push himself up.

'No,' she ground out. If she let him recover he would tear her apart. She knew it. He had to be restrained.

She pushed his face back into the bedclothes, reached for her clothes of the day before and found the trousers of her cotton pants-suit. The legs wouldn't tear free. But she bit into the seam and then the stitching tore apart. She bound his wrists tightly behind and rolled him under the coverlet. Part of her shredded blouse was bundled inside his mouth and secured by a gag from the remaining trouser leg.

'Don't die on me,' she whispered fiercely into his upturned face, and in the dimness saw the whites of his eyes reappear.

Behind the gag he made a furious grunting sound and she knew if he got free he'd have no mercy. So she tore a sheet and tied his legs to the bedposts. If she left him spread-eagled there in her bed they would know what he'd intended. Perhaps it would be enough to delay any organized search after she'd gone. Maybe they'd even understand how desperate she'd been.

And now there was no choice. She had to go down, fetch the powerboat's key and steer it through the storm waters across the lagoon. She dressed quickly in warm clothes, stuffing money and any valuables into her shoulder bag. Then, shoes in hand, and with the rest of the torn sheet over one arm she stole down to let herself over the salon balcony, on to the jetty.

15

Claudia Dellar stood by the telephone, her mind seething. Gus's boy Jake was an unmitigated scoundrel. She knew as well as if she'd been listening in, what had prompted him to ring up with his offhand, insolent admission about the petrol.

It had been Matthew's doing, exercising his authority over him and knowing exactly the manner in which Jake would comply, aiming to give further offence to herself.

All these years later, and Matthew couldn't pass up an occasion to insult her. She could still see the mocking eyes, deep-lidded like a vulture's, as he listened to Carlton announce his engagement to herself, aware, as they all were, that he'd set it up to unload her now that he'd landed Joanne.

She had been humiliated, livid that he was in a position to do this to her. She had played into his hands by passionately threatening to make public their affair. Their head of chambers then had been a desiccated puritan who, she realized too late, would automatically ascribe all blame to the woman. She'd have been sacrificed anyway. It had been a question of accepting either the older brother or professional disgrace.

And Carlton, another of Matthew's pawns, had played along with his younger brother's wishes, because he was weak and because, never having any gift for making money, he'd always needed subsidizing. It had suited him over the years to have her tied to him in the same financial dependence.

But in the end she had succeeded where Matthew had expected her to fall apart. She was the one now with the whip-hand over the pathetic poet. And she had never declared a truce with the man who'd cast her off.

His time would come, she promised herself. As for the crass and despicable young Jake, she could get at him through what he held most dear, the offensive motorbike he'd fawned over his stepmother to buy. Madeleine, being as stupid as her dead mother, was as easily won round. Otherwise why in middle age marry the womanizing Gus? It was ironic justice for Matthew that Joanne's fortune would be steadily dwindling away through that pair of wasters.

On the phone just now Madeleine had said where they were going for a family dinner. Claudia knew the restaurant, always the same one because they assumed they had a right to the very best on offer. Madeleine, Gus and

Matthew would go by car, Madeleine driving because she didn't drink on these occasions. Jake, as always, wouldn't deign to be transported, insisting on following by motorbike.

Over the years Matthew's tastes had become set in stone. On the few occasions when she and Carlton had been included in these outings to Windsor they would arrive at eight, go straight into the restaurant, dine and remain there until the stroke of ten. Then by car straight home to Ascot and lights out at a quarter to eleven. Jake, whatever his condition, was expected to follow on within the hour, wherever he chose to sneak off to after that.

Well, tonight, Claudia vowed, he should pay for his contempt, and at more than the cost of the petrol. She tucked the note with the Kawasaki's licence number under the base of the phone for use a little later.

★ ★ ★

If Kate Dellar still harboured any idea of Stone's unconcern about Jessica, it was dispelled with the arrival of Roger Beale. He arrived while she was still at tea; a small, dynamic man with darting eyes and an unexpectedly gentle voice.

Stone's introduction of him as his man-of-affairs carried unintended irony. He had clearly been instructed to drop all business matters and concentrate on this single problem of Jess's disappearance.

The little man slid his briefcase on to a table beside the central window and removed from it two yellow envelope files. Kate, invited to take a seat opposite him and Stone, saw that Jess's name was on the cover of each. Without her reading glasses she couldn't read the sub-headings upside-down, but noted they were of differing lengths.

'You keep files on my daughter?' she queried, offended on Jess's behalf.

'On all our employees,' Beale replied evenly.

'I didn't realize she *worked* for you, Mr Stone. May I ask for how long?'

'Since the week after she left College. It was a confidential posting, but she would have told you sooner or later, I'm sure.'

He was trying to let her down lightly. *Confidential*: what else did that imply but barring her from knowing? It was insufferable. He must have been a party — its instigator most likely — to Jess's dropping out of university. She had never fully understood why. Did nobody trust her with being told what was going on?

Kate felt she was blundering blindly in a maze, outside others' relationships. She'd only recently learnt that Jess was already acquainted with Dr Marion Paige. They had met in Michael's office at King's: another association — with her own husband — which she'd been ignorant of. And apparently the meeting had set the two women at odds with each other.

It seemed that she'd been stumbling blindfold among inter-related strangers, truly the odd one out, as the Dellars had always implied.

She sat back, unable to cope with more revelations, momentarily unsure whether Jess had invented the story of being Stone's lover, as an exaggeration of her professional connection with him. Had she, working for him, girlishly been longing for a more intimate relationship?

Surely not. That wasn't Jess's way. Or hadn't been until now; casual as she'd been about other admirers. Kate was almost sure they were close. The man's distress over Jess's disappearance seemed real enough. And when she'd accused him he hadn't denied Jess was his mistress. She'd been convinced when he said he was in love with her.

But was she deceived? The man was an enigma. His apparent caring could cover something else: perhaps no more than concern for business secrets at risk if Jess found herself among the wrong people?

She found she was shaking again. He reached out a hand and touched her arm. 'Mrs Dellar,' he said. 'Kate, would you rather not . . . '

'I want to know everything,' she decided suddenly. 'It's time everyone was straight with me.'

The two men exchanged glances and Stone nodded. It was left to Beale to explain.

'We have been making inquiries with everyone known to us who had any connection with her. So far no lead has come up. There have been no sightings, no phone calls. Her credit cards have not been used. Her passport is still in her desk at the office.

'The police have been equally unsuccessful. We're working in parallel with them and to some extent sharing investigations. They are about to pass her photograph to the press, asking for witnesses who may have seen her in the past few days.

'Also we are hopeful that your son will soon be well enough to give us some idea of what was in his sister's mind that night of the fire.'

'The two of them are close,' Stone said, 'as

twins often are.' He seemed to be thinking aloud.

She stared at him with sudden suspicion. 'You know Eddie too, don't you?' It came out as an accusation.

He nodded, calmly. 'I have done for several years; from his later school days. It was Eddie who first introduced Jessica and me.'

Here was yet another extension of the network where everyone was interconnected, except herself. Kate shook her head in denial, eyes closed for fear the tears might squeeze through. This nightmare was developing, growing like some monstrous germ under the microscope, dividing and combining until it filled every corner of her mind.

She had to make a stand, find some clear path ahead. She drew her hand away from where Stone's covered it, reopened her eyes and stared into his sombre face.

'Nothing matters,' she said wearily, 'except to find out what has happened to my daughter. I want her back.' And Eddie, she breathed silently; and Michael.

'Wherever she is,' Stone promised, 'we will find her.'

★   ★   ★

It wasn't until they were through Padua on the Strada Statale 16 that Jess dared to feel safe. The arduous night had exhausted her physically and she longed for sleep although her mind was nervously alerted to everything around her. She was still anxious that the blow to Stefano's head might prove fatal.

Two of the intended four had dropped out. The truck's main body, covered by heavy canvas stretched over a frame of tubular metal, was roomy enough for the three girls, and anyway Goldie had elected to go up front in the driver's cab. There were bales of woven material to lie on, which partly compensated for the vehicle's primitive suspension. With the back canvas rolled up to allow air in, Jess watched the sun's slow rising, and colour seep into the pearly sky. Held by its calm beauty, it took her a moment to realize they must be heading almost due west.

'Where did he say he was making for?' she demanded of Carla. 'We're turning inland.'

'He said Bari. That's the far south, isn't it?'

It struck Jess that her own scanty knowledge of Italian geography wasn't to be of much use. She forced herself to relax and eventually the sun removed itself from their view of the outside world, sliding properly round to their right as they continued staring out. From up front she could hear the usual stabs of conversation you get between two people ignorant of each other's language, then argument, the voices shouting to get above the engine as they roared uphill.

Eventually the pair must have reached a compromise because Goldie turned in her seat and shouted through the cab's sliding rear window, 'Breakfast in five minutes.'

'*Dové?*' Jess shouted to the driver.

The man's rumbled reply sounded like *Monsélice*. At least she'd heard of that town. Perhaps it was large enough for her to buy a map there.

Last night, when she had rifled the kitchen cupboard for the motorboat's key, she had come on the First Aid box. One of the packages in it contained a roll of wide elastic bandage, the sort once used to support painful varicose veins. With a silent apology to Rosalba's swollen legs and a hope she'd not have urgent cause to need it, Jess had stuffed it in her shoulder-bag.

In the dark, before she'd set a course across the stormy lagoon she had stripped off her sweatshirt and wound the bandage round her waist, slipping the large denomination notes inside. Now her only money that anyone might glimpse was small stuff, enough to cover costs of the journey. If she'd underestimated, then she'd miss out on a meal, to keep cash for necessities.

Already they were in narrow town streets with ancient, crowded buildings. The truck rattled over an uneven surface like large cobbles or a cattle grid, ran on another fifty feet and pulled up. The girls heard the two cab doors slam and then Giorgio's face came over the tailgate. 'You and me,' he said, pointing at them both. '*Andiamo, si?*'

They got out and Carla looked round in disgust. 'Where's the sea, Goldie? You said we'd skinny dip.'

They were high among hills in the sort of ancient fortress town that tourists would flock to for the architecture and churches. Not a glimpse of sea, but to reach a *trattoria* terrace they had to pass a bookshop on the corner. 'Order for me,' Jess said. 'I'll only be a moment.'

They chose coffee and *frittatas* for which Giorgio paid, impressively flexing his muscular arms to make his snake tattoo writhe as he chucked out his sweaty chest in its dingy string vest. Goldie snuggled up to him, required to demonstrate their joint gratitude. Her sideways glance at Carla had sly understanding in it. Carla smirked back, giggled and switched her mocking gaze to Jess.

They were up to something involving

herself, Jess guessed. Somewhere along the way she was going to be stripped of her belongings and dumped. The only way to counter that was to drop off unexpectedly first. But not here, without reach of the sea.

'*Mare?*' she demanded of Giorgio and spread her hands hopelessly.

'*Si, si. Piu tardi,*' he said impatiently, and followed it with a voluble flow of Italian, waving an arm to embrace the town around them, the little café, the sky, the sun. She was expected to enjoy what was on present offer.

Ah yes, the sun. It still glared pitilessly down. Last night's storm had done nothing to ease the temperature. Jess sweated and itched under the crepe bandaging. She didn't intend swimming when the others did, and leave her belongings unguarded.

She pressed open a page of the little Italian road map to find where they were. Giorgio, peering over her shoulder, planted a thick forefinger on the place name, leaving a smudge of sweat as he traced the route south. '*Grazie,*' she said sweetly.

While he made a delivery and picked up three sizable crates of ceramics, the girls were free to window-shop. Jess found some foreign newspapers but the British ones were dated three days back and she didn't want old news, being more uneasy at present about the situation she'd just walked out on.

There was no way Stefano could guess which direction she'd taken. If they recovered the motorboat it could be anywhere east of San Marco, even of Murano by the time the fuel ran out. She hadn't been happy about turning it loose with the choke wedged full open. A hazard to shipping, at least it had its front spotlight on. She hoped it could be avoided as it crossed the marked lanes, and not end as pulped fibreglass.

Their journey resumed unbroken until Comacchio, just short of Ravenna, where Giorgio had further stock to pick up. It was there Jess decided to disappear. The farther south they went the wider the crossing of the Adriatic, and she wasn't sure just what territory was opposite. Yugoslavia was split up now and Croatia still sounded like dangerous country, although some bold tourists had started returning to the west-facing coast.

According to notes in the map book, on Comacchio's Venetian-style canals the fishermen could sail down to open sea at Porto Garibaldi. After that, international navigation by the limp little tourist guide would be optimistic in the extreme. Columbus had had less to go on, she consoled herself; but then America was big enough not to be missed.

She slid over the tailgate, telling Carla

251

she'd go for Coke and cream cakes; anything to make the journey pass more quickly. The other girl shrugged, impatient to move on to somewhere they could swim from.

Jess's priority was to get herself a solid meal as prelude to any imposed fasting on the next stage of her journey. She made her way towards the lagoon and picked on a small cafe close to where fishing boats were moored. Scanning the faces round her as she waited for her order to be made up, she wondered if any of these men were involved in the steady trade in illegal immigrants. If she happened on the right one, chances were that he'd even prefer to take human cargo in the opposite direction.

She didn't want to stay here overnight, but was prepared to be patient until the right kind of face suggested a likely accomplice: needy enough to be tempted by a few hundred euros, but not venal enough to take everything she had and drop her overboard to save himself fuel.

I'm crazy, she admitted: travelling farther from home; banking all hopes on a totally unknown, war-ravaged country still fired by age-old enmities. This time she'd gone too far. For a brief instant she feared she might not make it. 'Except,' she said aloud, 'that I have to.'

That evening, in Ascot, a slight but significant spat broke out between Madeleine and her husband. It was Gus's appointed duty to check on the stable-yard when the girls had left after watering the horses for the night. He was supposed to pick up the keys, padlock all gates and hang the keys in Madeleine's office. She, fussily double-checking since they'd be going out for dinner, couldn't find them and had to chase him to the bathroom.

'Try my trousers' pockets,' he shouted from under the shower, but didn't apologize.

They weren't to hand because his clothes were already in the laundry basket. Ruffled at having to search through dirty linen, Madeleine was even less enchanted to discover a number of betting slips alongside the truant keys.

Gus could get away with a lot, but this time he'd chosen a bad moment to display his ineptitude. She burst in on him again as he towelled down, and read the riot act. At which he, already looking for some excuse to avoid the family dining-out, took umbrage and shouted back that he'd get himself something to eat at the local pub instead.

It upset Maddie, accustomed to mediating as pig-in-the-middle between him and her father. She couldn't recall just what had made Matthew so irritable tonight, but he had already been hatefully sarcastic to Gus, implying he was a worthless hanger-on and his job as an estate agent mere face-saving.

She couldn't let her father get away with that when Gus was the only one she could expect any real kindness from. There had been an unpleasant stiffness all round, but she was sure Gus would eventually relent and fall in with the evening's plans as arranged. However, when she went down again to the car after returning for her driving gloves, she found the rear seat empty.

'That husband of yours,' her father said in a voice of disdain, 'is a diva in his own right. He has presumed to take offence and gone off in high dudgeon.'

In her driving mirror Madeleine saw Jake, wearing his leathers, wheeling out his Kawasaki from the second garage. As she let in the clutch and the car moved off, Gus appeared from the house and went down to speak to his son.

Plotting? She devoutly hoped not. These little squabbles were best fast forgotten, not mulled over and blown up into a lasting atmosphere. She guessed it could end with Jake too deciding to fall out of the family party.

She was never the smoothest of drivers, preferring her own Land Rover to her father's Mercedes, and the disagreements had been enough to set her nerves on edge. She ground the gears as they left the driveway, causing Matthew to remark that he should have bought an automatic since she couldn't manage the clutch.

It didn't augur well for the rest of their evening. She had no idea then how true that would prove.

16

Next morning Chief Superintendent Perry summoned Yeadings to his office, pursed his small mouth and treated the Superintendent to a fixed stare. 'The ACC asked me to have a word with you about the Dellar case. He isn't very happy about the apparent lack of progress.' Perry took seriously the passing on of dissatisfaction.

Yeadings waited po-faced, saying nothing, watching his senior's eyes. The man appeared to have aged since they'd met up a fortnight back, before he went on leave. Now the cheeks sagged more puffily, the broken veins showed an even plummier red, his forehead was more creased. It seemed that the ACC's quoted unhappiness was a catching condition round here. Poor old bugger. Perry was looking forward to retirement. Just another three months to go.

The prolonged silence made the DCS uneasy. He preferred his comments to be dutifully punctuated with murmurs of agreement or, even better, of apology. 'A complicated case, it seems,' he prompted.

Yeadings considered this. 'I think we shall

find it gets more so. In fact that's what I should prefer.'

'How d'you mean? As you describe the situation there are already a number of unexplained factors . . . '

'Which so far appear unrelated. Links are missing, or being deliberately concealed. To recognize a pattern we need something adhesive. It could be that we have more than a single crime here, with two or more independent instigators: arson and murder, also possible abduction. And I'm pretty sure there's yet more to come.'

Perry blew out his cheeks, a habit the other recognized as denoting reluctance to be persuaded. 'Then you must contain it. At all costs we must avoid a long investigation. I need to hear of some positive progress by the weekend at the latest. I don't need to stress to you that there are influential people . . . ah, er . . . '

' . . . involved?'

' . . . who need to be satisfied that all possible is being done.'

And so on and so forth, Yeadings silently agreed. Now just potter off for a cup of tea. Let me get on with my work.

'The inquest,' Perry said, making it sound like a question.

'Is at three this afternoon, sir. No

conclusions can be drawn. I'm expecting a fortnight's adjournment. You will be fully advised.'

'And by then I hope . . . ' Perry raised both hands and left them suspended in the air. He wasn't very good at ending his own sentences.

'Right then,' Yeadings said briskly, rising, gathering his papers from the desk between them and turning on his heel. 'If that's all, thank you sir, and I'll wish you a good day.'

★   ★   ★

The Coroner's Court was a clean-lined modern building separated from the police station by its own car park. Across the access road and about five hundred yards farther was the Fire Station marked out by its operations tower of red brick with blackened openings used as practice windows. As Yeadings strolled into the forecourt he could hear a deal of splashing and shouting from beyond the sheds.

He found the Station Officer in his upstairs office, busy with paperwork. The same sounds of horsing about came in through the open window. 'Sorry about that,' he excused it, getting up and lowering the sash to cut the row. 'Got a coupla new lads on the watch.'

Yeadings walked across and looked out.

One, in clinging boxer shorts, was sitting on the concrete, grinning foolishly in a pool of water. The other, on a fully extended ladder was up the tower and being tilted on to the vertical. Watching, he realized it was a girl. Well, why not? They demand equality. With this lot initiation is initiation. She could thank her stars they'd left her full uniform on.

'So, anything spectacular you'll be throwing at us this afternoon?' asked the Station Officer.

'I'll leave the eye-openers to you and pathology,' Yeadings offered, accepting the proffered chair. 'Professor Littlejohn will take the stand after you. My DS will kick off with negative identification. We've little enough on offer. How about you?'

'Evidence of discovery of the body. Then it's up to the pathology people to describe its condition. I understand now that that will reveal how the man died. Manual strangulation, wasn't it?'

'So it seems. The hyoid bone was broken and throat cartilage damaged. If the coroner picks up on the way vinyl flooring was fused on to the underside of the corpse, your expert may need to explain how he came to be found on the stone-floored cellar.'

'That's straightforward enough. During burning, the kitchen floor dropped through on to the flagstones, and the body with it. Then the upper walls, collapsing almost immediately after, cut off further air, stifling the flames; so the cellars were the least affected part of the building. Apart from being filled with debris.

'One interesting fact we did find: cellar access from the kitchen was by a heavy oak door lined with steel. Formidable lock on it too. It would have done for a bank vault.'

Yeadings remembered this detail from the SOCO's report. 'Not modern, though. It would have dated from the fifties. I understand the late Frederick Dellar put down a considerable quantity of valuable claret years ago. Maybe he didn't trust the servants.'

'Strangely enough, some of the wine has survived the fire.'

'That should increase its value if it ever reaches Sotheby's. Amazing how a murder detracts from house prices and puts hundreds on portable mementos. Not that I'd care to taste it after such heating. Actually there's a witness statement I'd like your views on, Bob. A technical point. It's about the moment when Eddie Dellar is supposed to have forced his way into the burning kitchen.'

The senior fireman grunted. 'Can't say I

saw any such statement. Got enough of my own to shuffle.'

'The witness, Augustus Railton, claimed he was at the door to the kitchen when Eddie pushed past. He tried to restrain him but came off the worse. Then while he staggered back an explosion inside the kitchen hurled him back against the wall of the hall passage.'

'That could have been caused by an inrush of fresh air. A classic fireball. Maybe that happened when the windows blew.'

'Or air surged in from the cellar door being opened?'

'Could be, equally. Especially if the coal chute had already been forced open. I wouldn't give much for the chances of this Eddie in that case. According to the press, when found he appeared to have been in a fight. If it happened when the windows blew then he'd look all of that, catching the full blast face-on. He should have landed out in the passage on top of your witness.'

'Unless the blast hurled him right on through the way he was heading.'

'That's possible too. He'd have been on fire, of course.'

'His clothes were singed, but there was almost no smoke-blackening up his nostrils and none in his lungs.'

The Station Officer stood up and took a

precautionary squint through the window. Apparently matters hadn't got totally out of hand in the rear yard. He turned back to Yeadings. 'Makes me wonder how far the fire had taken hold on the kitchen, Mike. And how long your witness stood outside the door waiting for something to happen.'

Yeadings nodded. 'We seem to be thinking along the same lines. One thing does seem likely: if Railton wasn't lying, then the door to the cellar can't have been locked. Eddie Dellar could have held his breath and barged through like a Rugby forward. And maybe the 'restraint' offered by my witness was faint-hearted in the extreme. A touch of the Munchausens in his heroism.'

'Nobody likes to admit they turned tail in a crisis. But why did this Eddie head for the cellar in the first place? The natural instinct is to get out in the open.'

'That's what we have to find out,' Yeadings admitted. He glanced at his watch. He needed to note something in his log before returning for the inquest. And for that occasion he'd be in the background. Let Zyczynski testify. She was more involved than anyone and there was mighty little that the coroner had to go on at this stage. It would have been different if they'd got the victim's ID.

'I'll push off,' he said; 'and see you at three.'

*　　*　　*

The fire scene continued to fill his mind as he drove back. When he reached his office he opened the relevant file and again checked Gus Railton's statement which he'd quoted to the Station Officer. Then he ambled into the Analysis Room and consulted the diagrams pinned to a pegboard. Eddie Dellar had had some desperate reason to go through fire to get to that cellar. And nobody had suggested an overwhelming passion for claret.

Larchmoor Place, undamaged, was shown there as three separate floors, and in front and rear elevations. On the ground floor he visualized Railton in the downstairs passage and Eddie Dellar thrusting him aside to get to the kitchen.

They had only Railton's version of how it was. He'd implied the place was an inferno. But Eddie Dellar's survival argued against that.

So when the young man plunged in, to get to the cellar, had the body already been on the kitchen floor? Could he, in the smoke, have overlooked something so bulky? Or had he run into the unidentified man still alive;

they'd fought and that was how Eddie got his ribs kicked in?

In which case Railton's story was a tissue of lies. The timing was all wrong. Minutes must have elapsed before the fireball which he claimed had hurled him back. So had he known there was a dead man/intruder in there? That might have been his reason for keeping everyone out until fire destroyed all the evidence.

Whichever way, it made Railton worth far more than a second glance as the potential arsonist-killer.

Yeadings closed his eyes and stood rocking gently on his heels, scrolling back through recollection of other statements. Somewhere Railton had been mentioned as others were being herded out.

Yes. Mrs Kate Dellar had stated that he was the one who woke her. He'd come banging on her door, and she'd found it hard to wake because of taking a sleeping tablet. So she'd been the last one to leave upstairs.

Her statement had been detailed. She had seized a few belongings to pack in a bag, dropped — and had to grope for — her reading spectacles, then made her way out on to the landing. Someone — perhaps Robert Dellar the journalist — had shouted reassurances that the young people had been evacuated from the top floor. He was standing, waiting for her, at the top of the front stairs. But they'd left it too late and flames suddenly came roaring up the stairwell. The back stairs had already gone, as well as the kitchen. In desperation they'd both escaped by an open window from the upstairs library, dropped on to the roof of the front porch and waited for a ladder.

So Gus Railton must have gone downstairs after calling Kate. Or had he come back upstairs to wake her after the incident at the kitchen door?

Yeadings looked at his watch. Time he should be on his way to the inquest. Except that he could safely leave it to Z and DI Salmon. It would be more rewarding, he decided, to stay and work out a more exact sequence of people's comings and goings on the night of the fire.

He returned to his office. Almost immediately the internal phone rang. He listened, nodding; asked for full details to be sent up immediately.

That morning he had warned Chief Superintendent Perry that there was yet more to come, not knowing that events had overtaken his expectations.

The message was from Traffic. Last night Sir Matthew Dellar and his daughter had been involved in an RTA. His Mercedes, driven by Madeleine, was in a pile-up at a roundabout between Windsor and Ascot while returning home from an evening out. Both were in Intensive Care in Windsor Hospital, their condition critical. DI Salmon had been informed this morning, but nobody had been able to reach Yeadings, since his mobile wasn't operative.

Switched off for peace and quiet while he was with Perry, the superintendent admitted silently. It looked as though his team would have plenty on their plates once they emerged from the inquest. Meanwhile it was up to him to look in and check on any witness statements for the accident. He assumed that a uniform officer would be posted at the hospital.

This had happened too soon after the fire at Larchmoor Place. Sir Matthew had survived the first incident, but the arsonist-killer might succeed with a second attempt on the retired judge's life. Too many of the same family were ending up as serious surgical cases.

Traffic Division had had the damaged Mercedes plastic-wrapped and removed for scientific examination, doubtless on Salmon's insistence. Like Yeadings, the Inspector wouldn't have overlooked that the crash could have been fixed. One thing he had omitted, though, was to leave a written note for Yeadings to find on return to the station. If Traffic hadn't been wised up on his interest in the family it might have escaped his notice.

Inform Perry, he told himself, and reached again for the phone. The DCS made a small explosive sound at the news. 'You were wanting a development,' he said, breathing heavily. 'Now you've got one. Let's hope it's going to lead somewhere.'

★ ★ ★

The inquest was swiftly dealt with and adjourned for a fortnight as Yeadings had predicted. Later, DS Zyczynski found his office empty when she took up her list of convicted criminals known to have threatened Sir Matthew Dellar's life. There were five, three of whom were still serving life sentences. One had since died, and the last was given an exemplary report by his Probation Officer whom Z knew to err normally on the side of scepticism. It looked as though the erstwhile judge had little to worry about.

With no further duty allocated to her, Z opted for a quick visit to check how Kate Dellar was weathering her misfortunes. She wasn't at home, and at the library they told her Kate had phoned in to ask for the rest of the week off. Afraid this meant some deterioration in Eddie's condition, Z made for Wycombe hospital to join her there.

The surgeon who had operated on the young man's pierced lung was in the unit office as she passed. He stopped in mid-flow of an amusing story and, recognizing Z, called after her. She went back. 'How's Eddie Dellar?' she asked.

'Have you suddenly become family?' he asked with mock severity.

'I'm a concerned party,' she told him.

'Well, there's no more cause for concern than yesterday. Sister can probably tell you more.'

Sister emerged from the group. 'Maybe even a little less cause for concern. He's stable and we're keeping our fingers crossed for signs of some improvement. But don't tell his family. We don't want false hopes raised. And there's absolutely no chance of any police getting closer to him than that bulldog out in the corridor.'

Her cheeks were slightly flushed and she was more vivacious than Z had seen her; almost frivolous. Maybe some personal therapy was at work, and it could be connected with the entertaining doctor. 'Is

Eddie's mother here?' she asked.

Kate wasn't. In fact she had phoned in at midday to ask for news and said she couldn't get in until the evening. Z grimaced and looked at her watch. 'I think I'll hang on here in that case. Maybe catch up on a meal.'

'Staff dining-room. Be my guest,' said the surgical registrar with alacrity.

She wasn't sure, but it was ten hours since she'd had breakfast and she was feeling empty. So yes; it seemed a chance not to be missed.

'You carry on,' Sister said. 'I'll tell Mrs Dellar when she gets here, and phone a message down to you.'

So Z joined the doctor, whose name was Oliver, and quite enjoyed the substantial lasagne with broccoli tips and a large cappuccino.

'It really should be decaff at this time of day,' Oliver advised, having fetched it for her. 'Believe me. I'm a doctor.'

'Nothing interferes with my sleep,' Z assured him. 'Believe me. I'm a copper. When we come off the job we could sleep on a clothesline.'

'As bad as being a junior medic,' he said, grinning. He was pleasant company, and if flirting with her was likely to make Sister more determined, then Z was happy enough.

They were walking back to Intensive Care when Oliver's pager went off. He read the message. 'Your lady has arrived,' he said. 'If you can find your way to her, I'll drop off on the way. There's a case I should take another look at before I go home. It was good seeing you again.'

Eddie had two visitors. Kate was accompanied by a tall, handsome man in his thirties who looked vaguely familiar. Z doubted she had met him before. It was more likely she'd seen his photograph somewhere — but not on police records.

They were seated on the same side of the bed while a nurse made some adjustment to the saline drip on the other. When Kate caught sight of Z at the door she rose and came across. 'There's someone I want you to meet, sergeant,' she said.

The name, like the face, was one that Z had to search her memory to recall, but unsuccessfully: Charles Stone, she was told. Someone important, she was almost sure. Not a politician. Not an entertainer; and yet surely it was on television she'd seen him. No more than a glimpse as she changed channels. In an interview perhaps. On some specialists' panel? Kate had introduced him as though he required no explanation.

'Jessica's boss,' Kate added.

He had risen. They shook hands.

'How do you find your son?' Z asked moving closer to the bed.

Kate hesitated. 'He — I think there's been some kind of change. His breathing seems different. More as though he's asleep.' She'd picked up on it, as possibly only a mother would.

The man spoke quietly. 'Mrs Dellar will be staying with me for a few days, helping in our efforts to trace her daughter. I think you should have my address.' He passed Z his card. She noted that he lived only ten to twelve miles away. Under his name was written simply Import-Export: no company name. So he was a businessman. That would account for her having skipped his programme. Apart from the news, she only followed TV that had a storyline.

'I'm glad you've someone with you,' she told Kate. 'It's no time to be on your own.'

She left them to their vigil and returned to write up her day. As she pulled into the station car park her pager sounded. The Boss wanted her upstairs. She glanced up and recognized his outline at the window. He'd been expecting her return.

'Something's happened?' she demanded, knocking and entering in one movement.

'Sir Matthew and his daughter were

seriously injured last night in an RTA just a short way from their home,' he said tersely. 'And an anonymous caller reported a biker driving erratically at the same time a couple of miles away. We were given a partial licence number. It could belong to Gus Railton's son Jake.

'I want you and Beaumont to chase him up and bring him in. He could have gone to earth somewhere. He has a lot to explain. And we can't risk any more of that family going missing.'

17

In the ICU at Windsor the bleeper sounded urgently from where Madeleine Railton lay unconscious. Gus was hustled from his wife's bedside as the crash team raced in to resuscitate her. He sat in the corridor, head in hands while they fought to keep her alive. Despite their desperate efforts there was no response

Madeleine's death was confirmed at 7.10pm. When Zyczynski arrived she couldn't deny Gus was deeply shaken. There was guilt too because he hadn't been with her when the car crashed.

'It wouldn't have helped,' she tried to console him. 'You'd have been badly injured too, sitting beside her.'

'No,' he said bitterly. 'Maddie's father always took the front passenger seat. Claimed his legs were too long for the back.'

In an outsize Mercedes? Z doubted it. Sir Matthew would be exercising his authority over the family. Theirs could have been an uncomfortable home, as three-generation setups often are.

'How was it you weren't there?' She already

273

guessed there'd been a family falling-out, but she was curious to hear him explain it.

'Look,' he said, 'I don't want to think about it now. It was my fault, only Maddie was already stirred up over something her bloody father had said and she rounded on me. She didn't normally, but there's only just so much you can take from a fucking — well, someone like him. He shoves everyone in the dock.'

'Then maybe you weren't at fault. There are times we all get pushed into silly situations.'

'It was about locking up the stables,' he burst out, deciding to unburden himself after all. 'I'd let her down.'

Z listened, nodding while he explained. His usually high colour was more pronounced than usual. She thought she saw the beginnings of tears in his eyes. But tears from grief or frustration?

Later she passed all this on to Yeadings as the team met in his office, joined by Percival from the Branch.

'How far ahead do you suppose Railton's looking at present?' the Boss mused. 'Losing his wife — undoubtedly his financial stay — is going to change life fundamentally. If his father-in-law survives, can you see the three men settling down to domestic bliss together?'

'I expect Madeleine will have covered that risk,' Z supposed. 'Seriously horsy people must know that accidents happen; circumstances can change overnight.'

'Well, Railton's learnt it now,' Salmon put in sourly. 'We'll need to take a look at her will in case there's been some fiddling with the car.'

'So who would you pick as the potential fiddler?' asked Yeadings mildly.

Salmon's eyes narrowed into slits. Invited for an opinion, he stretched his stocky legs to their full extent on the carpet before him and fell into lecturing mode. His voice dropped half an octave as he tucked his chins into his chest.

'It's suspicious, Railton falling out at the last minute. He could have cooked something up with his son — owner of a high-speed motorbike. There's that anonymous call-in about a crazy biker just a mile farther on. The partial licence number given could fit young Railton's. Two other cars were involved in the pile-up. I want statements from all survivors on just how the incident occurred.'

Yeadings nodded. 'Inspector Wright of Traffic is collating material from the scene, but apparently none of the initial statements mentions a biker. All we have on that is the anonymous caller. One major factor regarding the crash is considerable oil spillage, pre-incident, on the curve which the Mercedes was taking. Skid marks suggest it made the driver lose control. They've retrieved a crushed plastic container with residue of used sump oil in it. We have to leave it to the specialists to report back on the Mercedes. Meanwhile we wait for Sir Matthew's recovery and any account he's able to give. At present he's barely conscious and frequently drifting. You'll have copies of the other survivors' statements as soon as they're available.'

'If Dellar dies,' Salmon supposed with crude satisfaction, 'we get to see his will.' He looked round at the others. 'No need to be mealy-mouthed about it. To my mind this is no accident. If both Dellar and his daughter had died at the scene before being found, then legally it'd be accepted that Sir Matthew died first, being older. Well, it's happened the other way about and the old man is hanging on. Which could be less in Railton's favour. As it stands, whatever Sir Matthew had intended leaving his daughter will go elsewhere. The Railtons will inherit only whatever Madeleine intended leaving them.'

Yeadings grunted agreement. 'We don't yet know the intricacies of the wills in question. But Sir Matthew's an expert in law, and if he has a poor opinion of his daughter's husband and stepson it's unlikely he'd have wanted them to benefit unduly.'

He pushed his empty cup and saucer away. 'One thing I'm pretty certain of. He'll have everything covered to his own satisfaction. As was the case with his late wife's will.'

'You've seen that, sir?' Beaumont interrupted.

'I took a trip to St. Catherine's House today,' the Boss admitted, 'and obtained a copy. It seems Sir Matthew married an heiress. When she died their daughter Madeleine and son Robert were left a considerable sum in trust, but Sir Matthew received the lion's share outright. We can safely assume he'd advised her on drawing up the provisions.'

'If — ' Salmon pronounced, and paused. He screwed his mouth tight, then continued. 'If the Railtons set up the car crash, we're agreed, aren't we, that it's gone sour on them? Their big meal ticket's gone, with the old diehard surviving. Not what they'd have intended at all. Let's interview them in depth while their wounds are smarting.

'Beaumont, get after them and find out exactly where both were at the time of the accident and an hour before and after.'

'Say, nine to midnight?'

'Better make it that. And then check up on any witnesses they use for an alibi.'

'And Zyczynski?' Yeadings queried.

Salmon considered. 'She can liaise with Traffic.' He turned to her. 'See what the Fire Service can turn up regarding the oil spill. Small ones aren't uncommon, but it did disable two other cars after the Mercedes. I know that road. There's a fairly irregular traffic flow at that time of evening. Since earlier vehicles weren't affected, the spill must have just happened. Maybe a can fallen from a lorry taking the roundabout at speed. But I'd put my money on the contents being deliberately spread there. Could be by our biker.'

'This roundabout,' Percival muttered. 'Is that marked on the map as Woodside? It all looks like open country round there.'

'Country, yes. But heavily wooded. There's a lot of cover,' Yeadings explained. 'The other thing about Woodside roundabout is that it isn't round. The island's central to a complicated intersection, elongated and shaped like a hide.'

'Hide? You mean like a shelter for watching animals?'

'No, hide as in an animal's skin. Imagine a sheep's fleece, its forelegs pointing roughly north and its back legs south.' He sketched it roughly on his notepad and pushed it across.

'The Mercedes, leaving Windsor Great Park, approaches it from the northeast, to come off at the second exit. The central reservation is woodland, offering plenty of cover. If I meant to set this up that's where I'd be waiting, with a clear view up the curved approach. There'd be time enough then to identify the Mercedes and sling out the oil.'

'Only at that time of night it's dark, and there's no lighting except low reflections on the road signs. There was no moon then,' Salmon argued. 'The traffic's light at that hour, but it's almost continuous. The Merc's headlights would look much the same as any others.'

'Except by infra-red. There's enough curve to offer a side-on view. Night glasses are something we'll search for when we've someone in the frame.'

They all considered this.

'The car's a wreck,' Percival put in. 'I've been to see it. The wheels were locked to the left, as if she tried to steer into the skid. But it could be she saw something to avoid on the far-side and overdid it. Perhaps a person moving on the edge of the reservation, or the oil being thrown. It would be instinctive to recoil. The first impact was on a yellow road sign for Legoland. It probably knocked them both out. Then the next two cars piled in at the back and side. With that they hadn't a wax cat's chance in hell, poor sods.'

Salmon rose to his feet. 'I'll interview survivors from the other two cars myself; find out what they saw. If the biker's identified as the boy Jake, then he'd be close at the right time and far enough ahead to set it all up.'

'Good,' Yeadings said, nodding. 'I'll expect to have something in writing before you all go home tonight.' He watched them leave, then turned to his logbook. There was plenty more to add. The last entry covered a conversation with Z before the whole team met up. It referred to Kate Dellar's being befriended by Charles Stone, her daughter's boss. She could be contacted at his home address for the next few days.

Stone was a big fish. Could that account for Special Branch nuzzling in on this case? Nothing extraordinary for the man to query an employee's disappearance, but why should he take such a personal interest in the widow Dellar?

Yeadings would welcome an excuse to talk to Kate again himself, and at the same time take a look round Stone's country house.

He began to hum under his breath, recognized the tune as Coward's *Stately*

Homes of England, grinned and broke off. Not more than ten or twelve miles away as the crow flew. He rather fancied the trip out there. He'd get an official car laid on.

★ ★ ★

It was a little after nine-twenty when Yeadings' driver was confronted by the closed gates to Charles Stone's estate. 'Find a bell or something,' the Superintendent instructed him shortly. 'Give it a good yank.'

The instruction proved unnecessary, as a thickset man dressed like a gamekeeper came out of the lodge to confront them, with a twelve-bore shotgun under one arm. Yeadings lowered his window and nodded across. He dangled his warrant card, giving name and rank.

'I'll have to speak to the house,' the man said, unimpressed. He moved away, produced a mobile phone and spoke into it. After a short wait he growled some reply, then came across to the car. He bent and gave Yeadings' face a searching inspection. 'Mr Stone will see you. You can go ahead in one minute. Take the left fork and park by the front door.'

They waited while the man disappeared into the lodge, then the twin gates sighed open and they drove in. There was a single bend and the house came in sight on a grassy knoll, three storeys of warm red brick in an unpretentious William and Mary style. The left fork took them a further semicircle and up an incline to reach the ground floor. Under the white-pillared porch three people stood waiting.

Yeadings took his time getting out. It gave him a chance to form a rapid impression of the little group. Stone, slightly ahead of the other, smaller man, was easily recognized from press photographs. He was youthful-looking, tall, well built and erect, rather more handsome than in print. His Armenian ancestry showed in his sleek, blue-black hair, strong profile and assured stance. His manners were English public-school, casually correct. Beside him the woman appeared small, a slighter, younger Judi Dench, with the same short nose and determined little chin. Her hair was cut ear-length and was as fair as his was dark. They stood close. But for her being the elder, Yeadings would have taken them for a couple.

'Superintendent,' Stone said, 'it's good of you to call.' He introduced the other two and they all shook hands. The man, Roger Beale, was described as Stone's assistant.

Even before the superintendent could be invited indoors, Kate Dellar asked anxiously,

'Have you any news?'

Yeadings knew she meant about her children. 'I'm afraid not, Mrs Dellar.'

'Let's go through,' Stone said, and led them to a small salon off the hall. Crushed cushions on two chairs and a sofa showed where they had been sitting. Yeadings made for a spare seat. They appeared to have been drinking fruit punch. Stone indicated a half-empty glass jug on a table between them. 'I'll get some more. The ice has melted.'

Before Yeadings could demur, a tall woman had appeared at his side with a tumbler and fresh juice on a tray. Stone nodded but didn't introduce her. So not the wife. She left as silently as she had come.

'We heard about the dreadful accident last night,' Kate Dellar said. 'How are they both?'

'I'm sorry,' Yeadings told her. 'Mrs Railton didn't pull through. She died earlier this evening. Her father's condition is still critical.'

Kate was shocked. The men were unsurprised. Yeadings was left to assume Stone had his own means of gathering information.

'So much has gone wrong,' Kate said, distressed. 'You'd think there was a curse . . . '

'An unlucky family?' Yeadings asked softly. 'Certainly one that seems at risk. So much

283

has happened just lately. Where do you think it all began?'

She had shut her eyes and now all the colour left her face. She seemed unable to speak, both hands clutched tightly against her chest.

'Michael,' she managed to get out at last. 'My husband. I can't believe any more that it was random. Someone — someone is picking us off, one by one.'

Stone, his face severe, moved across to sit beside her on the sofa. 'Kate, there could be other reasons for — '

'He was attacked,' she insisted, 'on his way home. He always walked down Surrey Street to the Underground. Everybody knew . . . '

'It was the Met's case,' Yeadings put in. He had reviewed the report, dredged up when trawling the name Dellar. 'They would have investigated thoroughly; but without any witness coming forward they had to accept he was mugged for the money he had on him. You know that at night the Strand has derelicts sleeping in doorways. They get less and less from begging as the public tires of supporting their drug and alcohol habits.'

'No,' Kate said. 'First Michael, then Eddie and Jess. They tried to get at Jess on her boat first, remember? But she wasn't there. So they followed her to Carlton's and set fire to the place with us all in it. Now it's Matthew and Maddie. This is more than coincidence. What have we done to deserve all this?'

'Nothing,' Stone said sharply.

'You believe someone outside your family is carrying out a vendetta against you all?' Yeadings questioned.

Kate's chin came up as she faced him on it. 'I do. I know it seems beyond belief, but I believe one of us — ' She paused, took a breath and went on, ' . . . one of us has done something terrible to cause this indiscriminate attack on the rest.'

This was illuminating. Yeadings stared at her, then away, unwilling for her to guess what was in his mind. She thought one of the Dellars capable of provoking an irrational passion for revenge. Her anger was because she and her children, possibly her dead husband too, had been included with the others, considered guilty alongside whoever she suspected of this undefined outrage.

'So who in the family do you think ultimately responsible?' he asked quietly.

'Any of them,' she said bitterly. 'They're all monsters.'

★　★　★

285

This, when he reviewed it with Salmon, was meat and drink to the DI. Rather than shifting suspicion to outsiders, it gave greater credence, in his mind, to a conspiracy by the Railtons. What alternatives were there, inside the family or out? He couldn't see an octogenarian poet proving a master criminal, even after arson at his home. He'd hardly have torched it for his own gain, since it belonged to his brother. And he could have had no hand in the car accident that killed his niece Madeleine, because he'd moved away down to Sussex.

The theory of revenge wreaked on the younger brother by some criminal he'd sentenced harshly had been followed up and led nowhere. It still seemed the best bet to Salmon that both these crimes targeted at Sir Matthew were based on personal greed. Railton, as a drifter and a possible sponger, was fortunately to hand as prime suspect. Every detail of his past would need to be investigated and analyzed. Since Kate Dellar's reported bitter outburst, Salmon felt quite certain who were the principal 'monsters' she'd ranted against.

Yeadings decided to give the DI a free rein on this. Or enough rope to hang himself. They'd know better how sound his theory was once Beaumont brought the Railtons in.

The delay was explained when the DS phoned in to say Gus was becoming increasingly anxious about his son's absence and they were going together to visit a biking friend who might have offered him a bed overnight.

While these interviews were held up, a fresh drama was enacted in the ICU at Windsor. The constable guarding the outside passage observed the arrival of the injured man's brother and sister-in-law who had driven up from Cooden Beach. Their identities were checked and a doctor admitted them to sit a while by Sir Matthew's side. A nurse was present, making up her notes at a table by the door.

Between the blind's slats the constable had idly watched the older brother seat himself and reach for the other's hand. For a while he seemed to be talking quietly to the comatose man. The constable lost interest, returning to the paperback book in his pocket.

A wild cry rang out. Startled, he sprang to his feet, turning in time to see the nurse lunge forward between the woman and the bed, obscuring his view of the patient. A metal dish fell clanging to the floor and rang on as it circled on its base.

Then he saw the injured man fighting to get out, the IV tubes tearing from his body as he struggled with the nurse. The constable hurtled through the door and caught the nurse as she was thrown aside. His legs tangled with the overturned chair where the other man had sat and he fell against the stand supporting the blood bag. The whole lot went down with him and tore apart.

Sir Matthew Dellar crouched like a caged creature on the edge of the bed, all his weight on trembling stick-like arms. 'Bitch!' he screamed frenetically. 'Murdering bitch! You won't get away with . . . '

His words cut off with the hideous rictus of his distorted face. The feeble arms collapsed. A stream of saliva bubbled over the tangled sheets. He shuddered and collapsed.

On the floor Constable Jenks gazed up in horror. The nurse pulled herself to her feet. The others appeared petrified, Claudia Dellar's arms spread wide as if to protect her husband; he cowering against the wall, mouth agape.

A buzzer was sounding persistently. The nurse was at the monitor, shouting over her shoulder for help. She wrestled the bedhead flat and pushed the others away. The room was suddenly crowded with staff.

To Constable Jenks it was all grotesquely familiar, even the words they were shouting at each other. He felt trapped in a sequence from *ER*. At home his wife Ethel, both hands over her mouth, would be demanding, 'He's going to die, isn't he?' And he'd be saying to reassure her, 'It's only a play. He's just an actor getting paid for it.'

But this time it was for real. He had to get himself outside and phone in a report. They'd order CID in here to find out what happened. And by the time they arrived he'd have to be clear himself about what he'd seen.

Only what exactly was that?

He'd thought he was on to a cushy break here, but what a God-awful mess it was turning into.

18

Samples of the oil spillage at Woodside roundabout had been sent on for analysis at the forensic lab, and DS Zyczynski could get no further on that until their report came through. At best it would be in a matter of days; longer if they needed to refer the inquiry to the research departments of individual production companies.

She was still pursuing details of the crash with Traffic Unit when summoned to report to her DI. She found Salmon in his office looking distinctly ruffled. 'Sir,' she prompted him, as he continued riffling through loose papers on his desk.

'I want you down at Cooden Beach. See the Dellar daughter there and get her statement on her parents' whereabouts for the past two days.'

'You mean the Carlton Dellars?'

'Of course I bloody do.' He looked up at her, scowling. 'They suddenly turned up here to see the judge and scared the life out of him. Literally. He woke up enough to take one look at his sister-in-law, swore at her and had convulsions or something. Anyhow he had a seizure and he's dead now, so I guess that makes the car crash a double murder.'

She stared at his flushed face. Why this sudden interest in the Carlton Dellars? With this recent event he seemed to be suffering from a rush of suspects. Hadn't he already settled for a conspiracy by the Railtons?

'Listen,' he said emphatically and loudly, as if to someone of limited intelligence and poor hearing, 'we've only their say-so that they came up today. It wasn't a normal reaction. The dead man went berserk at sight of the woman. He wasn't able to accuse her specifically but his reaction spoke volumes. Called her a murdering bitch. The constable on duty was a witness, and the nurse present confirms what he says. That woman's hiding something. If she didn't do the job herself, she bloody well knows who did, and probably put them on to it.'

'Why should she?' Z couldn't stop herself protesting.

Salmon glared at her. 'Don't ask me. Go and find out. I've enough to do this end interviewing them all over again. We have to go right back to the beginning on this. She was always in the best position to set up the arson. Find she lied about her alibi for this one and we've got a starting point to break her down.'

'Are you sure the daughter's not come here with them?'

'They've only one double room booked at their hotel.'

'Right.' At least he'd checked that much. Perhaps it wasn't a wild goose chase after all. She'd have more confidence in him if he didn't get so worked up every time something new happened. She'd agree that greed might have been Claudia Dellar's motive just as easily as for the Railtons. The milk of human kindness wasn't likely to have flowed very freely in her veins.

'Have you contacted the Sussex police?' Z reminded him.

'We've no time for niceties. Get there and get something on them, before they think to phone through and warn the girl.'

Miranda wasn't a girl, Z reflected as she manoeuvred her car out of the station yard where a dog-van had been parked half across her exit. Miss Dellar was into her thirties: a woman, if not an especially mature one. There was something wrong there, not badly, but enough to set her apart. Probably a lonely person, unless she found other people just weren't necessary to her. Perhaps her upbringing by elderly and old-fashioned parents accounted for any strangeness. It could be interesting to find out more about her.

It was dusk by the time Z's car nosed along the double row of seashore bungalows. The sea was calm and as flat as the coastal scenery. The total lack of wind meant no sails showed out on the water. Between the buildings a few dinghies could be glimpsed pulled up on the shingle and almost every driveway had a small powerboat mounted on a carrier. A strong smell of charcoal bricks announced the early stages of a barbecue, but there were no moving figures, no voices except an occasional snatch of television news escaping from open windows.

House numbers were clearly frowned on here. It took some time to locate *Mon Repos*; midway between *Genista* and *Shangri La*. Z guessed the choice of name wasn't the Dellars'. Perhaps retaining it had appealed to some wry appreciation of the poet's for the bourgeois awfulness of it. She guessed he must despise seaside society and the people who retired here.

This bungalow had all its windows shut, but a sound of music met her as she pulled into the driveway. It broke off abruptly as she rang the bell. There was silence for a moment, then a sound of muffled footsteps in the hall. The door opened on Miranda Dellar, embarrassed and defensive.

'Hello,' Z began. 'I'm Detective Sergeant Zyczynski. I came . . . '

'Yes,' the overgrown girl said, meaning she remembered her.

'I wonder if I may come in. There's something I need to ask you.'

'I'm not to let anyone in.'

'But this is a police matter.'

She considered a moment, then slowly smiled. It wasn't a welcome; more like a naughty child's pleasure at overriding a ban. She held the door wider and retreated a few steps. Z slid in and looked around.

They had plenty of space here, which was as well since the place seemed over-furnished. The L-shaped hall gave on to several rooms, three with open doorways showing equally crowded interiors.

'Was that you playing?' Z asked, glimpsing the boudoir grand piano and sheet music spilled on the floor.

'Yes.' She let the policewoman precede her and bend over the keyboard.

'Schumann, wasn't it?'

Again the single breathless word of agreement.

'Would you play me some more?'

'It's for four hands, but I've changed it.'

'That sounds complicated.'

'Not really.' She seated herself and spread

her fingers, then let them fly in a cascade of notes. She used no script. It was all in her head and she played as if charged with frenetic energy.

Amazing, Z thought. They'd said she was backward.

The music went on while the light faded, and when eventually Miranda stopped she was still aware of the other woman sitting behind her in the half-dark, almost companionable. 'I'm thirsty,' she said. 'Can you make tea?'

'If you show me where the things are. Don't you make drinks yourself?'

'I can, but I'm clumsy.'

Z thought of the strong, muscular fingers flashing over the keyboard. 'Now whoever told you that?' she asked.

The kitchen was simply arranged, probably left the way it was when they bought the place. Elsewhere there had obviously been an attempt to turn the bungalow into something much grander. Z guessed that much of the excessive furniture had come from the old house before the fire. Which would have set light to DI Salmon's little blue touch-paper and reinforced his suspicions of arson.

Z dangled tea bags in matching mugs and started making sandwiches with sliced ham from the fridge. 'Where does your father work?' she asked, imagining a poet must have some sort of retreat.

'Work?'

'Write his poems.'

'He doesn't. He sits in the garden. Mother writes. Upstairs.' She shrugged towards the trap door at the back end of the hall.

'How nice. You have an upstairs. I bet it has a ladder. Can I have a peep?'

Miranda stood stock-still. 'We don't go up.'

Z put down the tea tray and looked at her. She remembered Miranda's sly smile as she considered letting her in. 'It would be rather fun, don't you think? Let's go up. Shall we?'

The cajoling voice couldn't be resisted. Ever since morning, when Mother had had that phone call and decided to rush off, the day had been growing special; hours and hours of music and nobody to complain about it. Then this nice woman coming to listen, and just when she'd started feeling thirsty and wanting something to eat. Now they would be doing something quite awful together; exciting. 'Take our picnic up there,' she whispered.

The loft room with its knock-through attic window was nothing special, cheaply furnished with a softwood work-station, computer and filing cabinet. While Miranda sipped tea, Z booted up and attempted a search of the computer files, but they weren't accessible without a password. The box files of papers she skimmed through proved that Claudia's 'writing' wasn't so much with words as with figures. The listed costings and dates made easy sense. There were also a number of yellowed sheets headed with the address of legal chambers in Middle Temple. Some had scribbled notes on; others were blank. Z remembered those had been Sir Matthew's chambers when he was a QC. It seemed curious that he should have supplied his sister-in-law with legal stationery.

By now Miranda had dared to seat herself at the work-station and had begun to 'play' the keyboard, dismayed that no sound but clicking ensued.

'We have to get rid of that,' Z said, pointing to the gobbledygook appearing on the screen. She deleted the letters and closed the computer down. 'I'd rather have a piano any day,' she said. 'Wouldn't you?'

'Yes.' Again the breathless monosyllable. Miranda appeared to be tiring after so much excitement.

'Are your parents coming home tonight? How long have they been away?'

The double question must have been too much for her. Miranda hesitated a moment, glanced at the watch on her wrist and said,

'Thirteen hours and forty three minutes.'

The precision was unexpected. 'They were both here the last two nights then?' Z persisted.

'Yes. Since we came down from the old house.'

So much for the DI's new suspicions, Z thought. It was back now to Square One for him, with the Railtons still in the frame.

* * *

Salmon was having little success with separately interviewing Carlton Dellar and his wife. With the poet he met not so much stonewalling as having his questions returned from a sorbo surface which deadened any force of the attack. He failed to get the man talking freely about the family, particularly regarding relations with his younger brother, the judge.

'He did appear upset when he saw your wife,' the DI was obliged to prompt, eventually coming out in the open.

'It goes back a long way,' was all the man could offer. 'Claudia and Matthew. They have no time for each other now.' He was still speaking of his brother in the present tense.

'No love lost?' Salmon paraphrased.

At that Carlton paused open-mouthed,

gave a little choking cough, then agreed, 'Ah, I see what you mean. No love lost indeed.' And they had had to leave it at that.

Claudia, questioned about the dead man's sudden aggression, remained tight-lipped. 'I simply walked in. I never spoke,' she claimed at last. 'I don't think he even saw me behind my husband. I hadn't done or said a thing.

'Carlton was trying to comfort him, to hold his attention so that he didn't slip away again. Then suddenly he seemed galvanized, and shouted out my name. I tell you, it was one of those hallucinations they sometimes get at the end. He mistook me for someone from the past. His dead mother or such. I hadn't done or said a thing.'

'But it was your name he called out. He was angry with *you*. Nurse Pelham said he was furious. Livid and shaking with rage.'

'He just went mad. That's all I can tell you. Something snapping in his mind. Nothing to do with us.'

'So what *was* in his mind? Some remembered incident he connected with you?'

'That's highly unlikely. Is that all, inspector? — because we should get back on the road. I don't enjoy driving in the half-light and we've cancelled the hotel for tonight.'

'I need first to know where you both were

two nights ago between eight and midnight.'

'At Cooden Beach of course. Until we heard this morning about Madeleine dying, we hadn't left there since your sergeant stopped us on the way down. You should have a note of that somewhere.'

Salmon was plunged in gloom. It was much what her husband had said. There was only one ray of hope. When Zyczynski got back she might prove them both liars.

★ ★ ★

Superintendent Yeadings wasn't asleep although it might have appeared so. He was watching bright colours merge and transpose themselves on the backs of his eyelids while morning sunshine poured through the office window, warming his face and detaching his thoughts to drift like flotsam. It was his version of navel-gazing, and a process he often found rewarding when some of the floating material became so persistent that he was moved to open his eyes, sit up and take note of what his subconscious had on offer.

It was a memory of Kate Dellar's voice that flooded his mind now, low and husky with anxiety. He could hear the tone, the melody, but couldn't distinguish any words. Then the pitch rose, became impassioned. Quite clearly one phrase was replayed. The mention of Surrey Street. It remained in his mind long enough for him to question why it should be significant.

He knew it ran from the Strand down to the embankment. That was where Kate Dellar's husband had been attacked. He'd have been walking down to Temple Underground station, on his way home from King's. *Temple*, his subconscious reminded him. The word reverberated.

So what? Religious undertones? No, legal ones. Middle Temple: which was where Matthew Dellar's chambers had been. Now who did he know who might have been there as a junior when old Dellar had still been a QC?

Randolph Metcalfe, of course, and you might say old Randy owed him a small favour. Yeadings reached for his diary and ran a finger down the letter M until he found the barrister's telephone number.

Lunch at Simpson's in the Strand. That ought to draw him, if only from curiosity. The man was a natural gossip when it didn't involve one of his own cases. He would probably be only too happy to dish the dirt on a one-time colleague, and no respecting *nil nisi bonum*.

★ ★ ★

Only one of the crash survivors was considered sufficiently recovered to be questioned. A passenger in the rear of the second car to smash into the Mercedes, he was still confused about how it all came about. 'There was an almighty skid and a *thunk* as we hit the others,' he said. 'That's all I know. And I guess I was dozing just before it happened. It had been a damn good dinner.'

Which didn't much please DI Salmon. The police hadn't even the satisfaction of breathalyzing any of the drivers since they'd been guarded by paramedics when cut out of the wreckage. One remained on the critical list.

So when the crash scene SOCO phoned in with a preliminary report Salmon fell upon it avidly. Photographs of the ground inside the reservation showed clear indications of recent intruders. Earlier drizzle had dampened the peaty earth, making it and the soft pine-needle cover ideal for taking shoe prints. A medium-sized, narrow sole had left double tracks here and there across the wooded traffic island. At an opposite point a few yards short of where the first skid had started there was a confused stamping as if someone had spent time waiting and tramping about.

Specimens of soil from nearby had been retrieved and were thought to contain drops of soiled motor oil.

Extending the line of footmarks across the island — 'hide' in both senses of the word now, Salmon thought grimly — there was a point on the farther road where a car had been run on to the grass verge. Tyre tracks had been photographed and measured.

'Right,' Salmon declared. He ordered Accident Notices to be erected on that spot asking the public for information regarding cars seen parked there. 'Copies to local press,' he demanded.

Size eight shoes, narrow, with squarish heels. What were the chances of that description fitting the Railton boy's biking boots? He guessed Jake would be no more than five feet five, so he'd almost put money on it.

19

Beaumont had at last succeeded in running Jake Railton to earth. He was lodging at a student pad with the fellow-biker his father had spoken of. Both were found in sleeping bags on the floor and rather the worse for wear, having survived a night in the cells at West End Central. This had followed a wild round of clubbing that ended with a police raid to pick up dealers in a sleazy joint in Soho.

The combined experience had required a sixteen-hour sleep-off and provided a cast-iron alibi for the time of the RTA at Woodside. Jake, decidedly frail after a bad experience with Ecstasy and the subsequent humiliation, was further shaken when told of the deaths of his stepmother and her father.

Beaumont brought Salmon up to date by phone, and the DI took it sourly. This additional blow followed a check on Gus's own alibi of having spent the crucial night with a single mother of two teenage children, all of whom vouched for his presence at supper and breakfast. Salmon's pet theory crumbled totally when he learned that Jake's biking boots were size ten with corrugated sole and broad fitting.

'Bring both Railtons in, just the same,' he ordered. 'They may yet lead us to whoever the biker was.'

'If there ever was one,' Yeadings cautioned. 'All eye-witnesses were questioned on that point and not one of them recalls seeing a biker at any point on the route between Windsor and the roundabout. The anonymous phone call is all we have on him. I want a copy of that tape.'

When it was produced he listened to it along with Salmon and Zyczynski. The recording had a crackle of static and the voice sounded muffled. 'A woman?' Yeadings asked the others. On the whole they agreed. It was a high rush of words with no pause for breathing and had an unnatural reedy quality.

'Maybe,' the Boss said. 'Maybe not. Let's check.' He sent for Sergeant Boddy who had been a recording engineer and still put on gigs as a weekend money-spinner. He listened with the others and decided it was an amateur re-recording with the tempo speeded up. 'If I slow it down the voice will be deeper,' he told them. 'Let me take it off for a try.'

Beaumont, who had returned and left the Railtons in separate interview rooms to cool their heels, was there with them when Boddy brought the changed tape back and played it over. 'What do you think? Is that a man now?'

It could be either. 'Maybe a deep-voiced woman,' Yeadings suggested innocently, wondering if Salmon would pick up the hint.

He did. 'Claudia Dellar,' he declared with conviction, leaping back to his alternative suspect. 'She could have set up the crash and put this call out as a diversion.'

'Quoting a licence number that must lead us to Jake Railton? Spiteful, wouldn't you say? Now that he's got the Met to establish his alibi, it certainly looks as though he wasn't on somebody's list of favourites. If we ask the lady to come back and explain herself when she's barely had time to turn round at Cooden Beach from the last trip, she won't be best pleased.'

Beaumont was looking doubtful. 'I grant the old harpy's capable of spite but she can't have fixed the crash herself, and I don't see her putting out a contract on her brother-in-law. She's a tough old loner. Where would she get hold of someone to do the job for her?'

'Why not some member of the family?' Salmon sneered, eager not to have this possibility shot down.

'None of them would risk it for love,' Z protested. 'So she'd need to have a hold over someone. And anyway why would she want either of those two dead? Not for money, since she already had her scam set up for the insurance compensation.'

'Some people never have enough,' Salmon growled.

'But she'd hardly be likely to inherit from them.'

Yeadings decided the discussion was degenerating towards peevishness, but forbore to point out that there were alternative motives for murder. Pure hate for one. He felt the grim elderly wife of the poet might have a lot of that stored up over the years, whether or not she was behind the crash scene. And again the cause might well lie in the dead man himself. His daughter's death could have been incidental.

In a long career of pursuing others' just, or unjust, deserts, Sir Matthew would have handed out a helluva lot of grief. Besides those who made open threats of revenge, there would be others who stayed silent, nourishing their hatred, building rancour and resentment towards the final explosion. There was no knowing how many there were like that.

If Sir Matthew Dellar had been the prey of such a one, then the secret to finding the predator could involve a long and arduous task digging into legal history.

'We have enough to hold her,' Salmon pursued, still on Claudia's trail. 'Wasting police time for a start. Then we keep on at her. In a cell, isolated from the others, she'll break down eventually.'

'She'd get bail,' Beaumont complained. 'An old bird like that.'

Yeadings sighed. 'The phone call's peripheral. I'll grant it was an act of spite, and I'm persuaded she did it, but we're off the main track there. Bring her back by all means and I'm happy to drag the truth out of her, but don't expect fireworks. What's more she's astute enough to turn round and accuse us of undue harassment.'

He glanced at his watch. 'I've someone to see in London. And the Railtons are waiting to be finally sorted out. When you're satisfied, leave a note on my desk.'

★   ★   ★

Randolph Metcalfe had already been shown to their table and was more than halfway through a double vodka Martini. 'On your tab,' he said mockingly, raising his glass in greeting to Yeadings as he came across.

'Order another,' the Boss said. 'I'll have the same. Plus a litre of still mineral water. Have

308

you had a look at the menu? Anything inspiring there?'

They settled to old codgers' talk, covered the necessary inquiries about family and acquaintances in common who'd slid out of view for the one or the other.

'So,' Metcalfe finally demanded, peaking his quizzical eyebrows, 'to what do I owe this sudden retrieval from your past?'

'Funny you should say that,' Yeadings responded. 'It's the past I'd like you to wander back into. I'm hoping you'll recall some of your early days at Fairweather, Mottram and Sneel.'

'Nothing wrong with my memory,' the other man claimed waspishly. 'It's a question of discretion, though. Can't let the snoopers in on our sanctified history, y'know.'

But he was mellowing already. That hadn't been his first vodka while he was waiting for his host.

'Less sanctified that sanitized perhaps in some cases,' Yeadings dared to suggest.

The elderly barrister snickered. 'Recovered scandals,' he said, delighted. 'And with no eavesdroppers to pick up on them. What a fascinating invitation. I just hope we aren't being illicitly recorded.'

'No. I'm simply curious.' The man was getting too arch for Yeadings' liking. It was good that the main course had arrived, offering a solid base for all that swilling alcohol. Time to introduce the quarry's name. 'Sir Matthew Dellar.'

Metcalfe laid down his knife and fork. 'The recently *late* Sir Matthew Dellar in fact. Actually only *mister* in the days when we entered by the same front door.

'Now there was a shark if ever there was one. His was always the wig most likely to grow long side-curls. Done very nicely for himself one way and another, I must admit.'

Metcalfe applied himself to his food and didn't look up for some minutes. Yeadings was afraid he'd dried up; but apparently he was savouring in advance the titbits he was about to drop. When he was ready he unloaded.

There were a number of choice tales, mostly of cases where Dellar had craftily shafted rivals. Metcalfe was careful to omit his own name from these, but then he'd been considerably junior to the rising star.

Dellar's success was owed to more than the winning of lucrative cases; he'd been selective in whom he cultivated, and the Head of Chambers had seen him as his blue-eyed boy.

'Which required some skilled cover-up since the old fellow was a stickler for puritan wholesomeness,' Metcalfe related with relish.

310

'And any of us in the know were careful not to cross the path of a man in the ascendant.'

'What was the thin ice then?'

'Dellar wasn't married. In those days that was a bit suspect, although no one was likely to speculate on it openly. He kept everyone guessing, though a couple of young men's names did get hinted at. Then there was that poor cow Gilmour. God knows how many years he kept her dangling in the background. She was a young solicitor in the firm and quite a dish. We heard later they'd kept a love-nest south of the river — Balham or some such place — and she'd been expecting a child. Never heard what became of it, though. He probably made arrangements for it, since he'd defended a number of seedy medics.'

'You mean an abortion?'

'Illegal then, of course, but there was an unofficial trade for those who could afford it.'

'Where would this girl be now?'

Metcalfe gave a cackle of laughter. 'Some girl! She'd be a right old crone by now. Gave up completely, like the light went out. Got on the wrong side of old Mottram and disappeared from chambers. We heard later she'd married Dellar's brother, a writer of sorts but not much cop. Bit of a comedown after the big man himself. Matthew, of

311

course, pulled off a real coup in the marriage stakes and I guess that's what put paid to the Balham love-nest. Money, y'know. He simply off-loaded the mistress. Well, even he knew better than to shit in his own territory.'

'Gilmour,' Yeadings repeated thoughtfully. 'Claudia Gilmour; would that be?'

'You've got it. Tall girl, quite a smasher in a lanky, Virginia Woolf-ish sort of way. Lovely bones,' he admitted sadly.

★   ★   ★

Yeadings drove back to South Bucks with plenty to ponder. He had dropped Metcalfe off at his depressing basement flat in Kilburn. He was a boring old fart but the lunch had left him in a happy half-stupor. Yeadings was grateful, but not enough to make a further arrangement to meet up. He hadn't missed the scuffed shoes and threadbare cuffs of a long-divorced solitary. They reminded him of the delaying hand of the Ancient Mariner.

The story had given him a totally new slant on Claudia Dellar, wife now to the brother of her one-time lover, and a mother for a second time. It was too easy, in the case of elderly women, to overlook that once they had been different, young and irresponsible. Miranda, her gifted and strangely detached daughter, was aged thirty. How old would the first child be if it had survived its father's 'arrangement'?

Dellar had been a cold-blooded swine, Yeadings decided. How right he'd been to see the man as meting out grief. It wasn't clear how Claudia had reacted all those years back, watching her longtime lover move on to someone else, when she had aborted her baby.

What possessed her to settle for the older brother so much the opposite of the coruscating and successful Matthew? Metcalfe had implied that in that she'd passively submitted to her ex-lover's diktat, or been dismissively paid off. If so, with such a dominant personality as hers it must rankle even now, to have been summarily dumped, and for money.

Once it was passed on, this account would only serve to strengthen Salmon's conviction that she was behind an attempt to kill Sir Matthew Dellar. Money might still indirectly be a part of the motive, but Yeadings' gut reaction was to see it as a crime of revenge.

★   ★   ★

It hadn't taken Gus Railton long to repeat his account of how he had come to miss the

313

dinner at Windsor with his wife and father-in-law. Questioned, he agreed that he had passed on the story of his spat with Maddie to his son, who then also decided to drop out.

'It stands to reason,' he appealed to the hard-faced men across the interview room table, 'that he wouldn't enjoy an evening with the two of them under those circumstances. Dellar was in a twisted and withering mood and Maddie was nervy. I quite agreed with his decision to go off and join his friends. He's a decent lad at heart and he's had a lot to put up with of late. It isn't easy, you know, for a young man to live under the thumb of a killjoy.'

'But no harder than for you perhaps?' Beaumont suggested.

'I'll admit it was difficult at times. I dared not face up to the old bugger. It would have upset Maddie. He was her father after all.'

'Hardest of all for her, caught in the middle.'

'I guess so. And at her time of life . . . The change, you know.'

Pulling out all the stops, Beaumont thought. The sobbing strings now. He was sorry for the poor sod, but he'd only himself to blame, walking into a situation like that. He should have stood firm for a marital home without the live-in older generation. Or taken one good look at the family and run for his life.

'Right,' Salmon said finally. 'Go with the constable here and write it all down, then sign it. Remember we already have it on tape.'

'In which case a written statement shouldn't be needed,' Railton protested, bolder once he knew the questioning was over.

Salmon smiled nastily. 'They still prefer it in writing,' he said, 'once it gets to court.'

They let Gus go. He was passed in the corridor by his son looking apprehensive.

'Horsy, keep yer tail up,' Gus quoted and got a blank stare in return.

Jake had had more than enough of policemen in the last two days. He faced this new DI with a sulky scowl. DS Beaumont, familiar enough by now, didn't actually make him puke but he was filth all the same.

Salmon's disgust with Jake's use of the Met for his alibi translated itself into disagreeable quibbling over all details of the young man's statement and prolonging an interview that wasn't of first importance. Since by then Jake was wise to this, the DI's manoeuvre succeeded only in increasing his bad humour. He retaliated by adopting an upper-class drawl and a vocabulary which he judged, sometimes rightly, would be foreign to a mere detective inspector. As a result the atmosphere in the small, enclosed room became increasingly tense and heated.

Beaumont, however, accustomed to teenager-at-bay strategy, happily collected some choice phrases to pass later to his own occasionally errant son.

Eventually the mental jousting ceased, from exhaustion of material to fling at each other. Jake was entrusted to Beaumont to write his punitive lines and Salmon, uptight with frustration, retired to pass on his spleen elsewhere.

It pleased Jake to make an involved mess of his written statement. Beaumont, unmoved, scanned the first few lines over his shoulder and binned the paper. 'Can you manage a computer keyboard?' he asked mildly, knowing pride wouldn't permit making a hash of IT literacy. Jake gave a lopsided grin and gave in.

★   ★   ★

Robert Dellar had been in the West Country chasing the story of a rumoured supermarket takeover when news came through of the accident at Woodside roundabout. It took a few hours to find a substitute to pacify the city desk and he reached the hospital the next day only in time for Gus to inform him of Maddie's death. His fiancée arrived shortly afterwards and they had sat together by Sir Matthew's bedside for about twenty minutes waiting in vain for him to come fully awake.

The double shock had brought on an asthma attack, which Robert was subject to on occasions of sudden stress, and he retired to an outside stairway to use his inhaler, while Marion continued to keep watch. Their visit was duly recorded by the constable on duty outside the ICU. Yeadings, working through a mass of paperwork later, noted this and entered both names in his logbook with the times given.

It still worried him that no valid sightings of Jessica Dellar had come in. The photographs released to the media had drawn the usual outbreak of reports, both rational and fantastic. All had been investigated and proved mistaken. By now it seemed most unlikely that she would be deliberately ignoring requests to get in touch. Both her mother and Stone had been adamant that although impulsive she was responsible enough to avoid causing alarm. 'Especially,' Kate had said, 'since once she knew Eddie was injured she would have rushed to his side.'

Yeadings was impressed by the alliance struck up by Stone and the girl's mother. Kate was still staying at the man's house and they appeared to have pooled resources in trying to follow up possible lines of inquiry. Each appeared to be bolstering the other's courage in facing the total blackout of information.

He rang through to ask if he might drop in and discuss the ground covered, but was told by the housekeeper that they had just left, following an urgent summons from Wycombe hospital. It appeared that Eddie had twice shown signs of waking from coma. He had even muttered his sister's name.

This was too important to miss out on. Yeadings' Rover was parked close in the police yard. He left a message for Salmon and prepared to drive himself. There was the usual rush-hour clogging of traffic, with gridlock at the complex roundabout system when he reached central Wycombe. He fumed in a three-deep traffic queue while a fire tender and set of ladders were rushed out to head towards the Cressex estate.

In the hospital grounds he found he hadn't the right change for parking and cursed that he hadn't waited for a marked police car. It would be just his luck to have the Rover clamped or towed away.

Slightly out of breath, he reached the Intensive Care Unit in time to catch Kate binning her protective mask and apron. She looked neither dejected nor elated, but confused, and he hesitated to ask after her injured son.

'They say he's fallen into a natural sleep now,' Kate volunteered. 'Just for a moment it seemed he was going to come properly awake. He said something, but his eyes were still closed.'

'What was it he said?' Yeadings ventured.

'He was calling for someone called Nicola. She must be a girlfriend, I suppose, but I've never heard of her.'

'Where's Stone?'

'He went outside in a hurry. To phone, I think. He won't have gone far.'

They found him at the end of the corridor. He put away his mobile and turned to Yeadings with quiet urgency. 'We need to talk, Superintendent. Kate will have told you what he said. But it wasn't Nicola he called for. I believe it was Nicholas. He's an employee of mine and he's failed to report in.'

20

They all sat in Stone's car while he explained that he had employed a junior assistant called Nicholas Dukakis. In fact he still paid his salary although the young man currently worked in London for his wife Giulia as an accountant, facilitating her control of finances being transferred as part of the separation settlement.

'Normally,' Stone said, 'he contacts me twice weekly to ensure matters go smoothly, but since I left for Washington he has left no messages. I had assumed he was held up by some complex legal point and would get in touch when he had dealt with it.

'My ex-wife is a very devious and demanding woman, superintendent. Which is why I chose young Nicholas. He is discreet and utterly trustworthy. If he found it necessary to get in touch with Eddie Dellar, then I suspect it was somehow in connection with Jessica.'

'Why? What has he to do with Jess? And why Eddie?' Kate demanded sharply. 'Haven't you other employees he could have spoken to?'

Yeadings watched the other man hesitate, choosing how to reply. 'Nicholas and Eddie had met before, at my office. You understand, Eddie is young, but he has already gone some way in the Department. We have had dealings together over various licences for import and export. Also, Nicholas would have been aware of Jessica's relationship to us both.'

'I'm not quite with you,' Yeadings cautioned. 'The Department: am I to understand you mean the Department of Trade and Industry?'

'That's where Eddie works,' Kate put in. 'He's a civil servant.'

Yeadings turned back to Stone who held his gaze with a challenging stare. No comment, Yeadings warned himself. Civil Servant was a term that covered a multitude of occupations. He was one himself, for that matter. It struck him then that both Stone and young Dellar could have interests allied to his own, but possibly on an international basis. This was spooktalk, or else serious bluff; and Stone relied on him to keep the young man's mother in the dark.

'I see,' he granted, not really convinced that he did. 'Go on.'

'There's not much I can offer,' Stone said sombrely, 'since Nicholas has failed to report

321

back. I am seriously concerned that he's been prevented.'

Prevented. Like being dead, Yeadings supposed with a flash of intuition. Dead, strangled and left to burn in a house fire? The implication was there to be picked up. Jessica Dellar missing; the young man too; and Eddie seriously injured after an apparent attack. What the hell had the three of them been up to?

'It's puzzling. Kate, the answer rests with your son,' Stone said, laying a hand on her arm. 'Already he's showing signs of coming round. Soon he'll be able to tell us what happened and it can all be cleared up.'

Never so simple as that, Yeadings thought. How could it ever be cleared up for that poor woman if her daughter was dead?

'You said . . . ' Kate faltered. 'This Nicholas works for your wife. And Jess works for you.' She made it sound a question, full of apprehension.

'Nicholas works for me too, but on loan to Giulia's financial manager.'

'She . . . your wife. I imagine she knows your intentions regarding my daughter?'

Yes, the possibilities were getting through to Kate. Yeadings said nothing, folded away in his corner of the car's interior. How would the man deal with her now?

Kate drew a deep breath to steady herself. Deliberately she chose words that denied the panic inside. 'She wouldn't feel very kindly towards Jess. What would she be likely to do?'

Stone was holding her hand now. Yeadings watched closely.

'Giulia's a hard woman. She can be malicious, but she'd draw the line at real viciousness, too afraid of the consequences. She has a great instinct for self-preservation.' His voice was level, but under it Yeadings detected a note of some emotion. Exasperation? Anger?

No, he decided: it was bitterness. This man knew the woman he was speaking of. He'd been time and time again on the receiving end of her malice.

'Has she got Jessica?' Yeadings asked quietly.

'That's what I'm trying to find out,' Stone said. 'She'll have no direct dealings with me. Which is why I'm trying to contact my son.'

★ ★ ★

There was a great deal more Yeadings needed to know. He found it difficult to remove Kate Dellar so that he could talk to the man alone. She was too aware of his intention and determined to hang on. Stone, after all, had been her protector. But the mention of a son had sent a ripple of new apprehension through her: a recollection that there was so much about him that she was ignorant of, and it might go against all her held principles.

Yeadings wished he had Rosemary Zyczynski with him but, without warning, Kate surrendered. 'Superintendent,' she said almost tearfully, 'you'll do all you can, won't you? I must stay with Eddie and find out what happened.'

⋆ ⋆ ⋆

Franco felt the phone vibrate in his jeans pocket. Automatically his hand went to it, but Giulia had seen. He had to carry on with pulling it out and reading the text message.

'Is that Stefano?' his mother demanded sharply.

'My new jacket's ready. I have to pick it up,' he lied.

'That can wait. For God's sake what has happened to the girl? She couldn't have got far.'

Franco wasn't so sure of that. 'It was a mistake to send Stefano packing.'

'*Turdo! Bastardo!*' She was outraged at the reminder of where they'd found her young lover and the condition he was in, but Franco had more to worry about. Somehow his father had picked up on what Giulia had done. Not surprising perhaps, because his spies were everywhere. His message had been bald enough: *Where is Jessica Dellar?*

'He will have gone after her,' Giulia decided.

It took Franco an instant to realize she meant Stefano. 'Then maybe he'll bring her back as a trophy, with his tail wagging and be ready for you to throw him a biscuit!'

She glared at him. He was getting too big for his trousers. That was no way to speak to one's mother. Sometimes there was a touch of his father about him. She was reminded he was growing up. It was time to find a wife for him as a distraction. Perhaps she should have allowed him to go and study at Perugia, but it was too international. There would have been outside influences. And Carlo Massimo could reach him too easily there, if he wanted to claim him. Not that he'd bother picking up family if he was bent on cultivating that English hussy.

The very reminder of Jessica, so deceptively meek and malleable yet scoring the final point, enraged her further. 'He's welcome to her,' she said, almost spitting at the thought of her husband. 'She's a filthy little whore, enticing Stefano as she did. Under my roof!'

'He never needed encouraging. He was all over her,' Franco dared to claim. Habitual courtesy forbade his suggesting that Stefano had a nostalgic taste for younger flesh than he was recently allowed.

'If he finds her,' he warned his mother, 'there's no knowing what he'll do to her, after the way she left him. Then how will you excuse that to Father? We'd do best to contact him in London or wherever he is and explain that she's been a guest with us and now she's moved on.'

'He's in the States,' she snapped back. 'You know we don't speak together. And how can you explain her coming here anyway? No, she must be found before he returns to England or there will be almighty trouble. Mortimer must come out here and take her back.'

'If she hasn't found some way to get back on her own,' Franco considered. 'She's enterprising enough. Maybe she'll simply go to the British Consul and say who she is; plead she's lost her passport. They'll send her home, a Distressed British Subject. *Finito*!'

'Imbecile!' Giulia stormed. 'You are useless. Go away!'

'Yes, Mama.' He withdrew, no way so calm as he sounded, went up to his room on the third floor and booted up his computer. Anything could happen to Jessica, a runaway on her own. He was anxious for her. Whatever his father's likely wrath, he must be informed. He'd be the one to find her if anyone could.

★ ★ ★

Yeadings heard the other man out. There were still unexplained elements in the story, such as the connection between himself and Eddie Dellar. It smacked too much of how young undergraduates were trawled at university and enlisted in political or intelligence organizations.

So much depended on what Stone stood for. His interests were widespread. He spent as much time in America as here. Grandson of an Armenian refugee; he was British-born, but then so were a number of suspected terrorists. As a capitalist he was assumed to be politically right of centre, but again that was no guarantee of loyalty: look at that ambivalent spy, Anthony Blunt.

If it was through Stone's influence or agency that Eddie had been accepted for the DTI, it could make that young man a suspect cuckoo in the Whitehall nest. On the other hand, it could prove Stone an SIS recruiting agent.

Yeadings himself had once stood at a crossroads in his career, and he still was in touch with the senior spook who had urged him to move across into the alternative service. He needed now to ring a given number and request a check on young Dellar's provenance. During vetting, his link with Stone must surely have come up. There would be confidential files on them both. Not that he'd get to see them.

Quite apart from this question there was what Kate Dellar saw as the family being 'picked off, one by one'. 'Do you believe,' he asked Stone, 'that the recent deaths of Sir Matthew and his daughter, and the earlier mugging of Eddie's father, were in any way connected with Jessica's disappearance?'

Stone answered without pause. This had been uppermost in his mind. 'I don't. They would be of no interest to Giulia. But I do think that the break-in on the canal was the work of whoever abducted Jessica from Larchmoor Place. It was a first attempt that failed because he didn't have updated information on her.'

'And the dead man found after the fire?' Yeadings pursued.

'We shall find, I think, that it was Nicholas, and he did all he could to prevent her being taken.'

So, Yeadings reckoned, that is the real crime we have to tackle. The others are a maybe. There was still a slender hope that the spilt oil and the car crash were accidental.

'There's another thing,' he told Stone. 'I think you and I should take a look at where Eddie lives. Would you ask Mrs Dellar if she has a key? We'll go in my car, if you don't mind. I'll be waiting in it when you come back.'

Stone hurried into the hospital and reappeared shortly. From his face Yeadings could pick up nothing. It was immaterial whether they had a key or not. He wouldn't hesitate to call in an enforcer to deal with the lock.

Stone dangled a keyring with a Pooh Bear tag.

'Did she say if she'd visited there lately?' Yeadings demanded.

'Apparently she hasn't. She seemed a little guilty that she hadn't looked in to check on the flat.'

'I take it you've been there before?'

Stone smiled. 'I have. I even know where to lay my hand on the coffee.'

Yeadings let the other man open the outer door of the little mews. It seemed to take some fiddling in the thick wisteria foliage beside it. They entered on ancient quarry tiles and went straight through to the kitchen. The superintendent noted red glows high in the corners that denoted a security system. He waited but nothing went off. 'I thought the house was alarmed,' he prompted the other.

'I de-activated it as we came in.'

Nul points for observation, Yeadings awarded himself. The man certainly appeared at home in here.

'What are you particularly interested in, Superintendent?'

'What do you suggest?'

'That we unload the cameras.'

Something else he'd missed as they passed quickly through, but they were cunningly concealed. Yeadings put out a hand to stop the other. 'Unless you've new film to reload, don't bother. I'll send someone down to see to it. We don't want to make a break in his recording. 'I must say I'm impressed. Are these just boys' toys, or is there some significance in these precautions?'

'I could say it's a neighbourhood known for break-ins, or Eddie has a technical streak, but you have already picked up on the truth, superintendent.

'As soon as he was reported injured Eddie's boss ran a check on who would be Senior Investigating Officer for the case. We learned your background.'

'I'm not exactly reassured by the security services keeping a file on a police officer,'

Yeadings said sourly.

'It does mean I can be open with you. Or as open as I have been so far.'

Yeadings smiled grimly. 'I'm investigating at least one murder, Mr Stone. Those films belong to me.' He held out his hand for Kate's keys. Stone smiled and dropped them into it.

'Good. I suggest we later look at the films together.'

★ ★ ★

Robert Dellar and Marion Paige walked side by side down Windsor High Street, under the shade of the looming Castle. There was no attempt by either to touch. Both were wrapped in private thoughts which permitted no intrusion.

'Here?' the woman asked, stopping by the door of a restaurant.

'It'll do. I don't feel much like eating, but maybe some soup . . . '

They had avoided the Castle Hotel in case there were press photographers there. The first of the swarm had turned up at the hospital as soon as the news of Sir Matthew's critical condition was known. Now that he was dead the paparazzi were eager for gloomy shots of the grieving family.

As if Maddie didn't matter, her brother thought. She was worth ten of him, the wicked old devil. Their early childhood had been partly shielded by Joanna, but once his mother died he'd felt the full force of his father's severity. Boarding-school had saved him. At least there he'd been buoyed up by the experience of already having been bullied by an expert. Nothing new the other boys thought up could penetrate his techniques for sliding out of trouble.

He had resisted the pressure to study law, but finally Matthew had so doubted his abilities that entering journalism had been accepted as *faute de mieux*. Then, to avoid living under the same roof, he had rushed into an unsuitable marriage and paid the price. Within a few weeks his divorce decree would be made absolute. He would be joined in the desirable flat in Regent's Park by Marion Paige, who wasn't an empty-headed blonde as Shelley had been.

He glanced sideways at her now. Marion's mouth had set in a hard line as if she were immersed in unpleasant memories. Upset, no doubt, by the double death in her fiancé's family. 'All right, Mopsie?' he demanded.

She said nothing, smiled her enigmatic smile and flapped one hand towards a corner of the dining-room.

'There's a vacant table over there. Let's snaffle it before we're headed off.'

Seated, she chose lamb cutlets for her main dish, with duck pâté to start. Robert dithered, conscious that sticking with soup would leave him with time to fill when he didn't feel much like talking. Perhaps he should order the same that she had.

'So,' she said when they had been served, 'why are the police making such a fuss over the car crash? I heard they'd taken the Mercedes in for forensic examination. Is this some special show they're putting on because your father was a VIP?'

'I suppose they have to cover themselves. The oil spillage at the scene was unusually widespread. Maybe they're expecting us to bring a civil case against whoever's found responsible.'

'And who's that likely to be?'

'God knows. Some lazy slob who didn't fix the tailgate of his truck, I guess.'

'You think that's all they're bothered by? It struck me they were asking a lot of questions. As though they thought it might not have been an accident.'

Robert laid down his knife and fork. 'Vandalism, you mean? That's an inner city problem. Highly unlikely out there in the wild.' He snickered. 'No, it's a spectator sport. Why cause mayhem if there's no one there to see?'

'You're probably right.'

'I usually am.' It was said without a hint of humour. Marion looked sideways at him to make sure.

'So you can go right ahead with the funerals?'

'With my father's, yes. I don't know what Gus wants done about Maddie's. That's up to him.'

'M'm. I wonder how her death affects the wills.'

'It may simplify matters. Depends just how deviously my father screwed up the provisions. I doubt he'll have provided for the Railtons if Maddie pre-deceased him — as she did.'

'Poor old Gus. He won't be very happy about that.'

'He'll get whatever Maddie meant him to have. Which is probably the lot in her case. So he's been lucky. Another year or two and she'd have got wise to his womanizing and probably cut him out.'

'Do you think so?' Marion chased a smear of sauce with the last forkful of broccoli. 'I've yet to hear what you're expecting for yourself. As only surviving child, you must be old Matthew's heir.'

'Must I?' Robert looked flummoxed. 'We didn't really get on. It would be like the twisted old bastard to leave it all to a rest home for retired cart-horses. He played his cards close to his chest. There was never a whisper of what he intended. Except to go on for ever. I honestly believe he thought he was immortal.'

'Well, he wasn't.' Marion surveyed her neatly cleaned plate. Perhaps, Robert thought, that accounted for her tone of satisfaction.

★ ★ ★

'Mother?' Eddie whispered.

She had sat there holding his hand, talking quietly until sleep overcame her. His eyes opened on a glare of whiteness that was alien yet partly familiar. The sounds reaching him were of quick footsteps at some distance, quiet rushes of controlled movement with a purpose in them. Then, focusing, his eyes took in the bowed figure by his bed, the corner of an unlined floral curtain and its rail. There was a scent of something like pine trees but with a sweetness mixed in. Hospital, he told himself. Yes, he thought he remembered now. He had opened his eyes on something like it already. And before that

— something much more terrible. He groaned quietly, aware now of the intrusions on his body, the paraphernalia of sickness.

'Mother? Kate.'

She awoke in an instant and he felt the tremor of excitement from her hand into his own.

'Hello, love.' She was fighting emotion, but it was too much for her. She leaned forward and put her cheek against his, letting the tears run, wetting them both. 'Oh, thank God, Eddie.'

'Mother,' he said, turning his head away. 'There's something . . . Tell Jess.' He stopped. Hadn't someone said Jess was missing?

'Oh, my God!' It was a hoarse shout, bringing the nurses running. '*Nicholas!*'

21

Gradually they were building a picture of what had happened, or of as much as Eddie had understood at the time. He insisted on speaking. Despite the surgeon's veto on visitors other than his mother, Yeadings was there too.

He started with Jess waking him at Larchmoor Place and begging his help for someone injured in the garden. At first he spoke as if Nicholas was unknown to him, but when Stone quietly came in and took a seat alongside his mother Yeadings leaned forward and said, 'We know who and what he was. Go on.'

'Nicholas told me Signora . . . Sorry, it's a complicated name. Charles Stone's wife, anyway. She was behind it.'

He stopped to sip water from a tumbler which Kate held against his lips. 'Someone meant to harm Jess and was coming to get her. I thought she'd be safe there until morning. Then I'd get them both away.' He sounded shaken and ashamed.

There was another pause while he closed his eyes to assemble his thoughts. 'He'd been shot at; was shocked. Not much more than a flesh wound. We put a pad on it. The bullet had gone through. We made him comfortable in the cellar. It was warm down there. He couldn't get upstairs.

'I must have been back asleep a while, but the radiator started knocking. It had run dry, air building inside. Then smoke — in the passage. I started shouting for everyone to get out. Downstairs — the fire — had really taken hold. I — went — for Nicholas.'

This time when he stopped, Kate protested. 'No more, please,' and the nurse came between, ordering them all out.

'Just one thing,' Stone insisted. 'Did you see Jessica again?'

'No.' It was no more than a whisper as his eyes closed.

⋆ ⋆ ⋆

'And after all that?' Yeadings asked Stone.

The younger man shook his head. 'We can only speculate. The house was already on fire. Do we assume whoever broke in was responsible? And had fought Nicholas off and ended up strangling him?'

'If so,' Yeadings granted, 'and the body was left in the kitchen, Eddie would have found it as he burst in. The door to the cellar was left unlocked, as we'd supposed. Eddie dived through to escape the flames, or was blown through by the blast which Railton described. The intruder must have been down there, trying to get out by the coal chute. They fought hand to hand and Eddie was knocked out. Still no mention of Jessica. Had she left by then? I think she must have. Willingly or forced.'

Yeadings confronted the other man. 'You believe the intruder was in your wife's pay. So who did she know well enough to use for this?'

'A thug called Jack Mortimer,' he said tightly. 'I always warned her against him. His ambition makes him dangerous. He has a streak of madness when he's crossed. But he's been useful to her in the past. Now he's gone too far and must know it. I've had people looking for him since I first knew Jess was missing. He'll be lying low, or out of the country.'

'And your wife?'

'Lives in Venice. She's Italian. Mortimer works for her here in London alongside my accountants. That's how Nicholas would have got wind of what he was up to. If Mortimer went first to Jess's boat it gave Nicholas time to reach her before him. But he was just a finance man, not an operative in the field. He should have called in other resources.'

Yeadings digested his words. Stone, he decided, lived precariously on the thin line between the legal and the criminal. Only sanction from one of the intelligence agencies could be behind such confidence.

'How did Nicholas know where to find her?'

'He must have accessed my e-mail.'

'With use of a password?'

'I told you. I trusted him. It cost him his life.'

'And this Mortimer got wind of his interest. Do you think he had him followed to Larchmoor Place?'

'Almost certainly. After they missed shooting him down, Mortimer would have gone in himself. He's a powerful man. Maybe he never meant to kill, or he went berserk and then had to cover up his tracks. He almost certainly started the fire, using whatever accelerant was to hand. By which time he must have made sure of Jess, leaving her somewhere outside while he set about rendering the body unrecognizable.'

They sat in silence while Yeadings considered this. Only conjecture, but it sounded possible. Faced by such a vindictive woman and her unpredictable thug, hadn't Stone made any move to protect Jess? He said as much to him.

'It worried me, but I never thought Giulia would dare ... And Jess is such an independent young woman, I couldn't clip her wings. She wouldn't stand for that, and I love her too much. She insisted on living on the canal boat. What could I do, but see that her neighbour kept an eye on her? I gave him a mobile phone to use in emergencies.'

'He never mentioned you,' Yeadings marvelled. Stone had an unusual gift for acquiring discreet allies.

'He alerted my PA who phoned me in Washington. I flew back at once. It was still too late.'

Yeadings sat, chin on chest, and mulled over how this might connect with what had happened to Sir Matthew and his daughter. Surely a separate matter. As he'd suspected earlier, there was more than one villain behind the misfortunes that had dogged the Dellars. Stone's marital difficulties were recent. He believed a more ancient cause had brought about the death crash.

He rose and assumed a more formal manner. 'Mr Stone, thank you. You've cleared up a lot of débris we could have done without. I wish you had approached me sooner. We shall continue to make every effort to trace Miss Jessica Dellar and I expect you to share with us any information that comes your way. As, indeed, I'm prepared to do for you.'

He nodded grimly. 'I have the matter of the car crash to clear up now.'

'Thank you, sir.' Stone held out a card. 'I'm leaving for Italy this evening. I know now where Jessica has been staying. She is still missing, but she did leave there by her own choice.

'This is the number of my PA, Roger Beale. Please contact him if there is any news.' He turned to Kate. 'You will stay on at my place, won't you?'

'Thank you, but I'd rather get back home. I've things I can do there to keep myself busy. That way maybe I'll worry less.'

Stone saw her to his car and watched as the chauffeur drove her off, then he returned to Yeadings with a request to run through the films they had taken from Eddie's home.

Two of them were blank. 'The cameras are only activated by movement,' Stone said. 'It looks as though no one's been in those rooms since he was there himself.'

But the final film, taken from a point just inside the front door, showed Jess entering, walking the length of the passage and disappearing into the kitchen. With the door left ajar she came occasionally into view again, moving something to the kitchen table and a minute or so later removing it again. Shortly after that she returned via the passage and left. She hadn't entered any of the other rooms.

'What was she doing?' Stone wondered aloud.

'Helping herself to ice cubes from the fridge,' Yeadings suggested. 'Wanting a cool drink. Except that she put them all back. Now, why that?'

The frames were electronically dated. Jess had visited Eddie's mews three days before they were both to meet up for Carlton Dellar's eightieth birthday. There seemed no connection with her later disappearance.

'Eddie Dellar doesn't appear on any of the films himself,' Yeadings pointed out. 'But he had to be there, so I suppose he could de-activate the cameras as required.

'I'll send Zyczynski to check what's been put in Eddie's freezer,' he continued. 'In the meantime I trust you'll keep me informed of your progress.'

With Stone's departure he went down to the incident room which seemed disconcertingly quiet. The inquiry into the RTA at Woodside roundabout had reached an impasse. In the analysis room he searched the walls for fresh information. Only one item caught his interest: the report of a silver car having been seen parked on the verge to the far side of the island at about twenty minutes past ten on the night of the car crash. It had been pointing north and could have driven off without sight of the pile-up.

'Which doesn't help much,' said the office manager who had just followed him in. 'Silver is the colour of the moment. Everybody's new car is silver.'

'Have you shown photos of car models to the witness?'

'She's coming in this evening for that. She's a midwife and she had plenty on her mind at the time. Not that she's much up on cars. She's a Ford Escort lady.'

Which, according to him, must mean an inertia purchaser. Yeadings grunted and moved on. 'At least we have a silver car and number eight shoes, narrow fittings, for our Cinderella search. That's all that supports it being a deliberate attempt on the Dellars' lives. If nothing comes of that, and the oil spillage leads nowhere, we'll have to let it go as an accident. It's enough having Kate Dellar paranoid, without us going the same way.'

'That other Mrs Dellar's been in,' Sergeant Thomas reminded him. 'And senior CID are all out. She's getting more than a mite impatient waiting to be seen.'

'Ah, Claudia,' Yeadings recalled. Salmon had intended making her uncomfortable over the nuisance phone call. Well, he supposed he might take that on himself. Could even get some satisfaction from it.

But for Jake having dropped out of the family group at the last minute, that malicious phone call would have been taken seriously. They could have hauled the boy in as suspect for a major crime. Spite like that didn't make the handling of difficult youngsters easier for anyone.

Sergeant Thomas had understated Claudia's present mood. Grim-faced and inwardly seething, she stood in angular silence, black against the light from the interview room's high window. Yeadings was reminded of the witch in Hansel and Gretel, except that the crone was depicted stooped, and Claudia seemed to have added a further two inches to her rigid height.

'Mrs Dellar,' he said, sailing straight in, 'we are interested in the phone call you made regarding a motorcyclist behaving in a drunken manner on the Windsor — Ascot road on the night of your brother-in-law's accident.'

She denied it scathingly: she knew nothing

about any call; stared him out and expected him to wither. He overrode her protests. 'It seems unlikely that, however long-sighted, you should have witnessed this from a distance of some sixty miles as the crow flies, Mrs Dellar.'

'I agree it's impossible. Which proves I did nothing of the sort. On the day of the accident I was at Cooden Beach with my husband and daughter. Maddie could have proved that if she had lived, because we spoke on the phone earlier that very evening. I know nothing of any motorcyclist.'

'Because there was none. But you did make that call to the police. My colleague has checked it with the telephone company.' This was a wild misstatement, but he was sure of her now.

He watched as she controlled the tremor that ran through her body. She couldn't deny that she was caught out. Viciously she changed her stance. 'It was my civic duty to report him. I knew how it would be. How he always behaved, full of drink, racing home on that infernal bike. Irresponsible young people like that need to be caught and taught a lesson.'

'Not on a false accusation. You are guilty of a public mischief, Mrs Dellar. And can be charged with wasting police time. I'm surprised that you were incautious enough to let prejudice override your considerable knowledge of the law.'

She darted him a sharp glance, then stared defiantly past his head. 'I don't know what you mean.'

'It's some years since you practised, Mrs Dellar, but not long enough for you to have forgotten the basics of law.'

She had not dreamed he knew her background. It struck her between the eyes, but she had an answer. 'As you say, it was a long time ago.' She spoke bitterly, her cold, snake-eyes fixed on him again.

'You haven't asked how it is that I'm so sure Jacob Railton wasn't near the crash scene.' He waited but she made no attempt to speak. 'As it happens, he was in police custody elsewhere, for an unrelated offence. That might offer you some satisfaction, except that afterwards he was released with a caution.'

'To terrorize the roads again.'

'I hope not, but that is for him to decide. Meanwhile, I must warn you that you face a possible charge yourself, and will be hearing further about the matter.'

'Is that all? You have caused me to travel all this way here for that?' She was still fighting to put someone in the wrong. As he nodded she sucked in her lean cheeks, drew herself to her full height and swept out of the room.

'No,' Yeadings said aloud. He'd wanted her to be guilty of more than a malicious desire to put down a cocky young upstart. Since Z had come up with evidence of fraud from Claudia's files (taken illegally and so useless in court) he had fancied her for the arsonist at Larchmoor Place. But now it seemed almost certain that the intruder (possibly Stone's Jack Mortimer) had torched the house to destroy the murdered man's body.

He was satisfied now that Claudia confined herself to greed and spite. A domestic tyrant, she hadn't the stature to have engineered the business at the roundabout. And she wouldn't have dared set Jake up if she'd prior knowledge of an oil spillage which could cause a death crash. That, for her, was a complication too far. It would have turned an apparent accident into something suspicious.

She channelled her bile into little, mean revenges. However much resentment soured her against old Matthew for his callousness in the past, she was not suddenly into murder now. It took a more devious and dangerous mind to set up the manner of his death.

But for what? Not money. No, it took a need for revenge greater than had ever inspired Claudia Dellar. Yeadings admitted he'd no idea who had reason to hate the man even more than her.

Restless after that negative session, Yeadings resolved to return for another word with Eddie. He was anxious to learn the end of his story. Maybe the young man had needed only a short sleep, and now was ready to continue.

As he drove into the hospital car park, he observed Stone's car a few spaces away, with the chauffeur reading a newspaper against the bonnet. So Kate hadn't agreed to be driven home. She'd come here instead.

He hurried along to the ICU, to find Eddie's bed empty. A nurse directed him to a small side ward. 'He's still asleep,' she said, 'but doctor thought he'd like to wake up to different scenery. His mother's there. Maybe you could get her a coffee or something.'

She opted for tea and he carried two polystyrene beakers back from the vending machine at the corridor's end. Kate smiled as she took hers. 'I'm so thankful,' she said. 'He's going to be all right. I've been afraid that if he came round he wouldn't be able to . . . '

Her eyes filled with tears. 'He was looking after his sister. Like he always used to do, when they were little.'

But not carefully enough, Yeadings thought. He'd underestimated the risk. The fact of

Nicholas being shot at should have been warning enough. He'd gone back to bed, to wait for morning. Maybe if Stone hadn't been out of the country Eddie would have tried to get in touch, and the older man would have handled it better. Doubtless the outcome would serve as a hard lesson in whatever training the boy had signed up for.

Yeadings had barely settled again alongside Kate when his mobile trilled. It was Z reporting from Eddie's house. He listened with amusement, then said, 'Right. Just leave the keys on my desk. I'll return them.'

'That,' he told Kate, 'was my sergeant reporting on the contents of your son's freezer. Apparently your daughter baked him a cake before they went to your brother-in-law's birthday weekend and left it there as a surprise.'

'Jess did? Are you sure? She's no cook. She won't do more than pop fast food in the microwave.'

'So perhaps it was one she bought.'

Kate was still looking incredulous. 'Why on earth would she do that? What kind of cake, do you know?'

'A fruit one, my sergeant said.'

'Certainly beyond her skills,' Kate decided. 'What on earth was she thinking of? She must know Eddie wouldn't eat anything like that.'

It left Yeadings wondering. He hadn't seen her narrowboat himself, but he imagined the galley wasn't equipped for great culinary adventures.

'I shouldn't worry,' Kate said comfortably. 'I expect someone gave it to her and she decided to pass it on. Girls have such a horror of calories. She may have thought Eddie needed fattening up.'

Or maybe not, Yeadings thought.

Eddie gave a little snickering cough and his eyes came open. 'Hello, Ma,' he whispered. 'Who's your friend?'

Yeadings introduced himself. 'I was here when you woke before. Don't you remember?'

'Vaguely. Charles was here.'

'He's left for Italy. He seems to think Jessica may be out there. Can you tell us a little more about what happened in the cellar?'

As Stone had suggested, he'd come upon the killer breaking his way out. He'd jumped him but the man was burly, armed with a tyre lever he was attacking the chute doors with. A wild blow had laid Eddie out and he remembered the man kicking him aside while he made his escape.

'But for the fire,' he said weakly, 'he might have stayed to finish me off. I was almost blinded. I couldn't do anything for Nicholas; was cut off by the flames. Managed to crawl out and into the woods. Last to leave.'

He was wretched about his ineptness, and despairing over his sister's continuing absence. Yeadings gave what comfort he could and then suggested to Kate that they leave him. She had been listening in silence, suffering with Eddie as each detail came out.

'I'll be back soon. With Jess,' she promised, and bent to kiss his forehead.

Watching her leave in Stone's limousine, Yeadings reached in his pocket for his mobile phone. He pressed out the number of a colleague in the Met. There was a little job he needed done in London and the inspector, ex-Thames Valley, owed him for help with his placement.

Just a chance fancy, he admitted to himself, but sometimes you could hit the jackpot that way.

He hadn't a lot of faith in Salmon's new favourite suspect. Beaumont and the DI were at present chasing up Robert Dellar for his shoe size. Only medium height, he might get into a size eight, but, however keen he might be to inherit, Yeadings just couldn't see him with guts enough to tackle patricide.

22

Because the summons had seemed so imperative, and she hated driving alone, Claudia had chosen to travel up by train. Now, mortified by the outcome of her interview with the superintendent, she contemplated the return journey as an exhausting chore.

Instead of Jake being at least severely reprimanded, she had herself been on the receiving end of a humiliating accusation. Her return was not to be the pleasurable experience she'd looked forward to. She cancelled the intended notion of a celebratory meal and crossed the forecourt at Marylebone station, towards the tube to Victoria for her connection.

As she passed the newsstand of WH Smith, someone clutching an *Evening Standard* came hurrying towards her.

'Claudia, is it you? I thought you'd moved down to Sussex? How very nice to see you.'

It was Marion Paige, the young woman Robert intended to marry once his divorce came through. Unremarkable, was how Claudia had classified her; and this was no moment to be obliged to make small talk.

'I'm on my way there now,' she said dismissively. 'I've a train to catch.'

'What a coincidence,' said Marion. 'I'm driving down to Eastbourne. That's quite near you, isn't it? Why don't I give you a lift? Then you won't have to flog across London and risk not getting a seat.'

Although not in the mood for socializing, Claudia conceded it would certainly be less bother. At the far end Marion would surely feel obliged to make a little détour and deliver her to her door, thus saving a taxi fare. Much more convenient. She allowed herself to be persuaded.

It was some years since she had driven in London herself and she felt a grudging admiration for the way the other woman negotiated the traffic. 'Driving in town,' Marion said nonchalantly, overtaking a bus and facing down an oncoming taxi, 'you have to be an animal to survive.'

From then on she had little to say and Claudia was glad to be able to slump in her seat, make a pretence at dozing, and so keep her at bay. Her offer had been acceptable; the woman herself was not.

With the onset of dusk Claudia re-opened her eyes on countryside that was unfamiliar.

'I always drive by Guildford and Horsham,' she remarked, implying that any alternative must be an inferior choice. Nothing would have persuaded her to use the M25 with the likelihood of being held up on the Heathrow stretch. It looked as though Marion had the same disinclination.

She was slowing now, indicating to turn into a lay-by as she braked.

'Where are we?' Claudia asked.

'Quite close to your railway line.' Marion sounded amused. She pointed upwards through the opposite window and Claudia made out the shadowed embankment thick with trees and brushwood.

'I brought along a thermos. Maybe you'd like some coffee. I'm afraid it's espresso, but I find that keeps me alert on the road. There is milk if you prefer, but no sugar.'

On the train Claudia would have ordered something stronger, but the offer was welcome. It had been close in the car and she felt a headache coming on. It made her feel doubly disagreeable.

They sat sipping, and still Marion seemed in no hurry to move on. Her hands, on the steering wheel, were tanned and Claudia recalled being told that she had worked for several years in South America, doing whatever geophysicists did. She was wearing

355

quite a splendid square-cut emerald on her fourth finger.

'That's an unusual ring,' Claudia remarked. 'I suppose you come across a lot of gemmologists in your line of interest.' From habit she made it sound derogatory.

'Some, of course. Actually my fiancé had this mounted for me. It is rather fine.'

'Fiancé?' Claudia's fine eyebrow shot up. 'Surely that's a little premature? His divorce isn't made absolute yet.'

Marion laughed. 'Just another two months. Then, when all these family scandals have died down . . . I shall achieve my inheritance.'

That seemed a strange remark. Claudia looked sideways at her and saw she was smiling again, a wry little pulling at the corners of her mouth. That mention of family scandals was quite out of order. Surely she hadn't been referring to the Dellars? Misfortunes recently, perhaps, but never scandals. She should be more careful of giving offence.

A spurt of anger made her want to wound this smug woman in her comfortable car. 'Robert is certainly looking for someone different this time,' she observed in her authoritative contralto. 'His first was a trophy wife: a silly, addle-pated blonde clothes-horse. Men couldn't keep their eyes off her.'

'Whereas I'm a sallow, raddled older

woman with little to commend her,' Marion said almost gaily. 'Thank you, Claudia. I must plead guilty to some quite off-putting genes. And then I've had so much practice at lying low, in every sense, making myself a non-person, letting others, quite literally, get on top of me.'

Claudia felt a flush rising up her chest and neck to flood her face with colour. If she hadn't misunderstood, the woman's meaning was utterly salacious.

'I'm not sure that I understand you.' Stiffly upright.

'And I'm quite certain that you don't.'

Did she imagine then that there was menace in her tone? Claudia moved a little farther apart, conscious of the door frame biting into her shoulder. She hadn't taken that much notice of Marion when Robert had introduced her, but now there was no denying she was peculiar, possibly unbalanced. Why invite anyone to share the journey down, only to be outright offensive?

She drained the last of her coffee and the dregs tasted bitter against her teeth. Perhaps she should attempt to put the woman in a more normal frame of mind. She handed back the cap of the thermos. 'Thank you. That was timely. I'm sure we all hope you will be very happy with Robert.' It seemed an appropriate remark to mend bridges.

Marion chuckled, deep in her throat. 'Oh, that won't last long, I assure you.'

Claudia gawped at her forthrightness.

'Do you really imagine I'd make it permanent? — settle to a lifetime of being patronized by that bombastic little show-off? No, Robert will be glad to divorce me. But it will cost him. Oh, how it will!'

The woman was unbelievable. Once Robert got to know her opinion of him there'd be no marriage. Did she imagine Claudia had no sense of family, that she'd keep silent about a remark like that? Startled and incredulous, she almost missed the next words.

'Of course I shall be well recompensed for my trouble. It is still a crime after all. As a wealthy man by then, Robert will be most anxious to keep it under wraps.'

★ ★ ★

At about this time Robert Dellar was returning, late, to his Regent's Park flat to change for a rather classy reception at the British Museum. Since the impressive new courtyard development, it had become a fashionable place to throw parties.

He parked outside the house. In his haste

he was unaware of the two men who piled out of a nearby Toyota and followed him up to his front door. 'Mr Robert Dellar?' the heavier of the two demanded, producing a warrant card. 'I am DI Salmon from Thames Valley police. This is DC Arnold of the Met who is assisting me in my inquiry. You may remember we met briefly after the fire.'

'Er, probably, yes. Actually, inspector, I'm a bit pushed for time. I am overdue for an appointment and I need to change. Can we do this another day?'

'No, sir, and I have a warrant to search your accommodation.'

'You have what?'

Salmon produced the paper and held it under the man's nose. The dim light of a street lamp failed to make it legible, but it did appear to be an official form.

'I don't understand. With regard to what exactly? And what are you actually looking for?'

'With regard to the deaths of Sir William Dellar and Mrs Madeleine Railton.'

Robert put out a hand against the door post to support himself. 'You really imagine I should have anything to do with that? Are you implying it wasn't an accident? Surely a skid caused by oil spillage. They were my father and sister, for God's sake!'

'Shall we go in, sir?'

As Dellar shakily removed his key and released the door, Salmon pushed past him. 'I think you should cancel your appointment. This could take quite a time, and we require you to be here while we look around.'

Rarely at a loss for words, Robert found his protests ignored and retired to the kitchen where he produced a bottle of single malt and settled in high dudgeon while the contents of his cupboards were unceremoniously stacked on the formica-topped table. He trailed behind the invaders as they reduced his scrupulously ordered bookshelves into unalphabetical chaos in the sitting-room and searched among the purely decorative basket of logs beside the 'live flame' gas fire. The mock-Persian rugs were dumped on upturned armchairs whose depths had been plumbed, producing only some small change, a lost credit card and a quantity of grit. Elsewhere fitted carpets were allowed to remain in place but other flooring was examined for suspicious cracks concealing hidey-holes. Upstairs, cistern and tank were examined and a panel removed from the side of the bath. In his bedroom all clothing removed from wardrobes and drawers was flung in an unlovely heap on the bed. Two pairs of shoes, size eight, narrow fittings (one showing traces of dried mud) were removed and placed in plastic bags for forensic examination. When they reached the second bedroom, converted for use as a study, Dellar became histrionic about the threatened confiscation of his computer.

'For God's sake,' he shouted, 'that's my fucking livelihood you're taking. I'm a journalist. I need that!'

'I guess we could arrange for an expert to examine it here,' Arnold allowed. 'The station has a couple who work on identifying paedophiles.'

The shame of this implication, however unintended, completed the collapse of Dellar's resistance. He slid gently down the wall to sit, dejected, with bent knees, on the Berber carpet. Salmon, regarding him with disgust, was amazed that anything so gutless could be involved in murder.

'Right. We'll leave it at that then. You say you haven't a garage, but I'll need your keys to check on your car. You can watch from the window. We'll post the keys back through the letterbox. Good-day to you, Mr Dellar.'

⋆　⋆　⋆

Superintendent Yeadings was sliding a new filter into the coffee machine when his call came through from the Met. He halted in mid-operation. 'Bob, what have you got for me?'

He nodded, scribbling notes on his desk-pad as the info came through. 'Splendid. That's a lunch I owe you. Let's make it soon. Say next week?'

He listened again and laughed. 'Oh yes, now we've got this last detail it should be sewn up by then. Except for the paperwork, of course.' They groaned in unison, swapped family news briefly and rang off.

Yeadings reached for his log, noted down the time and wrote in this last entry under the previous note on the silver Nissan. Then he turned back to the filter paper.

★　★　★

In the leafy lay-by under the railway embankment Claudia Dellar stared in disbelief at the woman Robert Dellar was expecting to marry.

'*Crime*? What crime?' she repeated. 'What could Robert be accused of?'

'Marrying his sister,' Marion jeered.

It made no sense. Robert was still married to the fashion-plate Shelley. And his sister Maddie was dead. This woman was raving. Surely she wasn't safe to be with. If only she would stop talking this madness and get on with the journey. Her driving at least had been reasonable.

'Robert's sister,' Marion repeated. Then, emphatically, whispered: 'His *older* sister.' With the same wicked little smile flicking at the corner of her lips, she was watching the other closely now, tempting her to dare to understand.

Claudia had opened her mouth to deny there was such a one; then her voice dried up.

'His big sister. Half-sister. *Matthew's bastard by you.* So what does that make me to you — old woman?'

Claudia closed her eyes. 'No,' she said through cracked lips.

'Oh yes. It has taken a long, long time to catch up.'

She paused as much to exert control over herself as for emphasis. 'You will never know the hell you abandoned me to without so much as a thought. As far back as I can remember — passed from foster parents to care home to foster parents again — I was abused, a punch-bag, a rag doll. And finally I was sent to a man who said what he felt for me was love. Some love!

'Gareth Paige. His wife was slowly dying but she managed to conceal it from Social Services until I was formally adopted.

'I wanted to die too. The unspeakable things he did to me. Over the years.'

She leaned back, her clenched hands relaxing on the wheel. 'You could say he brought me up. He taught me all I know. And he was rich as Croesus; so when I was old enough and he was weak enough, I let him die too.

'I was all he had to leave his filthy money to Imagine that. I was free for the first time in my life, eighteen years old, wealthy and worldly-wise. I opted for real education, won a scholarship to Cambridge. I chose work that meant I could travel. But all the time I promised myself that one day . . . One day, guess what?'

Claudia shuddered. 'Can we go on now?' she asked breathlessly.

Marion took her time answering, She swivelled in her seat and stared back with those odd, coal-black eyes which now filled Claudia with dread. Just so must Matthew have looked as he handed down a life sentence.

'Oh no,' Marion said softly. 'This is as far as we go. This is the moment I have waited for all my long, wasted life.'

★   ★   ★

364

Driving back from London, DI Salmon answered his mobile phone with a snarl. 'Sir,' he corrected himself, recognizing Yeadings on the other end of the line.

'The shoes are narrow eights, so we've got the right one this time. Nothing else apart from them, no; but one of the Met's computer experts is seeing what they can pull out of his hard disk. His floppies all appear to concern his work, but they'll be going through those as well.'

'Right, so you can turn round and look up an address for me in St. John's Wood now. Can you take this down?'

Salmon suppressed an expletive, signalled left and pulled on to the hard shoulder. 'Ready, sir. Got it. With regard to what inquiry, sir?'

'The same. In fact much the same quest, but with no warrant as yet.'

'You mean *shoes*?'

'Why not? There's nothing about the sole prints that's specifically male. It could as easily have been a woman spreading the oil at Woodside. And the lady does happen to own a silver Nissan. It's possible too that a geophysicist might own a pair of infra-red goggles for night work.'

The silver car was sheer coincidence, Salmon told himself. The super would be stocking up the evidence room like a secondhand Russell and Bromleys. And whoever knew a woman with more than size sixes? Pointless, time-wasting.

He ground his teeth, complied, and started to look for a turn-off to get in the reverse direction. While he drove he pressed in the number DC Arnold had left with him. He'd have to drag the bloody man out of the canteen. The Met would think Thames Valley didn't know their arses from their elbows.

As for Marion Paige! — the Boss needed his head examined. She'd only recently got to know most of the Dellars. What kind of motive was he dreaming up for her? Unless he imagined she was an old lag Sir Matthew had once sent down for a long stretch.

⋆　⋆　⋆

In the lay-by below the railway embankment Claudia felt the car's confined space pressing in on her. 'I — I don't . . . I'm not well,' Claudia faltered, fumbling for the door latch. 'Need air.'

'Stay there. I'll come round and help you out.'

Marion appeared, slightly out of focus, beside her and put a firm, hard hand under one arm to bear her up. She stood, rocking giddily.

'There; now start walking. It'll help detox you.'

'Detox?' She wasn't up to arguing. Let it go. She wanted to let everything go, but it was second nature to keep afloat. Float — that was what she seemed to be doing, her legs swinging loosely under her supported frame. And the woman was forcing her uphill. She hadn't the breath for it. She let her weight swing her back and the pair of them almost fell.

'Oh, keep going, you silly bitch,' Marion hissed between her teeth. 'It wasn't a heavy dose.'

'Dose.' The darkened hill above was lurching up and down, swinging in on her and then away. She had never been as drunk as this in her life, even when . . .

'I can't. Must — lie — down.'

'Have I got to drag you?'

Marion let her collapse at the foot of a tree. Her face, where it slid down the bark, opened with a jagged tear. In the light of her torch the other woman examined her closely. 'You can do it. You know you can. You won't beaten by a little climb like this. Where's your spirit, woman? Tell yourself to do this; if it's the last thing you do.'

'Drink,' came the whisper.

'There isn't any more.'

'Poi — son.'

The answering laugh was rich with malice. 'Only the rape-date drug. You should be so lucky at your age, dear Mama! And in six hours not a trace will remain. They'll just find a broken old doll who tumbled out of the train and rolled down the embankment. Those slam-door trains should have been out of service years ago.

'But then, when you're found — ''The old girl was in trouble with the police, wasn't she? Maybe she couldn't take the backwash of what she'd done.'

'Gus rang me about the malicious phone call. They'd guessed it was you. Who else knew where Matthew's car would be at that time? But you were wrong about Jake.

'Come on, stir yourself. See the starlight up there? That's where you're heading. Maybe someone will see you on the track and you can get away. It's your only remaining hope.'

Claudia felt herself pulled to her feet again, an arm encircling her waist. Rag doll, someone had said just now — or maybe it was a long time back. That's what she was, sagging, forced onwards and upwards, her cotton-wool legs mechanically finding ground, but her knees gone to mush.

Beside her someone's heavy breathing was offensive. Like a pursuing bear she'd had nightmares of as a child. She had to get away. Uphill. Not be feeble.

It took an effort, but she could make it. Between the darker trees the open air ahead was jolting nearer. If she reached that level she'd be safe.

23

At the St. John's Wood address Salmon found the house in darkness. He pulled into the kerb, deciding to wait for Arnold to join him.

It was a tall, rather narrow building with two front gables and a large garden allowed to run rather wild. It stood to reason, with a job like hers she wouldn't be at home a lot, lecturing at the university in term time then going off on expeditions. She must be worth a few pennies to afford a place like this. Anywhere of any size in a decent neighbourhood could command an astronomical price at the moment.

She could be anywhere in the world. Salmon imagined the leathery face framed in the fur of her parka hood, eyebrows and chin silvered with frost as she grimly plodded the Antarctic ice floes. Or did she only go for solid rock? What was a geophysicist anyway?

A rum job for a woman, even if she wasn't all that feminine. Not the sort to provide a good slap-up meal at Christmas. But then she didn't go rabbiting on like some women. She knew how to stay stumm.

It could be she'd have something short and

sharp to say at the idea of having her house searched. Not that he had a warrant. It would be a case of asking nicely. So he'd leave that to the Met man. It was the other one's patch, and a bloody wild-goose chase of Yeadings' anyway. If she even chose to turn up.

Arnold arrived twenty minutes after Salmon, locked his car and knocked on the Thames man's window. Salmon let him in, sourly noticed the disguise of peppermint on the man's breath and was reminded he'd had neither food nor drink for a good six hours. His stomach rumbled hollowly at the thought.

'It's a no-go,' he said. 'We'll give it half an hour, then call it a day.'

So Sod's Law operated. The silver Nissan appeared just five minutes short of knocking-off time, and they were obliged to go through with the farce.

She wasn't a big woman and her shoes were size five and a half. There was no point in taking any of them back.

Infrared goggles? She appeared amused. 'I'm not in the SAS, constable. No doubt they could turn up a pair in the department at UCL, if you really need some. I thought the Met would have something of that kind themselves.'

Arnold didn't care for the put-down

treatment, so, instead of peeling off and letting Salmon get back home, he wanted to examine her car. It took all Salmon's glowering pulling of rank to dissuade him. By which time the inspector was ready to phone Control and put in a negative report, in case Yeadings was hanging on for news.

★   ★   ★

It wasn't until a little after midnight that a querulous voice was put through from a private number at Cooden Beach, demanding whether Mrs Carlton Dellar was still being questioned. Night duty sergeant Bill Thomson had no information on the matter.

Carlton explained. 'An Inspector Salmon asked her to call in yesterday and she left here mid-morning. She should be back by now. She went up by train, you see. On a day ticket. So it would be out of date by now. She wouldn't have cared to waste it.'

'Right, sir. But I expect you'll find she did decide to stay over. Why don't you ring around her friends and find out who she's with.'

'She wouldn't do that. There's nobody she would drop in on like that. And in any case, if she changed her plans she would have rung me.'

'I'm sorry, sir. It has nothing to do with us. I've looked her up in the visitors' book and she was checked out at five-fifty.'

The thin voice bleated on. An old chap, and more than a tad peevish from the sound of him. Not surprising that his good lady seized the chance for a few hours off the leash. Sergeant Thomson sighed, tempering tact with firmness, and got rid of the caller.

A note beside the woman's name showed that her visit related to the murder inquiry for which Superintendent Yeadings was SIO. He was the one who'd spoken to her, because DI Salmon had been out.

Better make a note of the phone call in that case. Yeadings was a stickler for having everything written down.

★ ★ ★

It was eight-fifty next morning when the superintendent checked his desk and found the note. He looked up Carlton Dellar's Sussex number and put in a call. Within ten minutes he had Claudia listed as a Misper.

Beaumont, dispatched to Victoria station, made inquiries of morning travellers. 'Wrong time of day,' he grumbled to the uniformed man alongside him. 'They're all in a blethering hurry. We'll not strike lucky until the same time she'd have been travelling last evening.'

They drew blanks at the newsstand and coffee stall where a change of staff was on duty. 'It's mostly runaway kids we look for at the stations,' said the constable disconsolately. 'They still think the streets of London are paved with gold.'

'More likely that the grass here tastes greener,' Beaumont punned. 'And the crack cracker.'

'So what's with this old girl then? I take it she's not a junkie.'

'Possible suspect in a double murder,' Beaumont said gloomily. It had been Z's idea first, he remembered: that when Sir Matthew died so dramatically, calling Claudia a murdering bitch, he might have meant it literally.

'And that may turn out to have been just an accident after all.'

'Less bother for everyone,' said the constable comfortably.

★   ★   ★

The same inquiries were being made at Warrior Square and West St. Leonards stations, at either of which Claudia might have alighted to take a cab home. Sussex police came up with the same lack of information. Railway police were searching the coaches of all trains that had run from Victoria to Hastings from 18.30 onwards. In view of recent attacks perpetrated on that line, special attention was being paid to lavatory compartments. Sniffer dogs were being employed to detect traces of human blood on doors, seats and floors. And news-hounds, alerted to possible fresh violence, were already hot on the scent.

Carlton, distracted, again rang round the family in case Claudia had, incredibly, taken it into her head to go visiting instead of returning home. His call to Kate came as she was answering the door to Roger Beale arriving to report on Stone's activities in Venice.

She tried not to sound alarmed. 'I'm so sorry, Carlton. No, she's not been here. Is there anything I can do? How are you and Miranda managing?' She listened until it seemed his spring had run down.

Kate replaced the receiver and turned to her visitor. 'That's awful. Now Claudia's gone missing,' she told him, relieved to be free of Carlton's complaints. If he'd wanted her to go down and look after them she'd have had to refuse. There was enough to take care of here.

'There can surely be no connection . . . '
Beale said.

'With Jess, no. But the other business
— the car crash which killed Matthew and
Maddie — I don't know. It's possible.' She
shivered. It still seemed possible to her that
the Dellars were being picked off, one by one.

'About your daughter,' Roger Beale said,
declining the offer of refreshments. 'There is
good news and not quite such good news.' He
explained that Stone was correct in his
surmise that Jessica had been taken to his
wife's home on Lido, Venice; but she had left
again under her own volition. Stone's son,
who lived there with his mother, had been
quite frank about the visit, which he hadn't
properly understood but was highly suspicious of.

'You say 'taken',' Kate queried. 'She didn't
just decide to go there on her own?'

'It was something rather less than an
abduction, according to the Signora. More
like persuasion. But I'm sure deception was
employed. And the man who arranged this
was Jack Mortimer, as Mr Stone guessed.

'Perhaps the Signora wouldn't have admitted to a connection if she'd known he was
wanted here for arson and the killing of
young Nicholas.'

'But why take Jess there, Mr Beale? What

did this woman intend with her?'

'She pleads it was out of curiosity, but there was certainly more. I think she would have done all she could to break up the relationship. Malicious, but not resorting to open violence. It seems she panicked when Jessica ran off, overnight, by boat.'

'To go where? Surely someone's seen her since? Or she's been in touch?'

'We know she crossed the lagoon safely, although the boat was later found wrecked. It seems she joined some other young people hitch-hiking south to Bari. Mr Stone has gone there himself now to hunt for news. There's every reason to expect he will pick up her trail. She could, of course, have boarded a boat in the south to return to England, or tried for a flight back. In which case you could expect her home at any time.'

As he'd said: some good news, some not quite so good. Kate didn't know whether to feel comforted or more anxious. 'When you're in touch with Mr Stone,' she said, 'please thank him for all he's doing, and tell him Eddie is getting stronger every day.

'And now I really do insist you stay for lunch. It's ready prepared and there's plenty for two.'

★   ★   ★

The retrieval of Claudia's body owed nothing to the precautions Yeadings had set up. It happened by chance. A motorist en route from the Midlands to Haywards Heath had an urgent call of nature, pulled into the lay-by and took refuge among the trees on the start of the incline. The discovery of a human shape grotesquely sprawled some twenty feet in was enough to override his pressing need. He put out an emergency call on his mobile phone before unzipping. Sussex police, already alerted for a missing elderly woman, had a patrol car there in twelve minutes.

PC Micky Poulsen, fresh from his college course, imagined he saw a flicker of the body's fingers. In view of the body's temperature and the amount of blood congealed on face and shoulders, PC Fennell, being more experienced, left him to it.

But Micky proved right. He detected a feeble pulse; enough to have them covering her with their uniform jackets and summoning an ambulance. On arrival the senior paramedic privately thought her chances were slim, but they'd tackled worse injuries than these and won through. It had been a warm night and she was sheltered between the young trees.

They worked on her there while PC Fennell alerted the station and Micky made his circuitous way up the embankment, properly mindful of preserving the scene. Within minutes he came crashing back down to announce that he'd found the spot where she'd hit the side of the track and started to roll. It accounted for the surface injuries and flints embedded in the soft skin of the face and arms. 'Jumped from a moving train,' Fennell was reporting into his mobile. 'Or maybe got thrown.'

There was no ID until the handbag was found by searchers on the bank. It had ended halfway down, and its leather strap was broken. Inside, together with money, a small diary, keys and handkerchief, was the return half of her train ticket. There appeared to be no doubt that she'd intended to return home as previously arranged with her husband.

★   ★   ★

'I'm distinctly averse,' Yeadings told the assembled team, 'to believing this is another case of ill luck pursuing the Dellars. There have been instances recently of similar attacks on travellers, but I want you to approach this as a further murder attempt in the present set.

'Accordingly I want details of the move-ments yesterday evening and night of everyone we have already been questioning. And, for a start, we'll have Dr Marion Paige brought in for questioning.'

He regarded his DI and the two sergeants. 'Z, I think this one's for you. Softly, softly. We want her to feel quite confident when she arrives.'

'What about Robert Dellar?' Salmon demanded. 'He had the right-sized shoes.'

'Good point,' Yeadings agreed equably. 'And he's the lady's fiancé. Let's have him in too. Separately, in different interview rooms. DI Salmon and DS Beaumont can sit in on both alternately.'

'Not you, sir?' Salmon queried.

'I might look in later. But first I'm off to Haywards Heath to see how Claudia Dellar's faring. She seems a tough old lady and I'm told she's putting up a good fight. She's barely conscious and kept incomunicado, but if I'm right about her she'll soon be rarin' to get her version of things aired.'

★ ★ ★

Bright as a new brass button, Yeadings decided. He envied Sussex force their newly acquired Micky Poulsen. He sat with him in the staff dining-room of the hospital, picking over the details of the young constable's blow-by-blow account of the discovery. 'And the main injury, you say, was to the head?'

'Above the right ear. It looked really bad, pulpy. I guess that's partly why PC Fennell thought she was a goner. There was an awful lot of dried blood.'

Yeadings decided he should take a look at the scene, but later. 'Have you ever considered jumping out of a moving train?' he asked conversationally. 'No? Let's do just that. We open the window, lean out and unlatch the door. Go on.'

Delighted with the challenge, Micky picked up on it. 'The door opens against the airflow, so it takes some holding. We jump and land, hit the flint track and roll in the direction of the train. The embankment's steep there. We continue rolling, downhill, hit a few small obstacles and pick up some surface injuries, end against a tree trunk.'

'How do you feel?'

Micky raised a hand to the side of his head. 'I think I'm unconscious.'

'Try waking up then. Change hands — since you say the woman's main injury was to the right side of the head.'

They stared at each other a moment. 'It was,' Micky insisted, recalling the sight of her. 'Definitely the right. So . . . '

'Yes,' said Yeadings, 'it needs explaining.

381

The injury could have been caused by something other than a fall. A blow from some heavy instrument, for example.'

The young constable waved an arm threateningly. 'That would connect with the left side of the head. Or else the attacker was left-handed.'

'Not necessarily. In my tennis days my backhand was always stronger than my forehand. I doubt anyone thought to photograph the wound *in situ*, since she had to be rushed to hospital. But it may not be too late. I'll request it when the dressings are changed. Enlargements may give us some idea of the direction of the blow.'

'So it's not an accident or attempted suicide? It's a major crime.' The young constable's eyes shone. 'And when she comes round she'll be able to tell us who did it!'

'*If* she comes round,' Yeadings warned him. 'It's all hypothetical until then.'

★ ★ ★

Back at Thames Valley both taped interviews were proceeding, building alibis for the previous evening and night. There were intervals, intended to be unnerving, when Salmon and Beaumont moved between the two being questioned. Meanwhile, SOCO from the Met were examining both cars at their respective houses. The results were phoned through and reached Yeadings as he arrived back at his office.

Robert Dellar's Vauxhall Vectra was almost suspiciously clean, but there was little chance it had been serviced overnight. He had claimed he put it in for valeting two days back and used only the Underground since.

Dr Marion Paige's bore signs of recent use. More to the point, a pair of green rubber boots were found under a tartan rug in the boot. Inside them were two pairs of woollen ski socks. The boot soles had traces of peaty soil. They were size eight and narrower than regular wellies.

Time to make a move, Yeadings told himself. He collected Beaumont and presented himself in the interview room where Dr Paige, watched over by a uniformed constable, was declining vending-machine coffee. The tape was restarted, the interviewers identified themselves.

'Dr Paige,' the superintendent began pleasantly, 'are you familiar with the workings of the barrier machines at Victoria station?'

'Why should I be? I'm not an electronics technician.' It was an attempt at scorn, but a little lame.

'Then you may not realize fully how they

scan date and journey on a ticket. We have recovered the return train ticket issued yesterday to Mrs Dellar, who, I'm happy to say is recovering in hospital and due to give my colleagues a statement explaining her serious injuries. Also, we shall be asking these technicians you despise to search the electronic system for the recording of her ticket number, to check if she was admitted to the platform for her return journey. Meanwhile your car is being microscopically examined for traces of Mrs Dellar's presence.'

He watched the blood leach from under the tan of the woman's face. Then he nodded to Beaumont to caution her.

When she had been passed to the custody sergeant, 'I never knew that about those ticket scanners,' Beaumont said, impressed.

'What about them?'

'That they record the numbers of every ticket that goes through.'

'I wonder if they do.' Yeadings smiled beatifically. 'I'm as ignorant of how they work as Dr Paige herself. Actually I never claimed that they do record. Only that a search is being made to find out if her ticket number was recorded. But, like you, Dr Paige seems to have assumed I meant something more.

'You can check that out when you run the

tape through. An occasional spot of bluff doesn't come amiss. If you're careful.'

★ ★ ★

Kate Dellar felt she had made a new friend in Roger Beale. The little man had shed his official dignity and shown a human side. While she saw to shaking the wok of frying peppers and assorted vegetables he applied himself to carving the cold roast chicken. They were having their meal in the kitchen, for convenience and because sunlight was pouring in while the dining-room would be darker.

When the doorbell rang Kate clucked, darted a glance at the kitchen clock and said, 'That'll be the egg delivery man. He's early today. Would you much mind seeing to it? His money's on the hall table.'

Beale ran his fingers under the tap, wiped them on the tea towel tucked into the waistband of his trousers and went to do her bidding. He opened the door to a pair of large policemen and a leggy young girl with shaggy blonde hair.

It took him a second to recognize her from the photograph on Stone's desk. 'Yes?' he said politely.

The girl pushed past him and he was left to

hear out the explanation. The police were from Heathrow with instructions to deliver her to her mother at this address. She had arrived on a flight from Croatia with a temporary passport from the British Embassy in Zagreb. It seemed she was a bit of a VIP.

24

'Better come in then.'

The policemen followed Beale into the kitchen where the two women were clasped in each other's arms, and the wok giving out blue smoke.

'Jess, whatever have you been up to? And your hair!' Kate managed to get out through tears of happiness. 'Oh, never mind. We can go into all this later.'

'Mrs Kate Dellar?' one of the policemen asked solemnly.

'Yes, I'm Jessica's mother.'

'I'll vouch for that,' Beale offered, removing the wok with one hand and firmly offering them the door. 'Thank you for escorting Miss Dellar home.'

When he came back from seeing them out, the girl swung round on him, took in the tea towel apron and demanded, 'Who's this, Ma?'

Kate told her.

'Beale? Oh no, he isn't! Roger Beale's an absolute hulk. I should know. He's the one who carted me away.'

'But I'm the real one,' he said. 'The other

would have been Jack Mortimer, Mr Stone's wife's man. He'd have used my name because you'd heard of it. And they're looking for him on a count of murder.'

That shocked the girl. 'Who?' she demanded, appalled. At Heathrow she'd been questioned unmercifully, but no one had explained what had happened in her absence.

So Beale sketched a summary to bring her up to date. 'The fire would have been started after you were removed to Mortimer's van. It was young Nicholas that Mortimer killed, and you almost came down to catch him at it. Then he set the house alight to dispose of the body. Eddie had to struggle to get out and he seemed to be the last. But then we discovered you were missing. Imagine what your mother went through after they found a body in the ashes.'

For a moment Jessica was speechless. She turned back to Kate and hugged her close. 'Oh, Ma! I'm so sorry.'

'Will you tell me something?' Beale asked as they finally settled to their lunch. 'A week or more ago, what were you up to in Eddie's kitchen?'

She held his eyes a moment. 'There was a security camera? It picked me up then? I had something I wanted to leave for Eddie.'

'A fruit cake,' Kate said dryly. 'DS

Rosemary Zyczynski has it in custody. What is so special about it?'

Jessica hesitated, but in the face of all that had happened, did this one detail have to be suppressed?

'Charles had just got back from Russia,' she said. 'He brought me a present. A bag of uncut stones, mostly rubies, I think. I'd nowhere to keep them on the boat and I didn't want to use my bank.'

She looked uncomfortable. 'I wasn't sure, you see, that they were legit.'

Beale grunted. 'You'd no need to worry. Since the Soviet Union broke up they're using all sorts of currency. This would have been payment for services rendered. And it doesn't have Russian Mafia implications. The authorities will have approved, Customs duty duly registered.'

Jessica gave a long sigh. Then, 'So is Charles still in America?' she demanded. 'And what exactly are you doing here in Ma's kitchen?'

Kate took it on herself to explain. 'In your — er, absence, Charles has been most supportive,' she said. 'He and Mr Beale — Roger — have been kindness itself. Right now Charles is in Venice settling matters there and . . . '

'You've met him? Do you like him?' The

words tumbled out of themselves.

'I like him,' Kate said, eyeing her daughter evenly. She drew a deep breath. 'What's more, I approve. He is just what you need.'

★ ★ ★

Marion Paige had held her hand up for the deaths of Sir Matthew and his daughter. She elected to make a voluntary confession.

'I had nothing against Madeleine,' she allowed, 'but she was rather a pointless person.' There was no regret there, simply cold comment. She seemed careless of her own future.

'The arson, though: that was nothing to do with me. I suppose it suggested something when an unknown man was found murdered at the house. It seemed that if I was going to set the account right it was a good time then to fudge the issue. The Doom of the House of Dellar, as Kate saw it.'

'You gained admission to the family through Robert,' Yeadings supposed.

'He was easily flattered. Gus Railton introduced us. We'd been lovers for some time.'

'He didn't object to your getting engaged to Robert?'

'Why should he? He'd married for money

himself. He saw it as much the same: the little woman, however independent-minded, craves security in later life. There was no reason that, married to Robert, I shouldn't continue with him as before. Better cover, in fact.'

Beaumont, wooden-faced, said, 'You haven't mentioned Michael Dellar. He was the first of them to be killed.'

'Michael? I met him through my work. Archaeologists often use me as a consultant. Michael, a historian, would sometimes turn up at a dig. I liked him. He was the only good one of the bunch, a true scholar, but sexy too.'

She gave a twisted smile. 'To be honest — and now that you know the worst I've done, why not confess this as well? — I more than liked him. I found him very attractive. Not that he seemed aware of it. And when one day his daughter turned up . . . '

'She guessed how you felt?'

'She warned me off. A very determined young woman, that Jessica. Kate has no idea what it is that I have against her.' She sounded wryly amused.

'I might have made a stand and pushed my chances with him, but fate decided otherwise. He was mugged and killed one night on his way to Temple Underground. What an abominable waste! He was a lovely man.'

Beaumont leaned forward as if to put a further question, but Yeadings moved a finger and he held back. 'You used Michael Dellar to get to your mother,' the superintendent accused her.

The woman's distant gaze returned to his face. 'On my birth certificate I was Marion Gilmour, father unknown. My mother was Claudia — not a common name. Even before I decided to track her down, every time I came across the name something used to stir inside me. A vicious little asp rearing to do what it was created for.' Her laugh was harsh.

'I don't remember what brought it up, but Michael happened to mention a sister-in-law called Claudia. Of course I assumed she'd be of much the same age as him. Then I saw a press photo of her husband, the poet. He was as old as Methuselah. So I wondered. Maybe this Claudia was the right age to be my mother. Just a shot in the dark.

'It isn't difficult to check these things if you know where to go. And Bingo! I'd found her. Claudia Dellar, née Gilmour. But I still didn't know who her lover had been before she got married all those years ago. There had been an interval of eighteen months between my birth and her taking to the orange blossom.' Her lips twisted bitterly.

'So, with that much information, you

followed up her disrupted career in chambers with Matthew Dellar. Was it Randolph Metcalfe who spilled the office gossip?'

'Ah. You tapped into him too, Superintendent? Yes, he was very forthcoming. A neat little arrangement between the brothers, wasn't it? And everything so well covered up in advance, so that anyone in the know would assume she had aborted the baby. I was *disposed of*. Passed to monsters!'

Her voice rasped with fury. 'Nothing, but nothing, is bad enough for someone who did that to me! She should have suffered all the fear and pain that I did.'

★ ★ ★

It was all sorted and they were holding a mild celebration in Yeadings' office. A fax had just come through that Jack Mortimer had been apprehended at a bank in Rotterdam, picking up the second half of Giulia's pay-off in the name of Joseph Ryan. An escort was being sent to bring him home the next morning.

'Tomorrow's Saturday!' Z wailed. '*The* Saturday. And I meant to buy a new dress for the wedding!'

'You still have time,' Yeadings told her. 'Why don't I send you off now on police business and see you in church tomorrow?'

'Thanks, Boss,' she said, rising and placing her coffee mug on his office windowsill. 'What police business?'

'We require another pack of that Italian espresso. And better sign the card for Angus and Paula before you go. Right; paperwork you other two. Off with you.'

He watched them dismiss, wondering how long he could put off announcing what the brass upstairs had planned for when Angus Mott finally gave up in Kosovo. It seemed a pity to dampen their present enthusiasm. Strings had been pulled to ensure Angus would return, promoted to DCI. It left the rank of inspector, in dispute between Beaumont and Rosemary Zyczynski, yet to be filled.

The trouble was, Yeadings regretted, the Olympian gods at Kidlington HQ had spoken. The price of retaining Angus Mott in his specialized team was to have Walter Salmon continue as DI.

You win some, he told himself. You lose some.

★   ★   ★

Rosemary Zyczynski dropped the sealed packet of Italian espresso coffee into the carrier bag with her new natural shantung suit for the wedding. She had one other purchase to make: a basket of fruit for an invalid.

She found Eddie Dellar in an open ward. He was still weak, but cheerfully optimistic. His mother and sister had just left after a visit.

'I've been downgraded from a private room,' he said. 'That's progress. Six of us in this section. This time I'm going to make sure. It's last in, first to leave.'

We do hope that you have enjoyed reading this large print book.

Did you know that all of our titles are available for purchase?

We publish a wide range of high quality large print books including:
Romances, Mysteries, Classics
General Fiction
Non Fiction and Westerns

Special interest titles available in large print are:
The Little Oxford Dictionary
Music Book
Song Book
Hymn Book
Service Book

Also available from us courtesy of Oxford University Press:
Young Readers' Dictionary
(large print edition)
Young Readers' Thesaurus
(large print edition)

For further information or a free brochure, please contact us at:
Ulverscroft Large Print Books Ltd.,
The Green, Bradgate Road, Anstey,
Leicester, LE7 7FU, England.
Tel: (00 44) **0116 236 4325**
Fax: (00 44) **0116 234 0205**

Other titles published by
The House of Ulverscroft:

A MEETING OF MINDS

Clare Curzon

On a cold November morning, Detective Superintendent Mike Yeadings and his team are called to a pub car park in Henley-on-Thames where a woman's body has been found. Detective Sergeant Rosemary Zycynski is horrified to realise that the dead woman is her next door neighbour, Sheila Winter, the owner of a local garden centre. Sheila lived with her ageing mother and didn't appear to have much in her life outside her work, so the discovery of her body, naked and wrapped only in a black fur coat, is a shock. Could one of Zycynski's new neighbours at Ashbourne House hold the key to the mystery? Or the garden centre manager, Barry Childe, who has just served time for a brutal attack on a young woman?

BODY OF A WOMAN

Clare Curzon

Called to investigate the death of a young woman found dumped in woodland, Superintendent Mike Yeadings and his Thames Valley CID team find the body in exotic evening dress, her face covered by a feathered, bird-featured mask. Yeadings realises he had once briefly encountered her, in quite normal circumstances. This was Leila, the dutiful if undervalued wife of Professor Aidan Knightley; owner of a little gift shop in a quiet Buckinghamshire town; devoted to her two teenage stepchildren; on good terms with her neighbours. The circumstances of her death seem totally alien to all who knew her.

COLD HANDS

Clare Curzon

A dead body is found on a railway line —
a straightforward suicide, or something
more sinister? When the dead man is
identified as a customs officer investigating
counterfeit currency, it seems like more
than just a coincidence. Superintendent
Mike Yeadings is suspicious, so he sends
his undercover team, including DI Mott
and DS Zyczinski, to Fraylings Court and
the heart of the operation

DEATH PRONE

Clare Curzon

Bachelor recluse Hadrian Bascombe has summoned his family to announce his imminent death. They learn that his fortune is to pass to a single beneficiary whom he will choose from among them that night. However, when the company leaves he has given no more than cryptic hints of his intentions. On their way home the two youngest guests meet with a serious accident. When further violence reduces the number of potential heirs, Superintendent Mike Yeadings of the Thames Valley Police follows an intuitive line, which ends in confrontation with an embittered killer.

THE BLUE-EYED BOY

Clare Curzon

From the author of THE FACE IN THE STONE. Blue-eyed boy Joel Sefton, handsome and attractive, was mugged and dumped behind supermarket trash bins. Yet there were less admirable traits underlying his charisma, and many had good cause to hate him. It was a secret in the past of a WPC that proved vital in penetrating the blue-eyed boy's activities, and their labyrinthine effects.

THE FACE IN THE STONE

Clare Curzon

Ex-Warrant Officer Class 1 Edward Mather died in his Cyprus villa from asthma — or so it seemed: two months later a post mortem laid suspicion of murder at the feet of his widow. Mather was an adventurer, with an eye for making a fortune — yet where was it and what had he been involved in? As the police investigation took its time, it looked likely that the stranger from Athens would crack the mystery first - but then the widow took an interest and the case blew wide open.

ABERDEEN
CITY
LIBRARIES